TRIGGER POINTS

BOOKS BY MARTIN MAYER

Fiction

Trigger Points
A Voice That Fills the House
The Experts

Nonfiction

The Builders
Today and Tomorrow in America
Conflicts of Interest: Broker-Dealer Firms
The Bankers
About Television
Bricks, Mortar and the Performing Arts
New Breed on Wall Street
(with Cornell Capa)
All You Know Is Facts
The Teachers Strike: New York 1968
Diploma: International Schools and University Entrance
Emory Buckner
The Lawyers
Social Studies in American Schools
The Schools
Madison Avenue, U.S.A.
Wall Street: Men and Money

TRIGGER POINTS

POINTS

Martin Mayer

HARPER & ROW, PUBLISHERS
New York, Hagerstown,
San Francisco, London

1817

TRIGGER POINTS. Copyright © 1979 by Martin Mayer. All rights reserved. Printed in the United States of America. No part of this book may be used or reproduced in any manner whatsoever without written permission except in the case of brief quotations embodied in critical articles and reviews. For information address Harper & Row, Publishers, Inc., 10 East 53rd Street, New York, N.Y. 10022. Published simultaneously in Canada by Fitzhenry & Whiteside Limited, Toronto.

FIRST EDITION

Designer: Eve Kirch

Library of Congress Cataloging in Publication Data

Mayer, Martin, 1928–
  Trigger points.
  I. Title.
PZ4.M469Tr [PS3563.A9525]   813′.5′4   78–20212
ISBN 0–06–013019–9

79 80 81 82 83 10 9 8 7 6 5 4 3 2 1

for Henry Mayer, very cheerfully:
Neue Kraft fühlend

1

The Sniper

The eight cheerleaders of St. Iggy's High came down the sidewalk into the soft light of a street lamp penetrating the river mist of a November evening in Hoboken, New Jersey. Though this was not their favorite street for evening walking—full of what they called "the slum stuff" that separated their school from the neatly kept blocks of row houses where they lived—they felt a safety in numbers. Nancy Murphy and Debbie Scholz, fifteen and sixteen, had both turned down resentfully their fathers' offers to come drive them home from the basketball game; they wanted to walk home with the boys.

They were noisy but decorous, paired off two by two, the girls wearing raincoats over their costumes, the boys in denim jackets or short coats over the bright-blue pants of their uniform. Nancy and Joe Michaels had trailed the group by a few steps. Joe was known to be serious about Nancy; Nancy

1

was known not to be serious about anything. As they came to the light opposite the deep vacant lot that ran through to Ninth Street, Nancy broke away from Joe and came skipping ahead to the others, laughing, two long brushes of brown hair bouncing high behind her head, pug nose gleaming.

As she came past Debbie, she seemed to trip (later Joe would think he remembered a slapping sound); and she fell, knocking Debbie off balance. Debbie thought it was funny. "Whadja do?" she called. "Get sweat on your sneakers?" Nancy didn't get up. Joe and Debbie were down beside her almost together in a shared onslaught of fright. Nancy's eyes were clouded; through her thin lips came what Debbie told the police was "a horrible gurgling noise." Joe began to lift her by the shoulders, and then everyone saw what the bullet had done, and began to scream.

By then the man in the Ford wagon on Ninth Street had removed the shell from the chamber of the hunting rifle and placed it in the ashtray he would dump out, two hours later and a hundred miles away, in the trash barrel of a gas station on the New Jersey Turnpike. With a smooth, single gesture, he stowed the .22 in the box that hung from the bottom of the instrument panel, and snapped the lid. The car was gone even before the screaming began; having stopped for two lights and slowly negotiated Park Avenue, it was on the curving ramp, climbing the Palisades with the flow of traffic from the Lincoln Tunnel, before the first police car reached the growing and hysterical mob around the girl, who was dead.

Since his divorce, more than six years ago, Harry Johnson had been an assiduous reader of newspapers. He had both the *Times* and the *News* delivered every morning to his bachelor apartment on the top floor of an eight-story 1920s building on East Seventy-third Street in Manhattan—the sort of building that has had a self-service elevator for forty years, has cream-colored halls floored with a patterned mosaic of hexagonal stone, doormats neatly centered in front of the doors, newspapers on all the doormats. An uncompanionable, uninquisitive community of childless couples and the unmarried middle class; had been so from the beginning, would be so world without end. Each had his work to do. An FBI agent, supervisor, counterintelligence, assigned to the New York headquarters, Harry was about five minutes' walk away from his office when he got out of bed, a convenience that still seemed to him luxurious after all his years in the suburbs. He was forty-seven, but looked younger: flat stomach, only the faintest touch of puffiness above the cheekbone, black hair still cut and parted as it had been when he got out of the Army after Korea—resigning a commission as captain at age twenty-four—and signed on with the Bureau.

The previous night's sniping across the river was of course the headline story in the *News,* and he noted it was on the front page of the *Times,* too, in a little box down the bottom: "Fatal sniping." They were always fatal, it seemed, unless you could believe all the people who were calling the police to say someone had just shot at them and missed. There were calls like that almost every night. This was the fifth murder of this kind since Labor Day—in Hoboken, a kid cheerleader; in downtown Manhattan, a Puerto Rican truckdriver; in Stamford, Connecticut, a housewife; in Concord, New Hampshire, a lawyer's secretary leaving work; in Allentown, Pennsylvania, a male ragpicker, out from one of the mental institutions the states were trying to empty. There were, Harry thought, reading the list in the boldface box on the third page of the *News,* too many people out of loony bins in this country already; here, as in some other things, the Russians really seemed to know what they were doing.

Harry Johnson was a political agent who had no politics— or, more correctly, thought he had none. He never voted, even in local elections. He was a listener rather than a talker, if only because part of his job, first in the Army and then in the Bureau, was to get along just fine with anybody. The conviviality he needed was an accomplishment, not a trait;

but he was a man who enjoyed what he achieved.

Some of the most relaxed and happiest times of Harry's life had been the evenings drinking and bowling with the left-wing shop stewards and their acolytes whom he had been paid to cultivate and observe during the three years when he worked under cover as an engineering draftsman for Sperry Gyroscope and then Republic Aviation. Like the Jew who had the dry-goods store back in Kentucky, where Harry was brought up, or the Italian plumbing contractor—or for that matter the faith healer who swept up the loose change across the railroad tracks—these fellows had a right to believe what they believed. Defend to the death, and all that; anyway, he would tell the young agents who were so hot for politics, if it wasn't for these fellows, where would *we* be? Because he had been lucky in his first months on the street, providing the first lead to a conduit between Sperry's duplicating shop and the Russian trade mission, Harry had been freed from the donkey work of "clearance" and pretty much left alone to form his own judgments. He had never produced or paid much attention to the tittle-tattle that passed for analysis in those days when "security" was "tight."

His war was not, in short, a war of ideas. He fingered for specific protection, and if that failed, for prosecution. His Korean experience had taught him distaste not so much for Communists as for Koreans. He knew, of course, that ideas could lead to actions, bad ideas to bad actions. Under cover, he'd been an active member of a union that years before, in the Stalin-Hitler pact days, had called strikes to halt production of the war matériel the mad dog Roosevelt was more or less surreptitiously passing to the mad dog Churchill. But you couldn't keep people from having ideas, any more than you could make people act on the ideas they had. The trick was to spot that small cadre in whom the link between ideas and action was short and strong. Then you hit them as hard as you could. The people of the country who wanted a quiet life were as entitled to that as the others

4

were to their ideas. They paid him to keep their world orderly, to keep the newspapers dull.

It was realized early on that agent Johnson had a rare capacity to turn people who had for one reason or another begun to be queasy about where their ideas might lead them, were leading others. He could recruit and run agents because—in the buzz word that became fashionable in the latter 1950s, when Harry was promoted and emplaced—he could "empathize." In the Army, his leadership ratings had gone off the scale; his outfit had been in the retreat from the Yalu but had lost no prisoners. In the Bureau, his efficiency reports recommended him repeatedly for advancement; but he was happy in his work, and he and his then wife had been happy in their suburban home. He was not tempted by the prospect of becoming a special agent in charge somewhere like the place he came from.

Harry had received and absorbed a full-scale conventional training; he could and did take assignments from the other divisions. He had helped nail down an embezzlement case at what was then the Franklin National Bank. He had been active in the investigation not only of the Malcolm X murder, which intruded on his bailiwick, but also of the Joe Colombo shooting, when organized crime sent an SOS for manpower. And he had been near the center of planning in the still unsolved Whitmont kidnapping. But even while carrying a full-time assignment elsewhere, he had continued to run his agents in counterintelligence. Nobody else could do that; nobody else knew who they were. And five, six, ten times a year they delivered something significantly useful.

When the very young became the subject of preponderant interest, it was thought that Johnson would have to be replaced, but his networks seemed to rejuvenate themselves. He did his homework and he had good judgment; he was trusted. As he explained once to a review board, most of the kids he controlled were looking for someone their fathers' age, not for a contemporary. Within a small leadership cadre of radicals, Harry Johnson was a feared and hated figure, but the world at large knew him not. Within the Bureau, there was an ebb and flow of regard for the importance of Johnson's work, but he had become a fixture: continuity itself provides payoffs.

So at seven o'clock on this morning as every morning, Harry Johnson carefully read the papers at the red Formica table beside the little kitchen window that looked north and east to the crenelated granite cornice across the street, high enough on the eighth floor to get the early sun. He had shaved and dressed immediately upon arising—he liked the feeling of being ready to go—but now he sat relaxed, taking the trace warmth of a bright New York November morning, refilling his glass from the quart container of orange juice, nibbling at a rich bakery Danish, reading the paper. The water had boiled, and in a minute he would make himself a small cup of the bitter espresso that more or less officially began his day. Campfire coffee, he called it on the rare occasions when someone was there to share it. Reminded him of what his father used to brew over the fire when they went out on the river together near Louisville; it had come up the river originally, his father said, from New Orleans.

Faint bells—Harry registered all faint sounds—told him it was seven-thirty. No hurry. He read the sports pages of both papers, the bridge columns and the chess column. The bridge columns were indispensable on the second Wednesday of the month, because his daughter always read them, and this was the day he and Sue played in the master point duplicate as a team the whole club thought was cute.

He set his cup under the gleaming chrome coffeemaker, put in the paper filter, the finely ground beans, the boiling water and the weight, and watched the coffee drip into the cup. Before turning to the political news, as he called it, he reread the story of the murder in Hoboken, and thought about it. A surgically disgusting story; the neatness made it worse. The coffee was ready. Harry took the cup, and as he sipped the coffee he read about the debate in Congress on defense appropriations.

Because there were so many evenings when he didn't get home for dinner, Tony Whitmont liked to take his second-grade son to school on his way from Harrison to New York in the morning. Usually the chauffeur drove the Continental, and he shared the back seat with the boy, but Wednesday was the chauffeur's day off, and he drove the car himself. His wife, Carla, in apricot Ultrasuede skirt and Givenchy blouse, came to the garage with them and worked the switch that opened and closed the garage door. She hugged them in turn and accepted a kiss on the cheek, not kissing anyone herself—Carla Whitmont put on her lipstick and eye shadow, and combed out the long black hair carefully, immediately after she brushed her teeth and washed the remnants of the previous night's oiling from her face. She was only thirty-two, a year younger than her husband, and if she had owned one of those wicked-witch mirrors (she did own virtually everything else she might have wanted), it would have told her that she was indeed the most beautiful woman on her block, in her world; lacking such supernatural assurance, she took care of her problems as she perceived them. She was fond of her little boy and of her husband, who still, really, amused her as well as took care of her; though now she knew there were many men who were rich. But first things came first.

"You have the envelope?" she said as Tony opened the car door. The boy crawled in first, under the wheel, and perched on the seat.

"Yeah. I put it in the glove compartment last night." They exchanged glances. "You riding today?"

"Sisenor. I have to be ready for Saturday. It is the last meeting of the season. Are you still certain you can*not* fly

7

me down tomorrow after my class? I would so much like to give Major his work myself on Friday. And then I would have time to speak with the caterers."

"Horsefeathers on the caterers—the only thing about our house they don't know after this season is how to stop breaking our glassware. You're not ready to let them use theirs, are you?"

"No. Everyone says they are the best caterers in Maryland."

"Most expensive, too. Look, honey, I just can't get off before Friday afternoon. I've got meetings, one of them a problem. If you feel you have to be in Maryland Friday morning, you can drive down tomorrow night, or take a commercial plane and rent a car. The only thing is, there's no way to get help in there before Friday; that's the day they've got on their schedules. I don't think you fancy being in that house alone Thursday night."

"Never," said Carla.

Tony shook his head, still persuading, because even when an argument with Carla was won there was no guarantee it would stay won. "Just impossible. Even if I could swing it, there's Jay. He can't miss school, and he wants to go this weekend."

"Sure do," the boy said. "You promised we'd go crabbing."

"Damn cold," said Tony. "But we'll go crabbing."

The wide garage door rose behind the car, and Tony backed it out, his son beside him, snowsuit jacket over school uniform, head turned like his father's to watch the backward progress of the Lincoln. From a distance, they were rather alike: both pudgy, bump of a chin, nose spread out above the full lips, high forehead; close up, the boy had his mother's jet eyes and blacker hair, and he was better-looking.

On the second Wednesday of the month, it was all but impossible for Tony to look at his son without thinking about kidnapping. On that day every month (forever: there is no statute of limitations on kidnapping), Tony and Carla paid off the FBI agent who knew the truth about the Whitmont case.

Unfortunately—who could have expected it?—people were still interested in the Whitmont case. Almost nine years later, the story occasionally regurgitated in the press. Newspaper readers whose minds were carpeted with the detritus of antique news stories would still remember that Tony was the son of (the now late) Julius Whitmont né Weissberg, proprietor of Monteblanco coffee brokers, headquarters in New York, offices and roasters in Boston, Baltimore, Cartagena and Santos; that he had been living in a commune on The Hill in New Haven, where he was a graduate student in sociology at Yale; and that $750,000, none of it ever recovered, had been paid to some nutty Latin radical group to secure his freedom.

The follow-up stories had been prominent, too, for Tony, a knockabout Maoist before his kidnapping, had not long after his release switched over to business school in New York, joined his father's firm, and before his thirtieth birthday, on his father's death, became its president. He was reputed to be doing well with the firm, though there was some question whether the credit was his or that of the professional and aggressive multinational staff his father had left behind. A faintly nasty "Businessmen in the News" note in *Fortune* had pointed out that Latins were used to having the boss's son succeed, whether or not his qualifications were demonstrable. Tony, known as something of a joker even in his Movement days, had distributed tear sheets of the page around Monteblanco with a note that the honor of the firm now required profit targets seven percent higher than those previously set.

Other stories had appeared when Tony married Carla only a year after the kidnapping, for Carla herself had once been in the news, "La Pasionaria of Vassar," as an irritated history professor had described her when she led the pickets who blocked access to the library to protest inadequate funding of a program for Hispanic students. A gossip columnist in the *News* had found it worth her while to speculate on Carla's supposed "links" to Castroite undergrounds, and to wonder whether she and "her new No. 1 man" had met while he was a prisoner awaiting execution or ransom. Then there had been yet another newspaper story when it was revealed that the Internal Revenue Service had denied old Julius Whitmont a tax deduction he claimed from the "casualty loss" of his expenses in rescuing his son. That case was still in the courts.

"Daddy?"

"Yes, Jay." The boy's name was Julius II; naming her baby after his grandfather had been a little gesture of peacemaking by Carla with her father-in-law, who had been accepting but upset by his son's public conversion to Catholicism. Carla was one of those people who truly and firmly believed that the quality of their intentions would govern others' feelings about their actions. She had no interest in learning that for Jews, even not very religious Jews, naming a child after a living relative was anathema. So Tony tried—and failed— to explain to Julius why it was okay for Catholics. It had been an amusing if arduous baptism. Carla's mother had enjoyed herself. Tony remembered the scene in the church, remembered also the weeks of waiting until Carla felt fit for him, thought of her long thighs and the muscles that swelled in them just before their joining. So she wasn't Jewish. After all that instruction and ritual nuisance, neither was he.

"Daddy?"

"I'm sorry, Jay. I've been thinking of things." For an irritated second, Tony thought he had driven past the turnoff to the school, but he hadn't.

"Daddy, when can I take the bus like the other kids?"

"I guess."

"What does *that* mean?"

"Soon."

10

"The kids all say it's fun, the bus."

"You know I like to see you in the morning, Jay."

"Yeah."

Tony laughed. "Soon," he said again. The boy looked straight ahead, stolidly, as the post boxes and hedges and driveways passed by. Tony was again overwhelmed with fear for him. Carla seemed untroubled; maybe he should take that religion of hers seriously. She confessed once a month— he wondered *what* she confessed, what secrets she had from him. Had she confessed the kidnapping? It worked so well— not just the money but the experience of losing and regaining his only child, which had reconciled Julius Whitmont to whatever craziness his son might reveal. A year later, even Carla could be swallowed into Julius Whitmont's new-found sense of family, and it was Julius who persuaded Tony's furious mother, herself Latino, from Argentina, a woman who had come up in the world by marrying the boss, and knew all about schemers.

"Are you afraid the sniper's going to shoot at me if I take the bus?"

"What?" Tony said, turning into the school driveway, at the end of which the bus stood accusingly. "Oh, no," he said, with a look to his son's solemnity. "No, don't you worry about that."

"Will the sniper shoot at Mummy?"

"Who's been talking to you about snipers?"

"It was on the TV."

"I'm sure it was," said Tony. "They put all those things on TV, don't they? It's sort of like *Kojak,* which I don't like you watching. Those things don't happen to ordinary people like us."

They were stopped now at the glass doors. Abe Fine's Cadillac was pulling up behind them. "Could we get a TV for the car like Simon's father?" Jay said, noting its presence.

"Maybe someday, Jay. We'll talk about it. You get off to class now."

"All right, Daddy. And I won't worry about the sniper."

Tony Whitmont watched his son greet Simon Fine, waved into the rear-view mirror at Abe, and went off for his second-Wednesday drill, which could, indeed, be on *Kojak*. He wondered when his son would learn about the kidnapping, and what it would mean to him. Ancient history, probably: Little thrill, my daddy was a celebrity. Well, he thought as he turned onto the Thruway, for some people life is boring.

"I know this is a busy day for you and I appreciate your coming," Craig Spitts of the Lawyers' Cooperative said in a bright, nasal voice. He leaned back in the swivel chair, his cowboy boot resting on an open desk drawer, blue eyes brightly focused on a young man perched on the old leather couch. The young man's shirt collar was slightly big for his neck; even after six months on a congressman's staff, he still wasn't accustomed enough to collars and ties to know what his size was. "But I do think this is a case that Congressman Barkham ought to take an interest in."

"I don't think he will," said the young man, but respectfully: for him, Craig Spitts at thirty-two was an honored veteran, one of the company of saints who had marched on the Pentagon and gathered at the fountain to shout down the bayonets in Chicago. The curly sandy hair receding from Craig's widow's peak he saw as a mark of honorable age. "And you know it's not at all what I'm in New York for; I'm supposed to be running down leads on wiretaps for the FBI hearings. But tell me about it." He flicked out a watch from behind the white cuff. "Fast," he added. "We've got three or four live ones to interview this morning." It was the contemporary royal—the staff assistant's—"we."

Craig looked out the dirty windows of the third-floor offices of the Lawyers' Cooperative, over the early-morning bustle of Union Square. "Let me call in Oscar Riskovsky," he said. "I think that'll speed things up."

"Sure, go ahead."

Craig pushed the button on the telephone and told his secretary. He began the presentation without waiting. "This is a case," he said, "of a young man who was moving from being a gang leader to being a real community leader—he organized the boycott of the Head Start program in that district because the books didn't have enough pictures of black kids. He was *disciplined;* that's what made people think of him as dangerous. No question in my mind but that the cops wanted to get him. I won't deny that there were some people in the neighborhood who didn't like him either. But that doesn't excuse what happened at the trial."

A large shadow appeared on the ground-glass door, which opened, and a heavy young man in a thick tweed jacket almost shambled in—awkwardly of necessity, for he had only a left hand with which to open the door, and he sought to keep the left side of his face toward others in a room. Shattered by a bomb explosion, his right arm had been amputated above the elbow, and six operations by plastic surgeons had not quite restored the jaw and cheekbones on the right side of his face. His brown hair stood up in a wild brush; the gray jacket was rumpled and gave an impression of not being entirely clean; the thin, pale lips seemed not to have smiled in a long time. Oscar was a Vietnam veteran, but his injuries had occurred closer to home, when a bomb that was being armed exploded among a group of radicals, killing two of them, in the basement of an East Village tenement. The government had put him back together in a V.A. hospital; a U.S. attorney had urged that his injuries were punishment enough for his involvement with the bomb; and the Lawyers' Cooperative, whose members knew him, hired him as a paralegal.

"I don't think you two know each other," said Craig. "Adrian Francis, Oscar Riskovsky."

Adrian stuck out his right hand, and was disconcerted when Oscar took it with his left in a practiced backward grip. Then Oscar sat in the high-backed chair across the desk.

"How far have you got?" His voice, the resonance affected by the plastic surgery on his jaw, was a kind of flat growl.

"We just started."

"I've spoken to four of the jurors," Oscar said, looking away from both men, "and I *know* they put a lot of weight on that crazy identification by the cabdriver. All four of them knew from the newspapers that the defendant had been involved in that firebombing at Brooklyn College during the school strike, when he was in junior high. If you'll talk with them—I've got the phone numbers—you'll find that's why they thought he was the kind of kid who would throw down on a druggist."

"Unless you've got some FBI misconduct in the case," Adrian said, frowning, "I don't see why the congressman should get involved—at least right now."

"I never told you this was an FBI matter," Spitts said, holding up a left hand to ward off the accusation. "This is a human rights matter. The congressman's on the Judiciary Committee."

"Damned Tom of a black judge," Oscar grumbled, "won't give bail on appeal."

"A *fifteen-year* sentence," Craig said, "for a first adult offense. Unheard of."

"Suppose he's guilty," Adrian said, still frowning. "Of murder."

"They've got to prove that in a fair trial," Craig said. "I tell you, he didn't have a fair trial."

"I don't think the congressman should get involved," Adrian said again.

Craig thought, Give the young radical a taste of office, he becomes an expert in realpolitik. This Francis was the sort who got it all out of books. You learned about the woes of the downtrodden by reading advocacy for them they couldn't possibly read themselves. Spared that suffering, at least.

His own advantage, Craig sometimes thought, was that

he was not radical, not by temperament and certainly not by upbringing on an Illinois farm. What had "radicalized" him, in a brief rage that left residues, was the discovery that he was being spied on, that one member of his group planning a Hiroshima commemoration protest in Argonne Labs was reporting all the details back to the FBI. So the police were all ready to block them and shovel them contemptuously off as soon as they arrived.

The faith that drove Craig was, simply, a belief that he knew injustice when he saw it. Give him the facts of a case, with real people, and he knew which side he was on. It was the reason he had his job at the Cooperative. "We've got enough lawyers who want to use their clients to improve the state of the law," the head of the senior board had told him when he protested against promotion, arguing that he wanted to try cases, not run offices. "The idea behind this outfit was to use the law to improve the state of the clients." It was a grind. Half the time his staff were off on frolics of their own. Too often you had to rejoice in ambiguity; and now the birth of Craig's second child, his first son, was making him a warrior for the working day. He was worried that he didn't think about the office when he was home. Still, when the trumpet sounded, the war horse heard. "How can your congressman lose by it," Craig argued, "when all he's doing is fighting for the right to a fair trial? All we want now is continuance of bail, which is almost routine in this town—but they won't give it to this boy."

"Look, I'm not sure you understand," said Adrian, working his fingers together between his legs. He looked down on the threadbare Oriental rug hiding some of the gray wood floor, turned his right wrist and glanced at the watch. "For you guys, the Committee's FBI investigation is very popular and makes the congressman a hero. But he's got a working-class Catholic district with pretty old-fashioned views about the FBI. He can't give those fascists a chance to say he's trying to spring a black kid who shot a white grocer."

15

"That wasn't some innocent grocer," Oscar complained. "He had a numbers book, remember."

"Yeah, but it doesn't matter. Why don't you go get Congressman Fitch? His son is one of the lawyers out in that community, isn't he?"

Craig nodded. "Forgetting that the two of them aren't talking to each other," he said, "the fact that his son was one of the lawyers means Fitch can't touch it with a pole. All I want Congressman Barkham to do is to start the ball rolling, make the establishment worry a little that there's going to be trouble about denying this kid bail. If we get a little respectability, we can get one of the columnists in the *Times* to make a fuss. Political prisoners in America: this boy is one of them. It's such a damned heavy sentence, fifteen years for a kid with virtually no record."

"I gotta go," said Adrian, and rose from the couch. "Didn't I read somewhere after the trial that one of the deacons in a black church out there said he was praising God that this hoodlum was going to be sent away?"

"I told you," Craig said, "there are some people out in the community who don't like him."

"Wasn't there some stuff about cutting up a subway token seller with a broken Coke bottle?"

"That was a juvenile charge."

Adrian looked at his watch one last time. "It's all wrong for the congressman," he said authoritatively. "All wrong. Matter of fact, he feels he's got to go the other way today— we were talking about it late last night, after listening to the news. He's going to put out a statement calling on the President to put the FBI to work on this sniper business. The guy's going from state to state; that's the kind of thing the FBI ought to be used for, not all this snooping. Now is just not the time for the congressman to get himself involved with somebody like your kid. You're not even saying he's innocent."

"It's not a question I ask," said Craig.

Adrian came around the desk and shook hands, only with Craig; once, Oscar knew, was par for that course. "Well," Craig said, "I tried. I do thank you for coming."

"No," Adrian Francis said seriously. "You've been useful to us. I know you're still keeping an eye out for FBI stories. I'd like to help. So would the congressman. Not on this one. Nice to meet you, Mr. Riskovsky." And the door closed behind him.

"What do we do now?" said Oscar.

"Dunno," said Craig Spitts. "You've got that building violations case, the slumlord, to work on, don't you? I have a lunch today downtown with Joshua Fitch and the guys on Wall Street who mother that neighborhood law firm. We're hoping for some good advice. Maybe Fitch *can* get his father into it. I'll let you know what we decide."

Promptly at eight o'clock, the tie line to the main frames in Omaha had clicked on, and in the conference–display room in Cherry Hill, New Jersey, the talented peripherals went up, announcing their readiness to receive instructions in sentences that appeared instantaneously—no typing out letter by letter—on the green screens. "The facility," as the planning memo had called it, was really just two motel rooms knocked together—shag rug, striped drapes, tweed wallpaper, acoustic ceilings with overbright fluorescent fixtures sunk in them. At twenty-eight feet by twenty, the room offered plenty of space for the three astonishingly heavy black boxes that interpreted between the large computer out West and the terminals placed in three corners, each facing two rows of four imitation Breuer chairs, cane seat and back connecting bright round steel tubes.

Nicholas Gilette, broad-shouldered in a handsomely tailored dark-blue pin-stripe suit, sat at one of the terminals and in plain English typed out a request for instructions on testing designs for a heat-sensitive servo system to reduce fuel use in apartment house boilers. The screen filled instantly with commands, all of which could be met by punching in brief nonsense syllables specific to this program. That produced another set of instructions; then a screen of questions; then a schematic of a hugely complicated electrical circuit; finally a three-dimensional graph, which flicked on and off in alternation with instructions as to how it could be sliced to produce maxima and minima on changing assumptions. Under Gilette's practiced fingers, wedding band on the left hand, the thing was in work in less than five minutes.

There were three other men in the room, all from the company, everyone in white shirt and tie, Gilette himself sporting a richly brown thick mustache, and a heavy shock of the same color hair carefully combed to the right. He had startlingly blue eyes some saw as deep and some as flat; when he smiled, which he did often, almost in a nervous tic of response to conversation, he revealed gleamingly perfect teeth and no temperament at all. "Thank you all for being so prompt," he said. "We can check the others out later; let's get me some breakfast."

"Tough drive down, Nick?" said the area sales manager, a long-headed engineer with a skin color that matched Gilette's mustache, a triumph of the computer company's affirmative action program.

"Difficult and boring," Gilette said in a clipped New England voice. "I hate this night driving, and I don't like your Turnpike."

"You ought to take one of the company cars," the sales manager said. "They're more comfortable than that old Ford."

"It's my workhorse," Gilette said, smiling. "It would take me months to get another equipped just like it."

One of the technicians locked the door behind them and they walked off through the lobby toward the coffee shop. They passed the newsstand, and Gilette noted again that the Philadelphia paper had a headline about the "sniper murder in Hoboken." He had been depressed all morning. "Murder"

18

and "sniper"—they were the wrong words. He pushed the shock of hair back over his forehead, took a cigarette from the case he extracted from the inside breast pocket of his jacket, and lit it with a high flame from a gold butane lighter.

"Exactly who is coming to this demonstration today?" he asked as they sat down at a window table and accepted menus from the hostess.

"Oh, I think you'll have the whole top brass," said the area sales manager. "And the three product designers and their electronics chief. We'll probably have to move some of those chairs around as we go—I think it'll be more than eight. Conserv-Control isn't the only company in that business any more; they're going to have to improve their product—and they know it. They've been waiting for our Generation Five line almost as impatiently as we have."

"They've done real good with their Generation Threes," said one of the technicians.

"And there's some story around that we've made a big sale to ERDA, which would be awfully important to them. Is there anything to that one, Nick?"

"I can't tell you," Gilette said. "You did see the story about the deputy director we hired from ERDA last spring, didn't you?"

"Sure."

"I'll have to say that's his field of fire, not mine."

"They like our price, too," the area manager said, waving down a waitress. "The only thing that worries them is availabilities, deliveries. . . ."

"I've come with some promises on that," said Gilette. The waitress came and took orders for four large breakfasts.

"Tomorrow," said the area manager as she departed, "doesn't look as good as today. I thought we had a great package for a big savings bank, and they're big enough to need what we have, but they're that used to IBM and Burroughs. I think they're just going to send us a technical team, no purchasing authority at all, and we'll have to do the whole show all over again in a couple of months."

Gilette smiled. "Maybe not," he said. "I have a weekend's duck hunting with the chairman of that board down in the Chesapeake, starting day after tomorrow."

The area manager shook his head appreciatively. The other technician said, "Say, did you read the story in the paper about that girl who got shot last night?"

"I saw the headline."

"Awful business."

"Yes, it certainly is."

"One of the things that really got me was that stuff about the bullet that spreads out when it hits. Horrible thing."

Gilette smiled. "I must say I can't see what you find so horrible about a bullet. A bullet's a bullet."

"I mean, it seems like she didn't have a chance—makes it seem, I don't know, extra cruel, sort of. Do you use bullets like that when you go hunting?"

"It all depends on the size of the game. You do no creature a kindness to leave it badly wounded."

The technician made a face. "I guess I just don't understand."

"Perhaps you don't," said Gilette, and stopped smiling; and the area manager returned to the subject of computer peripherals.

II

Harry Johnson's Profitable Mistake

The usual piles of periodicals and clippings were waiting on Harry Johnson's otherwise clean desk when he let himself into his office at eight-fifteen. The *Worker,* the *Guardian,* Socialist Workers stuff, *New China Newsletter,* broadsheets from Iranian students, Palestinians, Portuguese anarchists, Puerto Rican nationalists, Chilean exiles, Castroites, anti-Castroites, Croatians, dissident Koreans, American Nazis. And on the other side were some dozens of newspaper clips from all over the country, from the service that underlined the names Harry followed to see where they were, what they were doing that got them in the papers.

Harry pulled a yellow legal pad out of the desk drawer and began racing through the periodicals stack, occasionally noting a name or a place on the pad: Tilly would make the file cards and update the file. He was still at it when she arrived at nine, called good morning as she hung up her coat and shook her red hair from under her hat. She went off immediately for morning ablutions, and on her return came straight into his office. A plain girl with a good figure and a lonely life; serious and capable. Two years of college; quit and answered the ad that got her the FBI job to pay the bills while her new husband went through medical school; and soon after he got his practice established, of course, he divorced her. It happened the year after Harry's divorce, and for one rather uncomfortable month they had eyed each other with some surmise, both relieved when the time passed and nothing happened. She had been Harry's secretary for thirteen years, knew exactly what she had to know, and no bit of information more.

"Anything to do?"

"Not yet. I've got another half hour or so with this stuff. Heavy day." The wastebasket was filling up.

"Remember, you have that meeting at the UN at ten-thirty—you made the date last week. Jerry called yesterday, very insistent that you get there—the Croatian business. He's got the Yugoslav mission, the UN, the State Department, the New York committee, everybody on his neck. And you have that monthly Wednesday lunch of yours today."

"I remember," said Harry, and went back to his reading. He got only ten minutes of it before the phone rang. He heard a note of surprise in Tilly's "Yes, sir"; and she called through the open door, "It's Mr. Adams."

"Yes, Bill," Harry said into the phone.

"Can you step up for a few minutes? We have to talk."

Harry had very nearly but not quite cut out smoking. He took a stale, opened pack of cigarettes out of the desk, felt in his pocket for matches, and with a nod to Tilly left for the elevators. Adams had made no changes in the square director's office: same big mahogany desk with rounded edges, the fluorescent reading lamp implanted at its back and pencils on the tray that formed the base of the lamp, the director's chair flanked by flags on their heavy stands. Government-issue green leather couches on two walls, government-issue coffee table before one of them. Picture of the President on the wall beside the windows. Over the couches, more personal pictures, with Hoover, with Senator Dirksen, with Bobby Kennedy. There had been one with John Mitchell, but that was gone, and in its place was a staff photo of Adams with the Secret Service people who'd been guarding Wallace when he was shot. Adams waved Harry to the chair beside the desk. All business.

"I had a call from Washington waiting when I came in. The President's decided we can take jurisdiction in those sniper murders; and the Director wants you to manage our end of it."

Harry and Adams had worked together when they were both cubs in the 1950s. He said nothing and waited for the explanation.

"You've read the stories in the papers?" Adams said.

"Sure."

"You tell me."

"The President and the Director both think it's good publicity for the Bureau, and—"

"Cut it out, Harry. We're both too busy for this."

"All right," Harry said. He put an arm on the desk and leaned over it, looking past Adams through the window. "He's a hell of a shot, whoever he is. You and I couldn't do tricks like that, no way, and as agents go we're pretty good. So whom has the United States government trained to shoot that well? Answer: a certain number of people who work for the Company. So which of our agents is coziest with those boys, CIA telephone code number, knows his way around Langley? Johnson."

"Very good, Harry."

Johnson looked at Adams, thought, The man's had this job only about eight months; he's put on weight, puffy cheeks, his eyes are tired, he's less careful about lacquering the long, thin hair over the bald spot. Not the best time ever to move into a supergrade in the Bureau. But nothing's happened to that great, plummy leader's voice of his; you could cast him for a politician in a movie, any time. "You want me to get them thinking that maybe it's one of their people," Johnson said, "and see what happens. Suppose it is?"

"Becomes their problem," Adams said.

"And if it isn't? They can find that out pretty fast."

"Well, I want you to double-check. Can you get identities from them?"

"Maybe."

"Do that. But I want you to stay with this case to the end. We're going to have a shake-up in counterintelligence, no doubt about it; that House committee wants blood, and you've been there too long. Twenty-some years, isn't it? I know you've been careful, but a man gets exposed."

Johnson used the cigarette he had brought for the purpose, inhaled slowly, exhaled slowly. Harsh, it was. "I suppose that becomes a policy decision," he said. "You do understand," he added, choosing his words and his grounds, "that there's a number of the people I run whom I can't possibly turn over to somebody else."

Adams made impatient yet vague motions with his hands. "You've got seven, eight years under the new retirement policy," he said. "I don't want you to spend them throwing back grenades. A lot of these agents you run are going to get severed whether you like it or not. You're going to have to defend operatives whose names we don't know—even you can't do that. Your people, most of them, are in place to report on groups, and the A.G. has ordered no more informers about groups. Even illegal groups are legal. Only individuals can be illegal. Don't argue with me—all that's for later anyway. For now, you'll just carry the extra load."

Adams exploded with something like a chuckle. "Old buddy," he said. "You may find it entertaining, working with just plain cops again after all these years. There's a meeting at police headquarters at two o'clock today—they'll have the lab tests on that girl by then—and I've already told them you're coming. There'll be a bunch of people there from Jersey, Connecticut and Pennsylvania, too. They want guidance, I think, so you should have your process started and you should be ready to chair the meeting, more or less. Anything I can do for you?"

"Computer time. Big memory."

"First priority, all you want."

"Are we going to use police people only?"

"No, you'll have some of ours. We'll worry about that when you get back this afternoon."

"My own choices?"

"Not really; most of what you'll need are criminal division people, and you don't even know who half of them are. I have a hunch you'll want to do a lot of it alone. You always did."

Budgetary considerations, Harry thought, are never far from the suface of the mind of the man in charge. "What about my UN meeting today?"

"Pass. Just tell Jerry what he ought to say. Get out of here, Harry. Get to work." Adams pushed a button on his desk; the buzzer sounded faintly outside, and presently his executive assistant was in the doorway, obsequiously taking orders.

As Harry returned to his office, Tilly looked up questioningly, and he nodded. "Get Jerry for me," he said, "and then make me a reservation on the secure line to Langley. I'll go down to the communications room to make the call in fifteen minutes. Top priority."

Gerald Hanford was a studious, not very inquisitive bespectacled young Foreign Service officer, sent by the State Department to the FBI to help out on matters involving foreign diplomats; he was the sixth man Harry had supervised in that slot—the first black, but otherwise the same man. All of them were good at accepting supervision—wanted it, in fact. With Jerry, there was no reason not to be brusque, and Harry was:

"You're going to have to handle it youself, Yugoslav ambassador or no Yugoslav ambassador. You can tell them I've been assigned to work on that sniper case; even the Jugs will think that's important enough. All I could say to them if I were there is that we know *who* these Croatians are, we know *where* they are and we know *when* they meet with strangers. There aren't many strangers; if there were, we would know what they were saying, too. This is a very small crowd. They all—repeat: all—knew each other in the old country, and they don't recruit. You can't turn anyone inside. We've been watching them long enough so I think I know where they would stash any heavy weapons, if they got them. The Jugs have their own secret service working on it here— so many of them that they're treading on each other's toes. If in fact they want to work with us, that can be arranged— but not, obviously, in a meeting with Waldheim's people and the goody-goods of the liaison office and God knows who else. You can slip a word in their ear, and we'll see what happens."

The CIA call was more complicated. The line was open to Langley when he arrived at the communications center, but it took almost fifteen minutes to get through after he gave the code number to the operator on the other end. From the sounds on the wire he gathered his contact was not in the country, and was being in effect paged to a phone, probably at an embassy. There was the usual irritation of phase delay from satellite communications, faintly aggravated by the encoding step, and the voice at the other end lacked character. It said, "I suppose this is urgent."

"Yes, it's urgent. Look, Phil, I'm going to start with my maximum demand, and don't hang up, but there's a limit to how far down I can negotiate it. What I want is a list of the names of the marksmen you've trained over the years, and what they're doing now."

Harry waited until he could be sure that the silence was not just a matter of satellite distance, then said, "Have you been near enough to New York to hear about our sniper?"

"Yes, there was something about it on our news wire."

"We had another one last night that was virtually a trick shot, like something in a circus. You know, if you've got a rogue elephant on that squad, he's a menace to *you.*"

"Can't be," said the voice.

Now it was Harry's turn to wait.

"Well, of course, it *can* be, but it isn't," the voice said.

It made no sense to argue. Harry said, "I'm still here."

"Shit," said the voice. Then, "Harry, I can't strip these guys for you. That House committee's all over you. In a way, it would be like turning them over to the KGB. These guys are agents. You don't need to know who they are, you don't really want to know who they are."

"We're in the same business," Harry said mildly. "We're protecting the same public." Pause. "I can't just accept your verbal assurance, from God knows where, that none of your people has gone off the reservation. Before I'm done, I'm going to have a lot of names in the machine; there's no need to tag yours specially." Pause again. "We're in it at the President's personal request."

"For argument's sake, say it *is* one of ours. What would you want me to do?"

"Just give me the names. I don't want any active service people who weren't in the New York area often between Labor Day and now, but I do want those, plus all the people in that corps you've terminated by consent. What are we talking about? Five guys? Six?"

"More."

"You're kidding."

"No. This is talent we have a bank of, just in case. People

to ride shotgun on the rooftops when the President visits abroad, that sort of thing. Special arrangements with the host government. Sometimes even the Secret Service doesn't know who they are. You really think it's one of ours?"

"You know the old gag," Harry said. "I don't think— we've got machines for that."

"I can't let you cross-ruff my people in your machines," the voice said. Then, "There's a way, I guess. Here's what I'll do. Active people—I'll get the logs and look at them myself. That's a waste of time, but I'll do it. There's just a ghost of a chance that somebody normally in Buenos Aires or Addis Ababa got assigned to the UN for the session. If he's been in Addis Ababa, target practice on people wouldn't even strike him as strange. If that's what's happened—it isn't, but we're playing on your field—you'll hear no more about a sniper. I assume that's satisfactory?"

"As far as it goes."

"Veterans of the service—I'll get you the names of anyone in the New York area, on your promise to hand-process your-self, and to let me know what you find before you move."

"New York, New England, New Jersey, Pennsylvania."

"Okay."

"How about the ones you don't know where they are?"

"*Can't,* Harry."

"At least the psychological-profile people."

"For chrissake!"

Harry relaxed. "You haven't faced it, Phil," he said. "These fellows do get caught, you know. I'm not sure why, but they do. Suppose you don't know he's the guy, and we don't know he used to be one of yours. I need not remind you, I'm sure, of the degrees of sensitivity here. Fifteen minutes after the cops put their hands on this man, if we don't know about him, there will be no way, but I mean *no way,* to choke this story and any details associated with it. Whether you like it or not, you've got to trust me to protect your interests."

"I'm still listening," said the voice.

"Remember," Harry added, now enjoying himself, "the President wants it."

"Cocksucker."

"The President?" Harry said, looking up at the ceiling.

"When do you want it?"

"Today."

"Tomorrow," the voice said. "Afternoon. And careful with the data bank."

"On Mr. Hoover's grave," Harry said.

"An oath of mickle might," said the voice. "You'll get a call tomorrow at four o'clock, okay? On this line. It will be a woman calling, and she will speak only to you. Nobody else. The code word will be your number."

"Thank you kindly, Phil. Is there anything I can do for you at this end?"

"Yes. Catch some nice civilian sniper. How's your operation holding up under the new management?"

"Can't complain."

"Surprising."

"My nose is clean, hard and cold," Harry said. "I may not like the rules, but they abide. They look in those files, they find I gather intelligence. How I do it is all under my hat, my agents are mine, exclusive. The checks are to cash. No black-bag jobs, no unauthorized wiretaps; I run what they call a people business. And I'm a bureaucrat, Phil; bureaucrats survive."

"Well, we owed you one," said the voice.

"You still owe me," Harry said. "This one is a mutual-benefit job."

"Always nice to talk to you, Harry."

"Same here." And the line went dead. Harry nodded to the woman who was the guardian of the secure lines, signed out, and returned quickly to his office; he had a number of other phone calls to make. Tilly had coffee waiting for him. He made his phone calls.

The favor the CIA owed Harry went back to the Whitmont kidnapping. Harry had been called into Whitmont for counterintelligence reasons, because the kidnappers were self-advertised as leftist terrorists.

Young Whitmont had been living in a student commune, infuriating his father and amusing himself—Harry thought no more than that—by getting arrested in various demonstrations. The kidnapping was on all counts a peculiar business, somehow less grim than other such. The first indication of the crime had been the discovery of Whitmont's car, pulled into a dirt road before a farmer's gate, abandoned where it would quickly be found. Three days later there began a series of notes, always in Spanish. They arrived every other day, addressed to different employees of the company, making references to ingenious savageries that could be committed on a helpless captive, several of them including brief pathetic appeals in English, undoubtedly in Tony Whitmont's handwriting. But they were *taunting* notes, not in Harry's view truly menacing: "non-negotiable demands" for "agreement in principle" on a $750,000 ransom, after which instructions would follow. Each letter was mailed from a different country in or around the Caribbean; the police of seven countries were guarding airports; coast guards were boarding fishing boats to look for a captive gringo, and every other day the laughing letters came.

First attention was given, of course, to the various Latin liberation groups, but Harry's informants insisted nobody in those groups knew anything about Whitmont: the rumors current among the student groups said that the abduction had been planned abroad by former employees of Monteblanco. Nevertheless, Harry had gone around and interviewed personally half a dozen Latin students holding office in radical and Puerto Rican nationalist groups, just to look at how they reacted to a whiff of verbal grapeshot about the laws relating to kidnapping in the United States.

Nobody had become vituperative in response except Carla

Hunez. Harry watched her stomp about the bare little office the Vassar dean had put at his disposal, and thought the rising color of her anger was especially beautiful. He had seen pictures of her, but the actual presence knocked him dead—blouse tight on the ripe bosom, fitted pants, black hair in ringlets framing the rounded face of a classic Spanish beauty. She was a model looking for someone to paint her; but all those painters were dead. By herself, Harry thought, she denied Koestler's crack that you could tell what was wrong with left-wing movements by the appearance of their women.

Harry put through several specific queries about her, and from an informant at Bard College learned that there was a possible relationship between Carla Hunez and Tony Whitmont. They had met, it seemed, the previous spring, during a protest in New York relating to the American bomber that had crashed in the sea off Spain armed with nuclear weapons. Tony, who was fluent in Spanish—he had an Argentine mother, a father whose business was heavily Latin American—hung out with Latin groups. He had driven Carla back to Vassar after that meeting, and they'd been seen sitting next to each other at other conclaves, in private conversation. He was not important enough to notice from a movement point of view, but she was. Quite separately, there was some feeling among the informants that Carla, who was known for "bourgeois scruples" assorting oddly with her looks and costumes, had found herself a man. But she seemed so totally unconcerned about the kidnapping—almost supportive of it—that the story was scotched.

Harry saw another possibility, and went after further information about Carla. She was the daughter of a Puerto Rican grocer well established (two storefronts punched together) on Broadway in the part of uptown Manhattan called San Juan Hill; and except for eighteen months on a cousin's farm in Puerto Rico when the 1959–60 recession caught the family short, she had been brought up in an apartment behind

31

the store. A golden girl: pretty, very bright (access to school records was duck soup), a little vain, a little spoiled, a little greedy. She passed the entrance examination for the all-girls Hunter High School well ahead of any other Puerto Rican candidate of her year; won honor grades in history and Spanish, and in her last two years, in English, too; served as president of the Hispanic Society and held office in student government. Her English was just barely touched with an accent—a little refined for a New Yorker, as though she was imitating television announcers. Successfully.

Radicalism beyond the normal level of her high school (where several teachers, as Harry knew, were refugees from a purge of Stalinists at Bronx Science) had come to Carla only after her first year at Vassar, when she spent the summer traveling about Latin America as a walking delegate from New York State Hispanic Students, funded by the Ford Foundation. On her return for the fall term, she had made Puerto Rican independence one of the most fashionable causes on the Vassar campus, and had become a mutterer of demands about justice for urban rioters, power to the people, grape boycotts, community control, no exams for Third World students, and the like. The past summer, Harry learned with interest, Carla had made another trip through the Caribbean, this time without foundation support, for both publicized and unpublicized meetings with youth groups. He put through a check of airline manifests, and found that she had been in all the cities from which the letters demanding ransom for Tony Whitmont had recently been sent.

More. Father had died of a stroke soon after Carla went to college; mother now ran the store, working sixteen hours a day, no *comadres,* a cousin helping out, mostly on weekends, for bad wages. Older brother, Pedro, had attended Aviation High School but done only so-so. Eastern Airlines had hired him anyway, but had fairly quickly moved him from maintenance to a baggage-handling section of the training program; he was employed as a foreman in that section in the Puerto

Rican terminal. With the widow living alone in the apartment behind the grocery, there would be plenty of room to keep a stranger. A willing "kidnap victim" could be safely hidden there for quite a while.

At one of the meetings of the team on the case, the FBI contact with the Whitmont family told Harry that reply messages were being sent to the kidnappers via code announcements on the most popular Puerto Rican evening radio news show. Could this show be heard in New York? Harry inquired. You bet it could—it was rebroadcast every night. Were the letters specific responses to the replies? It was a new question; the agent thought and said, More or less— really, they were all sort of general and incoherent. Interesting, Harry said, and suggested that one letter from the Caribbean not be answered at all, to see what would happen. But the family was not up to playing that game.

It was now more than two weeks since the kidnapping, and some climax seemed close at hand: old man Whitmont was prepared to pay. Harry manipulated a wiretap request before a judge with Vassar connections who was known to be outraged about campus disruptions and their control, got the tap on the Hunez grocery, and assigned a pair of Spanish-speaking technicians to man it on a twenty-four-hour-a-day basis. Early in the morning of the second day the tap was in, Harry had an urgent call from CIA—from Phil. "We're taking that tap off the Hunez phone," said the voice. "Lay off the girl. She's one of ours."

"And what do you know about her?" Harry asked, playing for time.

"Enough," said the CIA man. "One of our women in Venezuela turned her two years ago, and she's been very useful to the ARA desk. She was a courier for us last summer, and she knows half the agents we have south of the Gulf. She's doing it one hundred percent for the money—her attitude was, Ask what your country will pay for you. I think it had something to do with horses. She'd learned to ride in Puerto Rico as a little girl, our woman took her out riding and learned she needed money if she was to do any horseback time at Vassar. There's always a danger when you use people like that; we have to cut our losses now. I don't want her talking to no lawyers, and we can't lay a glove on her."

"I have no authority to stop this investigation," Harry said. "You'd better have your boss talk to my boss."

"No," said Phil. "Then you get memos, things in files, telephone logs. This one is between the two of us."

Almost immediately thereafter, Harry got a call from the morning man on the tap: it had disconnected; somehow the wires seemed to have been switched. But just before it went dead, a man had called the apartment and said, "I'm here"; and Carla, who was supposed to be in Poughkeepsie, had said, "Good." No more.

Harry told his agent to pack up the tap, bring the recordings to his office, leave them with Tilly, and put himself back in the pool for assignment. He checked in with the team and found not to his surprise—they were reluctant to tell him, but couldn't avoid it—that the Whitmonts had caved in. The deal had been made. There had been a daybreak telephone call, probably from Puerto Rico, to Julius Whitmont's rabbi, giving him a message to deliver in person. The message told the Whitmonts to pack the money in a certain kind of suitcase they would buy at a store near the Monteblanco office, to go at eleven o'clock that morning to a certain telephone booth at Kennedy Airport, and await a call with further instructions. The caller had specified the employee of Monteblanco who was to carry out the mission—alone. It was an old, reliable, but somewhat dim-witted messenger. He was to have enough money in his pockets to buy a ticket anywhere in the Caribbean. The family would not tell the Bureau which terminal at Kennedy was involved, let alone which phone booth, and the decision had been made, reluctantly, not to track the old man but to pick up the trail at whatever airport the bag was off-loaded.

Harry called the motor pool and ordered a car. From his attaché case he took the minirecorder, put it in his pants pocket, and wired the miniature mike to his belt buckle. On consideration he took the gun, too, strapping it under his left armpit. He walked to the garage, took the car and drove to the grocery store on San Juan Hill. He circled the block, noting two shabbily dressed men sitting in a parked car across from the apartment house entrance to the corner building that housed the grocery store. Blended right in, they did.

Harry parked about a block away, and briskly walked to the store, through the front door, through an underlit corridor between shelves of boxes, straight through the curtain at the rear, ignoring a shouted expletive from the grayhead behind the counter in front of the windows. Beyond the curtain Harry was in a kitchen; from under the door to his right came a peculiar purple light. He opened the door, the shouting persisting behind him, and found himself in a small living room on an air shaft, stuffed furniture in floral patterns crowding the Oriental-type rug, niche with saint and candle in one wall, glass-fronted bookcase with dishes and silver ornaments—and Tony Whitmont, stripped to the pudgy waist, satisfyingly tan from the belt up, baking under a huge standing sun lamp. The door at the opposite side of the room opened, and Carla Hunez was framed in it, sweater and skirt and flat shoes: "*Quién es?*"

"Harry Johnson. We met at Vassar."

"Oh, God," she said, and kicked furiously at the end of the little Persian rug. "We don't have *time* for you; I have telephone calls to make."

The older woman from behind the counter was in the kitchen now, shouting in Spanish but keeping one anxious eye back on her store. "Tell your mother to go away," Harry said, and Carla did. Whitmont had said nothing. Now he shook himself and said, "You're the FBI? FBI . . . Look, this is really just a family affair."

"If it was just a family affair, you'd be on your way to

the slammer, right now," Harry said. "Turn off that damned sun lamp; it's too hot in here. We're going to have a little talk, and you're going to tell me what you're up to."

Whitmont turned off the lamp and moved it to a corner. He put on a T-shirt that had been draped over the arm of the couch and tucked it in his trousers. He and Carla sat side by side. Invisibly activating the tape recorder, Harry sat in an armchair across the small room; when both men stretched, their feet almost touched.

Carla said, "You *can't* arrest me, you know. I'm—"

"I can do anything I want to do. One of you tell me the story." They looked at each other, and it was Whitmont who talked.

They were in love, he said, putting first things first; they were going to get married. He'd been seeing a priest sort of behind everybody's back in New Haven, because Carla couldn't do that to her widowed mother, marry somebody who wasn't Catholic. All he had to live on that he really owned himself was two thousand dollars a year from a trust fund he couldn't touch, and his father was vicious to him anyway, would declare him dead if he married someone like Carla. His mother was maybe worse: German-Jewish from Buenos Aires, with a thing about Puerto Ricans.

Carla took over, and told Harry what he had to know. The money, in out-of-sequence twenty- and fifty-dollar bills, was to be packed in a red plastic three-suiter, the handles tied with a wire sealed in lead. The messenger was waiting in the Pan Am building. When they called, they would tell him to go to the Eastern Airlines building, purchase a ticket for Santo Domingo and check the bag through. Her brother had worked in the Eastern terminal and knew all the procedures. He had taken the dawn flight up from Puerto Rico on his day off, carrying a new bag identical to the one that would be checked through, and he had tagged it already for Santo Domingo. He was right now horsing around with old friends in the baggage assembly area. It would be easy for him to switch the bags.

Pedro would then take a taxi here with the money, take another taxi back to the airport and be home tonight. Carla was confident that the family would conceal from the authorities for twenty-four hours, or until Tony showed up, all information about what the messenger did; and even if the police did not honor the family's request to leave the messenger unobserved, the worst that would happen would be a stakeout in Santo Domingo over a suitcase full of newspapers.

All this was to be put in work at noon with the call to the phone booth in the Pan Am terminal. The plane on which the bag supposedly would travel left at twelve-twenty. There was a flight arriving from Puerto Rico at nine o'clock that night. Whitmont would be on that—or, rather, would be perceived to have been on it when he appeared, dazed and apparently frightened, and told a security guard who he was. She had arranged to borrow a car from a cousin at eight, and would drive Tony there herself, leaving him off in the mess of traffic on the arrival level of the terminal. There would be a lot of other people with tans like Whitmont's fresh off the jet.

"Very good," said Harry. "But there won't be anybody on the passenger list who was Tony Whitmont."

"Yes, there will be," she said. Her brother had bought a ticket in the name of A. Weissberg, and had sold it for half price to a Cuban refugee friend eager to come to New York, explaining that if it was ever discovered that he had abused his airline employee's right to buy tickets cheap, he would lose his job. The Cuban didn't know enough to read the status of what was in fact a full-fare ticket, or to query how Pedro got reduced-price tickets in other people's names. He could be trusted to disappear instantly on arrival in New York.

Harry regarded her with sincere admiration. "How long did it take you to work this out?"

"We made our plan in July, because I had to leave the letters with the people in August, when I was traveling."

"How could you be sure," Harry asked, "that they would mail those letters precisely on the days you told them?"

Carla eyed him for a moment. "You know who these people are. They are very meticulous. I am, too. I must make the telephone call."

The hands on the electric clock met at twelve, and Carla dialed. When the call was live, she spoke in a husky voice with a stage Spanish accent, and conveyed the instructions. As she hung up, she fell back onto the couch with her eyes closed. She was, Harry thought, almost human.

He turned off the recorder in his pocket. "I have it all on tape," he said.

Carla sat bolt upright, eyes wide. *"No!"* she said. "This is a very serious thing we are doing."

"We'll pay you," said Whitmont.

"Bribing an agent, are you?" But Harry's amusement faded almost as the words were spoken. He had been too single-minded—mission-oriented, as his CIA friends would have it—perhaps too pleased with the cleverness that had led him to this crowded little room, too relieved to find so much amiability at the heart of the matter. The call from Langley, the rumpled agents in the car outside, Carla's revelations that CIA contacts in the Caribbean had been mailing the letters—all this he had unwisely brushed aside, because he was "solving" a kidnapping.

What you do when a case is "solved" is all in the rule-book: the Miranda rights, the securing of premises and perpe-trators, the transfer of power to the prosecutor. For this situa-tion, there was no rulebook; what should be done here and now was by no means clear. Harry sought to maintain the tone. "You know," he said, "agents can't acquire large sums just like that. Nobody believes they have rich uncles. No place to hide; it gets discovered."

"I can—we can—find a way that will work," Carla said earnestly, and began to prowl the corridor between the couch and the door, Whitmont's eyes hungrily upon her. Figuratively, a lot of eyes were on her. Langley was watching, no doubt unhappily, but this was far from the first time an agent had cashed in a relationship. Arrested, on view, this hard, beautiful girl would have stories to tell; but if anything awful happened to her, some people in Latin America would be even more unhappy than they were scared. A decision had been made, by some committee, that Carla Hunez was to get away with it—at least for now, quite possibly forever— the capacity to swallow an unpublicized defeat being a prime quality of a well-adjusted spy system. Harry knew.

But the men in the car were not protecting Carla Hunez; they were protecting their employers. Exactly what they would do if he put this pair in cuffs and walked out with them was something Harry could not know for sure, but he had no doubt it was on their agenda. The chances were that their mission was to prevent Carla's arrest by any means. If Harry tried to call the Bureau or the police, the telephone would go dead.

All this passed through Harry's mind as a spasm of self-disgust for the failure to think sooner; the physical expression was a shake of the head, which Carla necessarily misinterpreted.

"I have a way," she said quickly. "No big sums. Every month we give you—we give you one thousand dollars. You keep your tape, you are protected."

"How would you do that?" Harry inquired, still abstracted. He did not listen seriously as the two of them, growing more animated and cheerful, threw ideas at each other. They obviously liked this sort of game; that was what had got everyone into this mess. But they were nervous, too, and Harry, thinking of what they still had to do that evening to carry out their plan, grew nervous for them. What was animating them now, clearly, was the thought of the safe harbor that would be theirs if they had an FBI agent as coconspirator. A final understanding thudded to the bottom of Harry's thoughts: just as he could not safely leave the building without them, he could not safely leave alone. He was condemned to be a coconspirator, to remain in this room through the afternoon and into the evening—to watch the money being delivered; and to take some of it.

"In this envelope, Your Honor, I have . . ."

"Marked as state's exhibit Letter E . . ."

Oh, shit, it would never come to that. And—suddenly he seemed to go over the hill, and see the sweep of peaceful terrain beyond—it would be great to have that money. The morality issue defined itself. To profit by status or skills as an agent was despicable; to profit by failure or stupidity was simply a windfall gain. One agency of the government compelled him to accept money for his inability to carry out his duties to another; so much the worse, so much the better. Every year he fought for more money in the cash fund, to be dripped out under vague headings of Agents' Compensation, and envied CIA for the torrent of money that ran unexamined through their hands. Now this entirely discretionary supplement, the Whitmont Fund, had been dropped in his lap, in a sense by the government itself, without appropriation, without the GAO. Liberated by a committee of colleagues, he could join the Now Generation, the community of those who looked at the world and said, "Why not?" Harry broke out in a laugh, disconcerting both his companions.

"Sir?" said Tony Whitmont.

"No, no," Harry said. "I was thinking of something else. Just go over it again for me."

The plan they had concocted rested on a single, simple guiding principle: to minimize contact between them and Johnson. They would leave the money somewhere, and he would pick it up. Under the seat of a parked car. Couldn't be Whitmont's own car—make it a rented car. Once a month, Whitmont would rent a car in New Haven, drive it to New York, and leave it where Harry could pick it up. Better— he'd have a friend rent it, so his name wouldn't be on it. Then Harry could take the car to the rental company's garage in New York and just leave it there—nobody asks who you are when you return a rented car. How would Harry get the car? Carla knew about post office lockboxes. Give Whit- mont the combination; he'd leave the car in a parking lot ("Make it an indoor garage," Harry murmured, just editing); put the parking ticket in an envelope; and leave the envelope in a post office lockbox. The FBI had such boxes, no? Yes. Harry noted that he couldn't compromise the security of one of his regular boxes by giving a civilian the combination, but he could always acquire another box. . . . Twenty fifties. ("Fifty twenties," Harry interposed. "I don't carry fifties.")

And so the deal was made, Carla delighted and Whitmont perplexed. Harry remained with them through the afternoon and early evening—out in the store posing as a National Cash Register salesman during the twenty minutes Pedro was in the apartment delivering the suitcase and downing a celebratory brandy; otherwise in the room with them, serving as chaperone. He learned a good deal about them: how they had met, the fun they'd had together at meetings where every- one else was solemn; he was able to confirm or refute some information that had been passed his way on organizations to which they belonged. What he most wanted to know, the missing piece in this puzzle, had to be approached carefully and circuitously: what had Carla been doing in the Caribbean so important that CIA would make this investment in her safety? And quite unconsciously, about five in the afternoon, Carla dropped it: she had been carrying "medicines." Harry, who had heard about proposals to use poisons in "selected" CIA operations, wondered but did not seek to discover whether Carla had any idea what was in those bottles or whose lives had been put at risk by her deliveries; more than likely, she didn't. A little later, Whitmont, who had expected Harry to leave immediately on the payment of his first installment from the suitcase, found the piece of the puzzle that had confused him. "You're staying with us," he said, breaking into a conversation on the personalities of the Puerto Rican independence movement, "because you think it might be dangerous for *you* if you just walked out of here alone."

"Almost as dangerous," Harry agreed, "as walking out with my hands on the two of you."

"You'd have stayed here even if you hadn't taken our money."

"Yes."

At which Tony shrugged his shoulders and looked to Carla and shook his head; but she said, "I feel much more safe with Mr. Johnson on our side."

At the appointed time, Carla went out to pick up her cousin's car, came back, and with a peck on the cheek to her mother, suitcase in hand, departed in Tony's company through the night to complete the game. Harry, the first thousand making lumps in his pockets, left two minutes later, and went to where he had parked the pool car. He opened the door tentatively but quickly, jumping back as it swung, and took the government-issue flashlight out of the glove compartment. Then he opened the hood of the car and shone a light to where the lever from the gas pedal came through the bulkhead. He thought he saw a gleam of new copper, and closed the hood quickly. He called his wife from the corner candy store to apologize and tell her he was on his way, and took the subway to Penn Station. He expected to go back for the car the next day, by which time no doubt it would be disarmed, but he never had the chance. About ten o'clock that night, while Tony was sitting at police headquarters with his parents, saying he was awfully tired and would like to answer detailed questions tomorrow, Angel Ramirez, "male Hispanic age 18, two previous arrests for car theft, one for burglary," attempted to steal the FBI pool car, which blew up and burned, "resulting in the death of the said Ramirez."

Phil reached Harry at home very early the next morning, "to make sure you don't worry about that car."

"Would have been neat, wouldn't it?" Harry said. "FBI man cracks kidnapping, makes arrests, crazies blow up his car and kill all three of them. No clues, no questions. Real shocker for the newspapers."

"That's history now," Phil said expansively. "You shouldn't have gone up there, but no hard feelings."

"Gee, thanks."

"It wasn't anything personal," Phil said. "I guess now we do owe you one."

Over the years, some of the arrangements had changed. The Lincoln Tony had driven down from Harrison that morning, for example, was a leased car, and the name on the lease was that of a subsidiary of Monteblanco in the land development business in Connecticut; a corporate treasurer had signed the contract. He still left the parking receipt in a lockbox Harry rented under the name of a nonexistent mail order house, and Harry picked up the car at whatever garage Tony had—by prearrangement—left it in. Then he drove it down to a Hanover Square garage where Tony had a monthly contract, and simply left it there with a wave to the attendant, who doubtless considered him one of his customer's team of chauffeurs. This arrangement had been suggested by Harry himself, after his daughter got a job as a securities analyst in the trust department of a downtown bank and he could use the car as transportation to a lunch with her.

Harry's first thought that he had not really been bribed, not *personally,* had gone by the boards during the awful and expensive thirty months between his wife's announcement that she wanted a divorce and her blessed remarriage. Once breached, the barrier had leaked again, to provide Sue with a first-class piano when she came to live in New York, and to cover the early stages of the learning curve when the bridge game to which he devoted half his evenings after his divorce transformed itself into a backgammon game. Other expenditures from what Harry described even to himself as a "special discretionary fund" were tangentially related to the work for which, in theory, he had accepted the money—six months' receipts, for example, had been spent to provide Oscar Riskovsky with plastic surgery beyond what the V.A. would provide or Special Services would approve for the rehabilitation of an injured agent. Still, Harry could and did console himself with the fact that more than half of receipts that had now passed $100,000 had been spent to comfort and support agents for whom the official cash fund provided only a pittance. Even that much, of course, he couldn't prove.

Picking up the mail in the lockboxes at the fake-Colonial post office down the block from the office, Harry noted that three of this Wednesday's four letters were from agents who had been beneficiaries of the Whitmont Fund. And in the small box up top, used just once a month, there was of course the envelope with the parking chit. Harry dropped the letters in his attaché case—he would read them at home at night— put the chit in his breast pocket and walked the six blocks to the garage he had chosen the month before. When the Lincoln arrived up the ramp, he settled in the driver's seat, opened the glove compartment and immediately switched a thin envelope with next month's typed instructions for the thick envelope with the cash.

It was all routine now; heading down the East River Drive, he was thinking about his daughter and about the meeting after lunch at the police department, not at all about the man whose car he was driving. The only thing memorable, and that only later, was a sort of standard New York near accident, when a damned fool stepped off William Street without looking left. He threw the fellow the motorist's traditional look of hate for someone his car had almost killed, and went on, left the car, and met his daughter at the usual time in the usual place, on the stairs to Sweets, still the best fish restaurant in town though the fish market had moved.

She was almost twenty-six now, born while he was in Korea, but it was still a little shock to see again how *big* she was, his daughter the woman, a larger edition of her mother, slim, very blond, high cheekbones, slightly thrust jaw, thin nostrils; not really pretty, but elegant. She had a lot of his temperament: the love for puzzles, the coldness—he'd learned to face it—that put a clinical emphasis on relationship itself rather than on the participants in a relationship. She'd been a music major in college—about the last cheerful experience Harry and Alice had together was a trip to Albany to hear her play a piano recital—and Harry had never quite understood how she wound up in the stock market. Not that she didn't enjoy it: she obviously did, and this was one of the days when the moment they met she began telling him of a recent coup, spotting a takeover candidate and putting some accounts into a stock that jumped thirty percent in two days. He wondered if that meant there was a man around again and she was forestalling any conversation that might bring it out; once in an anguished moment she had told him how careful she had to be in everything she said, because he was always looking around and behind her words.

That had been the night of the day Oscar Riskovsky blew himself apart. Harry had met Riskovsky because of Sue, who brought him home to dinner from a party of her piano teacher's students—very daringly, because she was a high school girl and he was a college boy, and that wasn't done in Wantagh. Harry already knew something about Riskovsky, whose grandfather had been one of the founders of the Polish Communist Party, and whose father was still active as an organizer for the United Electrical Workers, the last of the Stalinist unions. He was a bear of a boy, with a mouth full of rhetoric but not a mean bone in his body; and Harry as an FBI man was only marginally more foreign to him than anyone in his parents' generation. Anyway, his father had said not to worry about it, the Riskovskys had nothing to hide from the government or anybody else.

Oscar's confidence in his inherited politics was such that he could argue cheerfully, and at the house he had at Harry without rancor, both of them enjoying themselves, both of them, Sue once said rather pompously, learning something. Then about two years later he'd come to the house during Sue's first Christmas vacation from college, and he had forced a foul-mouthed, screaming fight about Vietnam, which was the end of that. It was so loud, the neighbors knew; Sue's mother said never again.

Sue had been out on her own in New York only a little while when her father called and came over one evening to tell her about Oscar's "accident." He was haggard and there was something in his voice she had never heard before; and quite suddenly she knew, he never admitted it but she knew, that the whole fight had been staged, that Oscar had gone to work somehow for Harry, had left her in a sense—for there had been, as Harry guessed, a physical relationship in her last year in school—to do her father's work. The whole thing happened at the time of her mother's remarriage, to a much older man, and everything was wrong at once. She went to see Oscar in the hospital, where he was bandaged into an object and couldn't talk. The object had simply looked at her and shaken its head.

It was some months before she saw her father again, and oddly enough she found herself stronger where the scar tissue had healed. They began the custom of playing bridge together, which they had done occasionally while she was still in school, forging a new, rather more distant relationship based on skills. Increasingly, her skills were at the center of her life as they had always been at the center of his, and of course she had the piano, which meant that in one sense she was never unoccupied, never alone. Harry had no more music than the dog in the apartment down the hall. There was one brief period—not so brief, almost nine months, but it seemed brief in retrospect—when she was living with a man from a block-trading house whom she had met in the course of business, and saw her father only as part of a couple. But Sue was a little much for Jim; his separation had itself dissolved instead of ripening into a divorce. Some of the deals she made with him after they broke up, when the sound of her voice on the telephone unhinged him with an unnecessary guilt, had come close to costing him his job and had won her not just a bonus but a considerable promotion.

So lunch was full of her business, with a serious detour at the end to discuss a wiggle on the convention they were using to overcall weak two-bids. She never expected Harry to talk about his work, and while he could have talked about both the sniper matter and the Yugoslav flap, it never occurred to him. "If you never tell people anything when you can talk," he once explained to a young agent he was breaking in, "you avoid dangerous speculation when you can't." He was not a news-bearer. He asked Sue if she had seen any good movies lately. . . .

They ate well, because that night there wouldn't be time—Belgrave Club tournaments started early. Anyway, a head and stomach clear with a little hunger does better, and they could buy a sandwich and a cup of coffee at the table while they played. Sometimes opponents got a little rattled when Harry glanced at his hand, put it face down on the table, and played the cards from memory while eating. Sue had wondered whether he knew they got rattled, and upon consideration had decided that he did.

The Manhunts Begin

Craig Spitts came back from lunch and sat on a corner of Oscar Riskovsky's desk, swinging his booted feet. "I damned near got run over on William Street today," he said, "and you know who was driving the car? The thought narc—Harry Johnson. Looked like he wanted to kill me. What the hell do you think he was doing down there?"

Oscar grunted distaste, then said, "You know, he's got a daughter who works for one of the big Wall Street banks."

"I guess she must make a lot of money," Craig said. "He was driving the fanciest white Lincoln Continental you ever did see."

"You sure it was Johnson?" Oscar said, studying Spitts. "Doesn't sound right."

"Got the license plate." Craig reached into the breast pocket of his jacket and pulled out a crumpled piece of spiral-book notepaper. "Could you get hold of Motor Vehicles and check who owns that car? That thing must have cost half a year's salary, pretax, and I don't care how senior an agent he is."

"I don't think I see the point of it," Oscar said.

"If this guy's on the take," Craig said, and whistled, "Christ, what a story that would make! Just find out about that number."

"When do you want it?"

"You know me, Oscar. I'm always in a hurry when I'm curious. Let's see if we can't get the word phoned down to us by Friday."

"Okay, if that's what you want." Before Craig could leave, Oscar said, "And what happened after you almost got run over? Anything interesting at the meeting?"

Craig was looking toward the door. Without turning around, he said, "They've decided they've got to get him out." He turned and narrowed a gaze at Oscar. "Fitch says there's no chance the Appellate Division will set bail; he has a pipeline to one of the clerks. The courts are just railroading that boy. Fitch says that whole section of Brooklyn will go up in flames if nothing is done for him."

"So what can you do?"

"They're going to get him out. Federal courts have ordered touch contact with visitors at High Hills. Fitch is going to go up and visit him, lawyer-client to guarantee privacy, and he's going to bring a gun."

"Jesus!"

"It was a pretty excited meeting," said Craig. "I'm not on the spot in Brooklyn; I don't feel competent to judge."

"What are they going to do with him," Oscar inquired, "after they get him out?"

"Wise guy," Craig said. "They wouldn't want to tell me that, and I wouldn't want to ask. Frankly, I think we're out of the case."

"Exactly when does this stuff come down?" Oscar said.

"Saturday."

"Do you think it would do any good if I talked to them?"

"Nossir. In fact, don't you dare. They shouldn't know you know."

"I'm surprised," Oscar growled, shifting uncomfortably behind his desk, "that you're willing to have them know you know."

Craig spread his hands. "Couldn't help that."

"There'll be cops all over this office on Monday," said Oscar.

"That's among the reasons I'd like to be out of the case," said Craig. "See what you can get me on Johnson's car."

They'd run out of money while building the new police headquarters beside the Brooklyn Bridge; the outside was architected but on the inside the ceilings were a honeycomb of painted raw concrete with clumsily installed fluorescent fixtures, the floors were low-quality asphalt tile, the walls were coated steel partitions that communicated sound. Still, there was money for the important things, the dignified, public things. On announcing himself to the desk man, Harry acquired an escort of two officers who obsequiously took him to the elevator (where a prominent sign enjoined him not to smoke, carry a lighted cigarette, cigar or pipe or make any flame or spark without prior approval of the commissioner), and he was led to the second-floor official conference room, two stories high with a ribbing of decorative teak slats on all the walls from floor to ceiling.

Harry was announced like a royal duke arriving at a ball and ushered to a long table assembled from ten smaller tables, a forest of steel legs at the front of the big room. Twenty or so men and one woman were crowded around the table, three of the men and the woman in uniform, the rest in the sports jackets that are, for some reason, what detectives wear. One of the younger men was in a leisure suit; one of the older men wore a zippered Eisenhower jacket. The rank ranged from the chief of police in Concord, New Hampshire, to detectives second grade from Manhattan South. As Adams had predicted, Harry was ushered to the place of honor, which turned out to be at the foot rather than the head of the conference table, facing down its length to the easel and the screen for the overhead projector at the corner of the room. There was a pad of lined white paper and a ballpoint pen at each place; Harry pulled his toward him and wrote the date at the top of the page. The pen worked.

The regional head of the Law Enforcement Assistance Agency, a mustachioed man in a vested suit, offered a welcoming statement, explaining that he had been responsible for calling everyone together, and that the President himself had requested the Director of the FBI to make the Bureau's facilities and personnel available to local law enforcement authorities. In a case such as this one, new modalities of cooperation should be attempted, and he was pleased to report that the LEAA lawyers had confirmed his view that the expenditures associated with interdepartmental collaboration in this case could be met with a federal conference grant. Voucher forms, which should be filled in septuplicate, were available on the table to the right of the door. They should be sent—he hoped someone from each police department would make a note—to Section LEAA stroke four stroke eighty-one stroke ten thousand four hundred seventy-three at the address on the form, and they would be promptly processed. The meeting was being taped, and a transcript of the tape would be sent to each participating police department as soon as it could be completed, probably within the week. He hoped there was no objection to the presence of the LEAA photographer; copies of the pictures of their representatives at work would of course be sent to the departments for whatever use they might deem appropriate. He had suggested that each department present in no more than fifteen minutes the essential information about the murder in its jurisdiction and the progress of its investigation to date, and that the presentations be made in the order of the commission of the crimes. This proposal, he was pleased to say, had met with general approval. Each department would identify its delegates to this meeting as part of its presentation, to save time. He greatly regretted that he could not stay for the meeting, but he was delighted that the federal government would be represented by special agent Harry Johnson of the Federal Bureau of Investigation, who was seated at the end of the table, and would undertake, he hoped, whatever functions might have fallen to his lot as the convener of the meeting, if he had stayed. Harry nodded. He remembered it well from the military. By the numbers: Everybody squat—shee-eet!

Among them, the five statements took a little more than an hour and a half. Each department had what seemed to be a competent map of the scene for the easel and a statement from a coroner or medical examiner on the cause of death; all but Concord also had pictures of the scene and blowups of the recovered bullet for the overhead projector. The conclusions were straightforward: though rifling on these bullets was inconclusive because of the deformation of the soft lead, there could be no question whatever that all these murders were the work of one man. From the trajectory of the bullet in the victim, it was all but certain that the perpetrator had been on the same level, not upstairs in some building. In three of the five cases, one could not be certain which way the victim was facing when shot, so that the placement of the perpetrator on the map could be no more than guesswork—but on every map there was at least one spot on a city street other than the street where the victim was struck which was a possible location for the perpetrator. No shells had been found, arguing that the rifle had been fired from inside a vehicle. The most likely hypothesis was that the perpetrator worked from inside an automobile.

The police work that had been done was much the same in each place. Queries on the streets and broadcast appeals had failed, not surprisingly, to turn up anyone who had seen a rifle barrel poking out of a car. Door-to-door canvassing of the blocks immediately around the scene had produced no one who had seen anything unusual, though a few people reported, most likely truthfully, that they had heard something like a shot. It was conceivable that some method lay hidden in the madness—that down the road this killer had a target whom he would murder after having established the random M.O. of these sniper attacks, covering over by confusion what would otherwise be a track of suspicion to himself. Harry doubted it; so did everybody else. What was entirely sure was that no link other than snuffed humanity connected those already killed, and that—with the possible exception of the non-union Puerto Rican truckdriver in Manhattan—there was no discoverable motive for the murder of any of them. The weapon was the most popular hunting rifle in the United States, owned and loved by literally millions of men and boys; the ammunition was available at department stores.

Some mail had been received both at the police departments and by the newspapers, which had for a wonder turned over the documents without printing anything. A few of the letters had accused neighbors; these had been quickly followed up without result. Most were scrawls of the stop-me-before-I-kill-more variety, none credible. Several of these were signed, and they, too, were followed up, on the grounds that (as the Stamford police inspector put it) there are people who will do *anything* for publicity. Canvassing of the neighborhoods was continuing, even where the crimes went back to September, but it was all make-work. The Hoboken people, new to the investigation, grew increasingly discouraged. Coffee was served.

After the break, it became Harry's turn. "First of all," he said, "I want to tell you that we *are* going to break this thing. Maybe because he'll make a mistake, maybe because he'll be unlucky, more likely because we'll come to know enough. Every one of you is going to have to make a major commitment of resources, but we can be a bigger help than

I think you realize. Let me tell you first," he said, rising from his chair and walking the length of the room to the front of the table, "what I've already done this morning.

"The Defense Department has a tape of all winners of marksman medals first class, and we've ordered a duplicate updated for our computer center. We purchase the mailing lists of the National Rifle Association and all the gun-oriented magazines, and we have in our library a merged disk bank of that material. As we're dealing here with someone who is clearly an extraordinary shot, I've also requested our research staff to feed into the disks the names of all winners of statewide, intercollegiate and national trap and skeet competitions who live in the northeast zip code areas. That work is being done this afternoon, and we have priority for the first computer run immediately on its completion, perhaps as soon as tonight, though I expect tomorrow morning is more likely.

"We will then have a tape of all members of gun-oriented organizations and subscribers to gun-oriented publications who have won distinction of some sort for skill with a rifle. The list will have names and addresses. Though our sniper may conceivably be an immigrant or a recluse who doesn't read much, I feel reasonably confident that the name of the man we want will be on the tape. Together with perhaps ten thousand other names.

"By tomorrow night, we will be able to deliver to you a list of names and addresses in your jurisdictions, so you can do a rough quick look and see if any of them is meaningful to any of your people. Meanwhile, we shall be carrying these computer processes somewhat further."

Harry leaned forward, resting his hands on the conference table and studying the police officers briefly, in turn around the room. There was only one man he knew: Vinnie Palio, once a detective sergeant in security, recently promoted a New York City deputy inspector. The pause heightened concentration.

"As some of you do and some of you do not know," Harry said, straightening up, "the telephone company maintains a subscriber data bank that tells you somewhat more about any householder for whom you have an address. It is not normally available for law enforcement use, and indeed its existence may be denied. There are legitimate business reasons for its maintenance. We have been very careful about the cases in which we have sought access to it, with the result that it has not seemed worth the while of congressmen who know dimly about its existence to seek more precise information. *Pro bono publico* in this matter—in confidence, as I need not tell you—AT&T has agreed to do a computer run that will supply us with social security numbers for all the names on our tape. From these social security numbers we will be able to ascertain the places of employment of the people about whom we might wish to know more. That information should be available by the end of the day on Monday.

"All these crimes were committed on nights before workdays. Though it is of course possible from the location chart that the sniper is a man who simply seeks out random shooting spots, the span is more than five hours' steady driving, and I find it far more likely that we are dealing with someone whose job puts him on the road. This could be a truckdriver, a salesman, an accountant, a securities analyst—there are quite a number of possibilities. By the use of job description banks in the federal departments, it should be possible for our people by means of telephone queries to discover if any federal employee should be investigated. For the rest, I think we are talking about several hundred names, by no means an unmanageable total. These will be your responsibility, but even here—"

In Harry's jacket, his caller made a penetrating beep, stopped, beeped again. "Even here," he said, resuming, "there are some elements of technical assistance we may be able to supply. If you'll all excuse me for a moment, I have to make a telephone call. I'll come right back."

He looked questioningly at Inspector Palio, who guided him out to a deputy chief's office down the hall. The message for him was a code number and a telephone number. Harry pushed the buttons for a telephone booth in the Great Hall at Cooper Union, where Oscar Riskovsky was sitting with the receiver hung on his shoulder, pretending to conduct a conversation while a plastic shim held down the tongue of the phone rest. When the phone rang, he took out the shim. "Mr. Johnson," he said in his gravelly voice.

"Yes, Oscar."

"I'd better see you tonight. Very important."

Harry held on. "Can't it wait a day?" he said finally.

"If it's got to wait, it can wait," Oscar said, the gravelly voice dropping even lower in pitch. "But you'll have to move in a hell of a hurry on Friday."

"Meet in Bay Ridge?"

"Sure."

"Seven o'clock, tomorrow. I'm sorry, Oscar; this is just a personal thing."

"It's all right. I may know a little more tomorrow anyway."

He was breaking a custom, more serious than a rule, but Harry felt obliged. "You know, this is the night I play in a bridge tournament with Sue. Once a month."

Now Oscar held on. "Give her my love," he said, and the unexpected word hung in the mouthpiece.

"I shall," said Harry, and cradled the receiver.

Back in the meeting room, the group had reached a consensus that the machines would indeed produce useful information, that Harry had brought the first beams of light into what had seemed an impenetrable gloom, but that a lot more would be needed. Especially, manpower—FBI manpower, not restricted, as the police departments were, to a single jurisdiction. On Harry's own analysis, it seemed unlikely that the sniper lived in any of the cities where he had committed his crime—so unlikely, the detective from Allentown said nastily, that the computer could better be programmed to eliminate names with those addresses than to flag them. That was fair enough: half of Harry's purpose in asking them to do legwork next week was to keep them busy. He had no doubt, he said, that at some point in the game they would have to call in other police departments to assist in some specific investigation. At the least, each of them should work out some arrangements with their own state police. He didn't, he added, know how much manpower the FBI would commit; but he would personally act as a clearing house for them, if they wished: "I can give you a telephone number where I can always—as you noticed a few minutes ago—be reached."

The meeting went on for more than three hours, and toward the end degenerated into amateur psychologizing, theories for predicting where and when the next crime would occur. Would the FBI provide the services of a professional psychologist?

"No," Harry said. "Nor an astrologist, either."

Harry got to the Belgrave in time to play a couple of quick games of Chicago before Sue arrived. He told her while they shuffled the cards and loaded the duplicate boards that he'd heard that day from Oscar, who had sent his love. At just that moment the waiter walked by, and she ordered a sandwich.

They played very well, got fixed only twice, set three contracts the declarers should have made, and were the only pair to bid a grand slam that not only made but should have been bid. Their 62 percent game would have been good enough to win most tournaments, but a pair of life masters who didn't usually play in club duplicates came in at 63.7 percent, and Harry and Sue had to settle for second place. As they sat over the last cup of coffee, analyzing their personal score sheet while waiting for the scores to be tallied, they talked about the possibility of playing together in a regional tournament over Thanksgiving Day. Now that she no longer went to her mother's for the holidays, they were both in need of companionable events.

"Are you going to be talking with Oscar again?" she said as he helped her out of the taxi at the converted West Side brownstone where she lived. No other man in her life, she thought, looking at her still young father, did things like that, actually leaving the cab and coming around to open a door; but, then, he was the only Kentuckian.

"I expect I shall," said Harry.

"Tell him to give me a call," she said. She seemed on the brink of saying something more, then thought better of it. As her father waited and watched, she climbed the stone stairs, opened the heavy door with her key, checked the ante-room "for boogies," and waved him off.

Somewhere it is written that the industrial salesman must sell during the day and party at night. The rule applies most strongly to the resident salesman and the visiting purchasing agent, but the fact remained that the senior vice-president of Conserv-Control—not to mention the area sales manager—expected Nicholas Gilette to be a host the evening after the presentation of the equipment, and he was. The area manager had made the arrangements, at a supper club in Philadelphia where the entertainment was a torch singer who was dressed exclusively in a thin gown that clung to her close enough to outline her belly button and who seemed constantly in imminent peril of swallowing a large round microphone. Colored spotlights kept splaying about the room with factitious excitement. They were a party of eight: the area manager and his light-skinned wife (both a little tense: these things were still not easy); the two vice-presidents of the customer company, one of them a long-haired design whiz still in his twenties, with their wives; Gilette, and a rather brassy blonde, her hair sculpted in gleaming tight curls and her eyelids pale blue, who during the working day was the software creator and tinkerer reporting to the whiz.

Like most people who are habitually bored, Gilette really did not have anything in mind that he would rather do if the fates released him from sitting in a Philadelphia supper club and during the breaks in the loud music talking chips, nanoseconds and Japanese CRT terminals with up-and-coming computer buyers. Many a night in Yugoslavia as a junior military attaché and member of an embassy team he had sat through evenings duller than this one. Life at home was no feast of wit and flow of reason, either, when you came right down to it. The blonde, who after he told her he was married had twice told him she was divorced, was wriggling her shoulders as the seven-piece band on the podium, twisting knobs on amplifiers, made a sound like a pitched tidal wave.

He should be cheerful, he thought to himself: they'd made a big sale today, and made it entirely on the quality of the machines and the programs. The sort of sale that brought more sales. Over the weekend on the Chesapeake, if not in the next two days of visits back and forth between the display room at the motel and the existing installations of the savings bank, he faced a chance for a truly spectacular step forward into a new market. This was civilian business. He'd been hired for his military connections, and he still had those—in fact, they were bound to become increasingly important as the men who had been lieutenants with him moved into jobs where they controlled more money. In effect a regional sales manager now—title: asst. v.p. for development—he had prospects. The company was diversifying. The foreign wife was liked; she was always a little aloof, withdrawn, but of course she wasn't—even after eight years really wasn't—all that comfortable in English. He didn't quite have the training of the younger men pressing up in the company: his math was some years out of date, and the machine was still a wonder for him, while there were people reporting to him, ambitious people, for whom the use of a terminal was as natural as the use of their feet. But all that could be remedied.

He danced with the blonde, not touching her; whatever he wanted, it wasn't that. The area sales manager, for whom today's results promised a bigger division, bigger money, had taken one drink too many. Prospects were harder to come by, there. Suddenly, a little drunkenly, he suggested that he knew a place nobody else at the table knew, a black club in Atlantic City, *raunchy,* he'd take them there; don't worry about it, that's one *safe* place, with the protection it's got. The light-skinned wife giggled, said, "Shucks, Joe, they wouldn't like *that.*" The Conserv-Control vice-presidents looked at each other; the whiz grinned wolfishly and said, "Ye-ah," the mousy wives made wide eyes and smiled tentatively, the blonde was excited. Gilette said, "Can you excuse *me,* Joe? I had that tough drive last night, and I'm older than you are."

"No, you're not. You just don't know how old I am."

"In spirit I'm older, Joe," Gilette said, smiling. "I need my sleep. Don't worry about dropping me off at the motel— I'll call a cab to here."

The area manager was sobering down, worried. Gilette said, "All right, Joe. We've got lots to celebrate. It's just me—you know, I have to keep my shooting eye. But if you guys are going to Atlantic City, you ought to get right out of here or it's going to be some late night. You head out, and I'll get the check."

A little awkwardly, consoled by Gilette's smiling, they rose and left, the area manager's wife deep in what looked like a firm discussion with her husband. Gilette ordered a cab, paid the bill, returned to the motel, where he didn't feel like going to sleep and didn't feel like reading. He had called home before dinner, thought about calling again but couldn't face it. He turned on the television, and didn't feel like that, either. A card atop the set announced a movie service, and the X-rated show was about to go on. Gilette dialed the

60

indicated number on the room phone, and stretched out on the bed to watch. The first scene presented naked girls licking each other all over. Gilette watched for a while, got restless, and went out to the station wagon for the long case that held the two guns and the equipment for maintaining them.

Back in the room, he lovingly removed the .22 from the case, tore off a corner of cheesecloth, oiled it, and began swabbing the inside of the barrel with the cleaning rod. On the television screen, there was now one girl with two men, giving a demonstration in the uses of orifices. Gilette sat in the armchair watching the television screen, cradling the gun in his lap, rubbing the barrel with a chamois cloth, thinking about the ducks flying in over the bay on Saturday.

IV

Names

The names were already pumping out of the printer when Harry came to work Thursday morning, and he went down to the machines to watch the large stack of folded striped paper grow depressingly on the table. There would indeed be hundreds and hundreds of names, sharing at least two characteristics—certain memberships or subscriptions and certain military or competitive awards for proficiency with a rifle.

Programmers put their faith in hierarchies. At the top of the list were the names of three men already wanted by the FBI; for them, presumably, Harry thought, the addresses on the subscription lists were no longer valid. Then came a solemn seriation by points, in the first group the seven names of men who turned up in six categories: marksman medals first class, winners of a regional or national shooting trophy, arrest records, membership in the rifle association, subscription to at least two gun-oriented publications, address in the inner triangle of New Haven–Albany–Philadelphia, which Harry had indicated he considered the likely area of residence. He was interested to see among the seven the name of one of his colleagues in the Philadelphia Bureau. Arrest records: the seven would turn out on investigation to have been picked up for drunken driving, adolescent joy-riding in a stolen vehicle, unseemly behavior while in service in a red-light district near a base (2), and urinating out the thirty-seventh-floor window of an office building during a Christmas party.

Harry could keep about a hundred names in his memory at any one time, and there were more than a hundred—probably close to a thousand—in the group that had four points or more. He ordered a Xerox of the entire set, and asked that another full set be sent to the New York police, to be posted on the walls where members of the homicide squads browse; a name might be recognized there. Tilly telephoned the other departments with the names of men in their areas who ranked high; the rest would be express-mailed later in the day.

Back in his office, Harry resumed his routine; he never allowed himself to be taken entirely off one case because another had become more pressing. The best soup came from simmering: what you put in the back of your head was always there. He went through the day's clippings and publications— perhaps a little more quickly than usual—and welcomed Jerry for a brief report on the previous day's meeting with the Yugoslavs. They had not been content; they demanded a meeting with Harry or, failing that, with Mr. Adams. The ambassador himself would attend. They were making a formal request through the State Department to supplement their request through the UN.

"That gives us some time," Harry said.

"Well, no."

"Oh?"

"Well, they pushed for a date. I gave them next Wednesday

63

morning, a week away—the best I could do. Their note to Washington will specify the Wednesday meeting."

"Thanks a lot."

"Gonna be done with this sniper job by Wednesday?" Jerry asked brightly.

"Sure I will," said Harry. "Why not?"

Harry made duty calls to the state highway police in four states, opening channels, soliciting information about road-block procedures and timing should a trap seem plausible. Then he called Adams and reported. "What are you going to do with the CIA names?" Adams inquired.

"We're committed to vet them ourselves," Harry said. "But I'm going to need soldiers."

"How many?"

"Five, to start—one pair, two singles, one of them with right-wing contacts, and a guy to drive me around and sit in on interrogations if I need him. I'd appreciate a podner with commando training: picking up this guy may be hairy."

"Frank Wu," said Adams. "Just took a week off and won a martial arts tournament in California. They made pictures of it for one of those Saturday sports shows on TV, which means we have to surface him all the way up anyway."

Frank Wu was a known quantity, and Harry had worked with him on some problems of Hong Kong immigrants with Maoist instructions. He had long wanted out of what he had called "the tong war business"—tong war being a phrase Hoover had once used in his presence—and he seemed to have found a remarkable way to get out. "The others?" said Harry.

"I'll have them at your office at five o'clock."

"Tell them they're safe for the evening," Harry said. "I have to get out tonight around six."

A messenger came staggering up from the computer room with piles of printout while Harry was on the phone with Adams, and Harry waved him to leave the material on the one clear corner of his desk. When his phone calls were finished, he began reading slowly through the names, searching for associations however far-fetched, marking some for investigation by the team he would acquire that afternoon, slowly memorizing others, mental doorbell-ringing that created a feeling of accomplishment Harry was much too experienced to believe. Still, there was only one needle in this haystack. Tilly brought Harry a delicatessen sandwich, and he ate at his desk.

Oscar, too, was on the telephone. The Motor Vehicles Bureau reported that the car and plate in question were licensed to a rental agency. Oscar called the agency, smoothly identified himself as a state trooper investigating a possible hit-and-run accident, and got the name of a Connecticut land development company. He called the company, identified himself as a salesman for a leasing firm, and got through to someone the operator said would know whether they rented any cars or not—she thought not, and so did the man to whom Oscar eventually spoke. People used their own cars; they got a mileage allowance, and preferred things that way. They were renting four bulldozers, at a stiff price: Oscar didn't have any bulldozers he wanted to offer, did he? A lawyer contact in a city not far from the company's headquarters had never heard of it—must be a subsidiary of something else, he said—and no information about it seemed available in New York.

"Sort of crazy," said Craig Spitts.

"Want me to stay with it?" Oscar asked.

"No, forget it."

"Are your friends going ahead with that thing we discussed yesterday?"

"As far as I know."

"I wish they wouldn't," said Oscar.

"Yup."

Tony caught Carla with a phone call just as she was about to leave the house. "Hey, my *linda,*" he said, "how big a bash is it that we're having Saturday?"

"About as big as you can with a sit-down dinner," said Carla. "I think I have thirty-seven, thirty-eight people said they were coming."

"Can you add three more?"

"If I must, I must. Who is it?"

"Carl Ensor and his wife. We have a cost overrun problem with the freeze-dried plant in Santos, and the *easiest* thing to do would be to get him to write up Commonwealth's loan. They're pretty near neighbors, the Ensors."

"The Ensors don't ride," Carla objected. "Everyone else at my dinner will be from the Hunt Club."

"Except for the Brazilian ambassador."

"He comes to every party."

"And me."

"All right, all right. And who is the third?"

"Ensor's got a houseguest. Computer fella—but Ensor says he's also maybe the greatest shot in America. They're going to spend the morning killing ducks, and they have no plans for the evening."

"Do you have a name for that one?"

"Yes—Gilette. Nicholas Gilette." He spelled it.

Carla wrote on the pad by the kitchen phone: Carl and Ann Ensor, Nicholas Gilette. "I'll add them," she said. "But let me ask you again for time: the earlier I get down on Friday, the less trouble everything will be."

"Talk to you about it tonight."

On her way out, Carla took a last look in the full-length mirror: boots, jodhpurs, lined leather jacket, peaked leather hat. She pushed a black curl out from under the hatband, nodded at herself, called goodbye in Spanish to the house-keeper and went out the kitchen door to the garage and the BMW.

66

St. Ann's Farm was about five minutes closer on the Taconic State, but Carla drove along the back roads that held the ridge line, big views up to Dutchess County and to the Catskills across the river. Most of the leaves were gone now, and most of what remained was a dead brown, but here and there Carla could see flashes of yellow foliage. Not so far off the pale green the trees would offer in the spring; Carla needed encouragement every year to face the winter. But the spring, of course, would be muddy, and not so good for the horses.

Carla's connection with St. Ann's was through a neighbor, who had a pimply-faced daughter at the school. It was a combination prep school and finishing school, grades eleven through fourteen; about half the girls in the high school program went off to a four-year college. What was first class about it, and justified it to those paying the highest fees in the state, were the creature comforts (every girl her own room), three separate menus (one for weight-watching) every lunch and every dinner, and the equestrian program. Something like a third of the girls had their own horses, and for the others the school maintained a stable of three dozen registered animals. The neighbor's daughter had seen Carla on horseback—Carla had chosen their house, in fact, because it backed onto a small state forest where she could ride whenever she wished, and she stabled two horses on the grounds. So the neighbor invited Carla to come and watch one of the Tuesday-Thursday afternoon classes at the 350-acre dairy farm the school had been given in memory of one of its least successful alumnae, a girl who (unbeknownst to a loving father) had drunk herself to death in Portofino at the age of twenty-eight.

This was shortly after Carla and Major had won their first ribbon at Madison Square Garden, and Carla when identified was invited to take a turn with the class. She rode bareback, declining someone else's saddle—"I am comfortable, you know, only on my own"—gave the horse a turn around the inside and then took him over the timber course like the wind. It made an impression, and three weeks later, after the instructor had been garroted in a freak accident involving a slack telephone cable to a nearby abandoned farmhouse, Carla was somewhat timidly approached by the school's headmistress, spinster daughter of one of New York's great names, and asked if she would fill in for the rest of the term.

A few weeks later, she offered to continue into the next year. Jay would be going to school and she'd have more time, she was enjoying the afternoons, and she got a kick out of the idea of doing volunteer work for the daughters of the women who were doing volunteer work for the Puerto Ricans of New York. Two of the mothers of her students told Carla they were themselves teaching—remedial reading and flower arrangement, respectively—at Union Settlement in East Harlem. It was known that Carla was "Spanish"— some thought Argentinian—and a suggestion was made that she, too, might be useful in the barrio, because she spoke the language; but she said she was doing more good with the riding class.

The farm, which earned its keep with the dairy herd, was bounded on two sides by state roads, white post-and-rail fences and oaks and maples with low branches that in summer and early fall allowed only glimpses of the timber course from the road. By November one could see through the branches easily and watch the girls and their horses rise to the fences—which were in fact light wood precariously attached to the posts so the horses could kick through safely. Carla now taught only those who were quite ready to jump— this year there had been ninety-one applicants, a quarter of the school, for the eight places in her class. Most of the class were young horsewomen of some accomplishment, who needed nothing from Carla but some tricks; a few wanted help.

Carla tooled the little car up to the stable, greeted the

farmer's wife, who took care of the horses, said hello to Captain (Major was now at the house in Maryland), and quickly saddled him with her postage-stamp saddle, securing, testing and refastening the belts under his belly. She mounted as effortlessly as a kite climbs in the wind, and rode out to the large paddock to see how the early arrivals were faring. Mostly, she taught from horseback, illustrating, suggesting, watching. For the jumpers, however, she sometimes dismounted to work hands-on, placing the girls' knees properly and getting their stirrups right. Even some of her better girls were hard to persuade that there was no need to grip a rising horse. They had been taught too often that "you become part of the horse"—while the truth of the matter, Carla kept saying, was that the horse became part of you, responsive to your will, your urging, your decisions. It was a problem for these girls: they did things all right; but they didn't make plans.

They worked one jump a day, usually back and forth (which added the discipline of the quick turn); and Carla arranged the placement and height of the hurdles. On Major—Captain one had to be a little more careful about—she had a technique that looked like a slow-motion jump, during which she could turn her head to the group, explaining as she went. This year she had three girls who were already riding in shows themselves, who spent most of their time stunting in the inner ring or flying over jumps on the other side of the course, wheeling, flying back. At the end of every class, Carla would choose one of the girls to go around the course with her in tandem. They were to watch her, not the course, and to do exactly what she did when she did it; and those who were capable of forgetting the perils they were inviting often could, in fact, finish the course. They could do that because the experience of watching Carla was special for them, so much what they wanted and hoped to be. That, of course, was the crown Carla wore: that these girls, whose older sisters had seemed to her residents of some fabled planet, now dreamed that somehow they might, if they worked ever so hard, become something like the Puerto Rican grocer's daughter.

Harry was in the communications room at four o'clock to take the call from Langley. The woman at the other end did not identify herself. "Here are the eight names," she said. "The addresses and the telephone numbers we believe to be good as of the first of October. These men are all resigned or retired. Their jobs are real jobs, not cover jobs, but in several cases the résumés with which the jobs were procured are substantially invented. It is extremely important that no action on your part cause any of these men to become exposed. The average paranoia level in this group is high, as you might expect. The identities are given to you in personal confidence, on the understanding that you will yourself conduct whatever investigation you consider necessary."

"Look, lady," Harry said, "I have not been brought into this to protect your ex-agents. I must assume that I will find this murderer with or without your help. My hunch is that I already have your names somewhere in my computer file, which is even now, as we talk, printing out for me. The most you are doing for me is saving me a few days' time. The most I can promise you is that my people and I will take the first look at these fellows ourselves—and that if one of them has to be picked up we will cooperate to the best of our ability in concealing your dirty secrets. I've been over all this with Phil, I think. We are the soul of discretion. You can tell Phil to cheer him up that my number two is going to be Frank Wu; your people have worked with him on Chinese agent questions. Now just give me your names."

"Only on your personal assurance," the woman's voice continued doggedly, "that pending authorization to release, you alone will know them."

"Only me and my best friends, subject to the qualifications

I have already given you. Cut it out now, and give me the names."

She did, and Harry's hand flew over the outsized pad of graph paper on which he took desk notes. He read the names and addresses back at the end, and they were verified. "Which of these," he then inquired, "would you advise me to look at first? Remembering that I'm in a hurry."

"Officially, we believe all of them are a waste of your time."

"Unofficially, which of them give you the greatest concern?"

"Unofficially, Kaganopoulos and Druck."

"Why?"

"The kind of jobs they have. They're failures. They work out of a car. Kaganopoulos has been in trouble, something to do with a threat on the life of a Greek political refugee. He got off without asking us for help."

"Anybody not on this list you think I should talk to?"

"I am authorized to say the list is complete."

"When does Phil get back from abroad?"

"I don't know that he is abroad."

"If I want to talk with you again, for whom do I ask?"

"You ask for Phil."

"Thank you, ma'am."

"Pleasure," she said.

Kaganopoulos was a name in the memory file: right-wing Greek-American, some black-shirt business with a residue of the fascists in Italian Brooklyn. Harry pulled the hard-copy file. Half Cypriot. Enthusiast for enosis and, not realizing that the two didn't mix, for the Colonels. A couple of parades, a demonstration or two across First Avenue from the UN, a picket line before the *New York Times*. Made a statement in a bar that he was going to kill Andreas Papandreou; when Papandreou came to address some civil liberties committee banquet, Kaganopoulos was arrested, charged with menacing, and quietly spirited off to a hotel in the Catskills for the four days the Greek resistance leader was in the country. A while ago, that. "The problem is," said a note in the file, "that if Kaganopoulos wants to kill a man, he can; the house is an armory." The name was on the basic list, with five points (but Druck's name, Harry noted idly, flipping, was missing). The Kaganopoulos address was not far from the restaurant where Harry was having dinner. He told Tilly to put in a call.

Waiting, he began to check the rest of the CIA names against the printout. Tilly buzzed him: "Busy." He said, "Keep trying." All but one of the CIA names were on the machined list, which meant his pledge to Phil had been busted already by routine procedure, which was just tough on the CIA, pompous bastards. He added the missing name to his personal priority schedule. The buzzer went again. "You've got him," Tilly said. "I dunno why you want him, but you've got him."

The earpiece was already going vigorously when Harry picked up the phone. "Fucking FBI. Whaddaya want with me? Ain't no fucking Papandreou coming; ain't no fucking big-shot Turks. We're doing nuthin'; nobody even comes to meetings any more."

"Just want to talk with you," Harry said. "Ask you a few questions, make sure you're not a man we're looking for."

"Ask me the questions."

"I'd rather come out and talk with you at home."

"Ain't got time," Kaganopoulos said. "Lots to do. I'm going out of town Monday."

"I'm pretty busy next week myself," Harry confided. "But I'm going to be only half a dozen blocks from your home for dinner tonight, and I thought that maybe if I could drop in, say quarter to nine or nine o'clock, we could get all this squared away."

"How do I know you really are a fucking FBI agent?"

"Well, I'll have credentials, of course. Or you can look

us up in the telephone book, and call the Manhattan switchboard number, and ask the girl to put you through to Harry Johnson. You'll get my secretary, and then you'll get me. Should I hang up so you can try?"

"All right, God damn it, I do that."

Harry hung up as promised, and returned to perusing the printout lists. He heard the phone ring; Tilly buzzed, said, "Your friend again. Remember, you have only ten minutes before the appointment Mr. Adams set up."

"Johnson here," Harry said pleasantly into the telephone.

"Whatcha want to talk to me about?"

"I'll tell you when I come. Look, Mr. Kaganopoulos, you and I have been on the same side of some things over the years."

"Long time ago. Fucking Ramsey Clark made faggots of all of you. Hoover's dead. They got Nixon. Got Papadopoulos. Fuck it. Come tonight. What you want to know, I tell you."

"Thank you. Quarter to nine."

"You got address?"

"From the same people who gave me the phone number."

"Yeah, sure. Gubbye."

Then it was Harry's turn to buzz Tilly, and tell her to come in with the men: this was a meeting of which, just possibly, Harry might want a record. Except for Wu, a stocky Chinese who had come to America as a boy from Trinidad and could work in Spanish as well as Chinese and English, the men Adams had sent were out of the mold: clean-cut and close-shaven if no longer crew-cut; vested suits, four-in-hands, sober look. Observant, but careful about asking questions. Myself when young, Harry thought. Veterans, and the Army training took. But where did they find so many of us?

The assignments had been seriously made: one agent had worked in Philadelphia, one in Hartford, they had their own contacts and could use them. By five-thirty, everyone knew exactly what he would be doing on Friday, and knew also that there would be no days off while the heat was on. Harry went home briefly, dropped the computer printouts on the kitchen table for later study, and by six he was in the subway to Brooklyn. He stood most of the way and read the *Post,* which had a long takeout, starting on page one, about "the psychological make-up of the sniper."

The Bay Ridge restaurant where Harry and Oscar met had been a Mafia hangout before a well-publicized killing had drawn too much tourist traffic, a good ten years ago. Now it was a neighborhood restaurant with a back room big enough for weekend family parties—say, twenty people. When there were no parties, the room had two square tables with four chairs at each, as in the old days when the capos sat at one and their men at the other. The floor was a lacquered oak, well kept. Three of the four walls were cream and green, divided by a plaster molding; the fourth was a very large watercolor of the Amalfi Drive and Sorrento, seen from an angle not even a helicopter could have managed. The food was every bit as good as it had been in the Mafia days. Harry was known as an FBI agent, but not under the name of Johnson. Management knew the name he used was wrong, but thought it better not to care.

Oscar was already at the rear table when Harry came in through the back door and gave his raincoat to the hovering Luigi. "How's it going?" he said to Oscar.

"All right. You?"

"Fine." Harry nodded to Luigi, who came over and recited the menu—nothing was ever written down here. After they had ordered—including the invariable "bottle of red" that came from somewhere in California and was the best bargain in New York—Luigi dutifully disappeared. "You've caught me at absolutely the worst time," said Harry. "What's up?"

And Oscar, interrupting his narrative to welcome the baked ziti and the wine, told Harry, in his growling, faintly defective voice, about the plot to smuggle a gun into High Hills—

chapter and verse, person, place and thing, including the rationale.

"Doesn't make sense," Harry said when Oscar had finished.

Oscar shrugged. "I know only what I'm told," he said.

"How guilty is this kid?"

"Very."

"Spitts isn't Kunstler," Harry said, rolling up the end of his napkin and straightening it out. "He doesn't get sick to his stomach every time a punk gets convicted."

"You've got to keep in mind," Oscar said, "what a big emotional investment everybody has in that Bed-Stuy project—and this kid was apparently one of the best things to come out of it. Nobody wants to think the kid conned him."

"Yeah. Even so. And of course I don't like hearing about it from you. All we need is for the judges to find there's a spook in that law firm. When you took this job, we agreed it was off limits. Your work place for me is the Vietnam Vets."

"You wanna ignore it," growled Oscar, "you ignore it." They had both ordered the veal chop, almost two inches thick, a baby steak; Harry ate it with a knife and fork, making thin slices; Oscar of necessity picked it up and gnawed.

"Can't ignore it," Harry said finally, and sighed. "Who knows about this, besides you?"

Oscar told him, and added, "I'm really pretty safe. I wasn't at the meeting. Young Fitch is a notorious blabbermouth. Those hot-shot young *pro bono* lawyers from Wall Street firms are going to be full of something so gloriously revolutionary as this."

Harry poured the remains of the wine bottle into the two glasses. "Just what I need. As you may not know, they've handed me the sniper case."

"I read the Bureau was in that. They didn't say it was you."

"There's no Goddamned profit in this one. I don't want Spitts, I don't want the *pro bono* kids, and I don't want you. I get a damned-fool congressman's son, which means it's all over the newspapers. Well, at least it's clean: you catch him with the gun. Maybe I can just turn it over to the prison people. Aah. I'll think about it. Thanks."

"There's something else," said Oscar, and waited while Luigi served the spumoni.

"Yes?"

"Were you driving a Lincoln Continental down around Broad Street yesterday lunchtime?"

"Why do you ask?"

"Because if you were, you just about ran over Spitts—" Harry snorted a short laugh.

"—and he saw you, got the plates on the car. From the way he described it, it's a very fancy car. Your driving a big Continental like that is like the fiddle student playing his exam recital on a Strad. You sort of wonder where he got it."

"So?"

"Spitts asked me to find out who owns the car."

"What did you find?"

"A rental company. Behind the rental company, a Connecticut outfit, tract developers."

"Behind them?"

"Couldn't find out in the time available. And Craig told me to forget about it. Too much work on something not our real business. It *was* you in the car?"

"I don't know," Harry said, smiling.

"Should I worry about what I might find if I *did* work on it?"

"*Such* a question!" said Harry Johnson, with raised eyebrows. "I have something else for you."

"What?"

"A request from Sue that you give her a call. Do you have her number?"

"No."

Harry had a slip of paper ready in his pocket; he handed it across the table.

"Thanks. I'd really like to know about the Continental."

"Spitts told you to forget it," Harry said, "and he's your boss."

"What do you want me to do if he tells me to remember it, and find out more about that car?"

"I said he's your boss," Harry said. "You find out what you can. Just don't expect to get your story from me."

"You son of a bitch," said Oscar, but not accusingly.

"Which reminds me," Harry said, looking at his watch and then putting his foot on the plank under the table that called Luigi. (Who else had it called, he always wondered, in the heyday of this room?) "I have an appointment around here."

"Do you want to let me know what you're going to do about High Hills?"

"No. Do call Sue, though, will you?"

"I'll call Sue," Oscar said, and got up. Harry moved to help him with his coat, but Oscar waved him away, humped into it in a way that was now second nature, and departed.

John—Jack, his father called him—was watching television, and Maria Gilette sat by the telephone in the narrow living room of the house in Croton-on-Hudson, reading a pamphlet Father Caffra had given her and waiting for the call. Her husband did call every evening when he was away; there was that comfort. And maybe—foolish, but maybe— it could be her father, out of Tito's jails, free to call her, free to come to her or at least to receive her if she came home.

The pamphlet was about the outrages committed against the Church by the League of Communists. Of course, her father would never have agreed with most of that: he was a good Communist. As a very young man he had been Tito's companion in the partisans; he had held high office in the foreign ministry after the war. It had been at Tito's summer island that she had met Nico, for her father was often part of Tito's hunting parties and after his wife died he brought his pretty daughter to Brioni.

She had been nineteen years old when they met, only recently emerged from what would in a less Communist country have been called a convent school—taught, in fact, by nuns in mufti, who had traded their services to the daughters of the Party leadership in return for freedom to keep a chapel and a priest, to practice their religion privately. She was sweet, small, round, rosy, her straw hair twisted in braids that wrapped around her head, wearing a peasant blouse loosely tied with a cord at the smooth round neck. Lively, too: the nuns had thought her mischievous. In the war, these nuns had been anti-Nazi; remnant enthusiasm as well as prudence led them to teach the romance of the partisans. Paired with the young American marine at dinner on Brioni, and told that he was the winner of a recent Yugoslav national rifle competition, she teased him in her school English to teach her to shoot like a partisan woman.

As they were leaving the table, a general in dress uniform had come to their place, sent with a message from the Marshal, placing at the disposal of the American lieutenant the practice range of the Yugoslav Army on the outskirts of Belgrade. Maria was most pleased; she would come with Lieutenant Gilette when he went, she swore it, and made him promise that he would invite her. She called her father over, and bade him give his approval. Mandragora caught the American lieutenant's eye and held it, smiled slowly, and said, "But of course."

The following Monday, Gilette checked with the ADM who handled protocol matters, who caused inquiry to be made and reported back the next day that Mandragora would in truth be delighted for his daughter to go to the rifle range with Lieutenant Gilette; and the embassy, which still in those days was permitted only restricted social acquaintance with the locals, happily made a car available from the motor pool. To demonstrate the seal of acceptance, she waited for him not at her home but on the steps of the foreign ministry, carrying her father's gun in its chamois case, its muzzle pointing skyward. Gilette explained to her as he led her to the car that one pointed a gun at the ground, and she agreed, seriously.

In the car, she asked him in slow, interrupted English how he had become a soldier, and he explained that he was a marine, that he had really studied mathematics, but in the Navy officers program at his university; and because of his success on the rifle team he was invited to "the soldier side of our Navy." She could not understand the idea of a university in the countryside or the military at it, thought the problem was her English, and was not very interested anyway; only the sight of the rifle range, her country's soldiers attending it, saluting both of them, restored her attention. She insisted that he shoot first, to show her—and she watched him change as he stood at the line, raised and cradled his gun, and nodded to the attendant to release the skeet.

The best teachers have a concentrated skill, but students cannot perceive it. This was the first time Maria Mandragora had ever in her life seen anyone exercise concentrated powers with complete efficiency. Twenty-five times he shot; twenty-five times the bird shattered into fragments. He did not look at her or at the soldier at the trap; only at his shells, his gun, and the targets shimmering in the wind against the green hills. His shoulders relaxed as he finished his set, and he turned to her at last. "Now it is your turn." He took her father's gun out of its case for her and loaded it, and she stepped to the line and lifted the weapon against her shoulder. He laughed. "May I show you?" It meant that he would hold her. She blushed, and composed her reply. "If I am not afraid," she said, "why are you afraid?"

First he set her in position, but she had no sense of the

need to lead the bird, and the third time she shot he kept his hands on her arms, turning her to the flight of the skeet. The shot kicked away an edge of the disk. Delighted, she pulled her head back against his shoulder to turn and look at him, and their lips almost brushed.

They danced at the annual ball given by the foreign ministry for the diplomatic corps, and with Ambassador Ensor's approval Lieutenant Gilette was invited for a winter weekend to Mandragora's country house. The deputy foreign minister arranged English lessons for his daughter from the teacher in charge of language training for Yugoslav diplomats. When Mandragora went to Vienna for a week to participate in trade discussions, he notified the American ambassador, who took the hint; and Ann Ensor invited Maria to dinner—twice in one week, with Lieutenant Gilette as her partner. First once a month, then every week, she went with him to the rifle range, "to study." She dieted, and gave her father firm instructions about clothes he was to buy for her on a second trip to Vienna. One warm weekend in the early spring, Gilette asked her to walk with him by the river, and her father said, Of course; and they sat holding hands while he told her more, now very interesting stories, about that exotic world in Vermont, the stony hills and stone fences, and the Canada geese that came through in the fall. He admired the improvement of her English. The great shock for her was the realization that the war in which his father died was the terrible American aggression in Korea, which she had studied in school; but she could forgive him even that.

One day her father said, "Do you love him?"

"Papa! . . . Yes."

"Would you marry him?"

"Yes."

"Do it," Mandragora said, turned away from her, then explained. Things were going to be bad. The Party was falling into the hands of a terrible faction that insisted Croatians could not be trusted, would never be full citizens of the new

Yugoslavia. He would be more loyal—to his leader, his country, his people, his past—if she were out of the country, somewhere safe. What she thought of—later, guiltily, she would remember the thrill of it—was Nico with his hands on her arms, her shoulders against his chest. Later, too, she would wonder not without some pride how she could have felt the confidence she knew that May weekend, for on Sunday by the river she simply said to Gilette, "Nico, if you want to marry me, my father says you can. . . ."

It had been blindness for her not to think of what might happen to her father afterward, how automatically it would be part of the accusation against him that his daughter had been "a habitué" of the American Embassy, had married not only an American, but a spy. He had schemed with the Americans, his prosecutor said, to break an independent Croatia out of the Yugoslav Republic, and restore it for protection to a new Austrian hegemony. Necessarily, she blamed herself. She loved her husband, she loved their son; if she was lonely now in America it was her own fault. She had not been so lonely when she came, and set up house, learned so much English, shared her husband's glee when the offer from the computer company released him from military service and doubled their income. But everything that had to do with their courtship had become anathema. She could not hate a person; she hated the paraphernalia.

Frankie Russell, her protector and friend, the wife of the man who had brought Nico his job, told her not to worry about resenting the guns that meant so much to her husband—any wife would be jealous of a hobby that took so much of her husband's time and care, and love. Father Caffra, on the other hand, urged her to accept her husband as he was, accept his talents with the guns as a gift from God, a gift that might even someday yield a great result to the glory of Him who had given it. But now almost five months had passed without word from her father, and faith was not enough. She needed magic.

There was no offering she could give the spirits—but Nico had a magic he could sacrifice. Now, she said to him, now when his work often took him away from home—now he should give up the weekend mornings on the firing range, the contests to which he traveled to bring back the medals and trophies that lined the walls of the folly room that made up the entire tacked-on fourth floor of the old house, where he spent so many evenings when he was home, the lathes turning, the lights bright under the microscope. She wheedled, she played on all the elements of his concern, the questions of what a father should do for his son and a husband for his wife; and she won.

As soon as he agreed to give up the practice and the competition, she knew, with a kind of satisfaction, that the sacrifice had been hers, too. He did not greatly reduce—he might even have increased—the time he spent in the upstairs room, and he put a new lock on it to keep her out when he was gone. There was a void in his conversation where once he had told her about improvements he was making in his guns or bullets or shells, about contests he was entering, the dream of trying out again for the Olympics. He was jumpy, and on the one occasion when he tried to persuade her to relent, he told her that he was thinking about shooting more than ever before, dreaming about strange and fantastic targets moving erratically and with great speed that he would hit as though he had some kind of magic bullet in an evil fairy tale. She pleaded that it was only temporary, he would get a promotion at the company that would mean less traveling, or—she blurted—she would hear from her father again and everything would be as it used to be. And he had simply nodded, worst fears confirmed, and smiled a shy smile that broke her heart, the remembered smile that had followed a triumph with the rifle, that spoke of a man behind the magnetic, terrifying skill.

The phone rang and it was Gilette, from New Jersey. "How was the day, dear?"

"Very good day, very good," she said. "John was allowed to play on the football field with the bigger boys. He was so happy. I went to White Plains and I saw Father Caffra, and I talked to Frankie Russell about the parent-teacher next week. I keep busy. Did your work go well?"

"Yes. We began our presentation to the Ambassador's savings bank, and all the terminals were on their best behavior. What did you talk with Father Caffra about?"

"Oh. Papa."

"Yes?"

"He says—he says there is someone coming out of the prison where Papa was being held last time we heard from him, and perhaps *he* will know—"

"Maria, you *know* these exile groups have no good information. You have to trust the embassy. It's now your embassy, too—you forget that."

"But they tell us nothing, Nico. Nothing."

"The man we have there now is no Ensor, that's for sure," he said, "but they have the channels. And Ensor can still activate them. He can."

"Yes, it was God's will that he called you after all these years," said Maria, and felt her cheeks become wet.

"But the person he really wants to see is you," Gilette said. "He can do business with me without having me down for the weekend. He said Madame Ambassador especially wanted to see you again. You could still fly down to Philadelphia tomorrow, or take the train, and I would pick you up. Frankie would take care of Jack; after all, it's business."

"But you go there to shoot."

"Our deal doesn't cover—"

"I am not saying you should not do it," Maria said. "But it is all so much like Brioni, Nico, I could not bear it."

"The Ambassador isn't much like Tito."

"I don't look any more like what Madame Ambassador remembers of me," Maria said.

"Nonsense. When you get dressed up, you look great."

"Oh, Nico, let me stay here."

"All right, dear," he said. "I won't push you. I agreed. Could you put Jack on the phone? I want to tell him how to cheer you up."

"I do try for you," she said. "I do." Then there was a rush of words: "You will not talk to him about guns, you promise me that you will not talk to him about the guns, the bullets, the hunting, the—what do you say?—rifle range, the medals, anything—"

"No, no."

"I get him"; and actively crying, Maria Gilette went to tell her son that his father was on the telephone.

V

Oscar

Politics for Oscar Riskovsky had been from his earliest recollection a matter of good fellowship—the men with their beer bellies sitting around the family dinner table late at night, listening to his bearded giant of a father, clearly the first among equals; talking, cursing, drinking, not infrequently laughing; picnics at the Party's place in the Catskills, with swimming and boat rides and a softball game, Sam at cleanup hitting home runs into the bushes. Campfires and singing: "Like a tree that's standing by the water, we shall not be moved." His grandfather, it said in the history books, had been a founder of the Polish Communist Party, and his father had grown up in the labor movement: the furriers, the Amalgamated for a while, then the UE, the breakthrough to the big machinery, the approach to the high ground of capitalist society.

But for the children, for Oscar's older sister, Martha, and

himself, only one year apart, the politics was second—or, rather, it was so much taken for granted that culture was always more important. Culture, Sam Riskovsky said to his children, was what made the Soviet Union "in the final analysis" so much more significant in the world than the United States—so many books they printed and sold, no trash, artists supported by the state, the ballet, the symphony orchestras in all the provincial cities. The reverence for Soviet culture had carried Sam through the horrible days of the Hitler-Stalin pact, when his friends fell away. His was a politics informed with the potential of the working class, Browder's communism, a vision of the Soviet Union as a model for a better America. Much better; Sam shuddered sometimes at his recollections of how the men in his outfit had amused themselves at Fort Dix, on liberty in Philadelphia, in North Africa, in Rome. . . .

So Sam Riskovsky wanted his children to be Americans, in the mainstream, where their example and their influence would count; he was as proud of Oscar's performance in Little League, and later his first-string status on the football team, as he was of his earnest proficiency at the piano. They were suburbanites. Sam had married late, after the war, when he was over forty, and the wife he found was not much under. The children were a gift—he could have said, almost, from God.

Martha and Oscar were brought up in Wantagh, well out on Long Island, not far from the socialist pleasures of Bethpage State Park and the lake and Jones Beach, to which they drove in the little Ford that was Sam's delight. ("Henry Ford was not a bad man—not a good man, but not a bad man; a *necessary* man.") Oscar was too young to have known the White Terror of the McCarthy days, when the American Legion tried to have Raia Riskovsky fired from her school secretary's job because she and her husband had rooted for the enemy in the Korean War—as indeed they had, Sam making a statement for his union "supporting for objective

86

reasons the need for the unification of Korea under the leadership of Kim Il Sung," though he never joined the chorus denouncing germ warfare by Americans, which he described as "a mistaken tactic." The attackers failed, because even with all the new people around in the tract houses, the town was still small enough that Sam was known: he might be a Communist but he was *our* Communist; a Purple Heart veteran; he paid his bills, mowed his lawn, borrowed a cup of sugar at the back door when Raia needed one and replaced it after the next shopping; and the people who came to his dinner table from outside were not unlike the people who lived in Wantagh, whatever their politics. Once or twice a year there were Negroes in the group, but what the hell, they weren't moving *in* or anything like that. Part of it, more than Sam could realize, more than Oscar could ever tell him, was that Sam was considered a character, a lovable town crank.

It was Martha who bore the brunt of knowing that her beloved father was tolerated because he wasn't taken seriously—and of sensing, obscurely, that Sam had begun to take himself less than entirely seriously. The decline in conviction, already well advanced before the children were in their teens, had started with the Khrushchev speech to the Twentieth Congress, the tearing down of Stalin. Sam could not believe that in the Soviet Union important officials were speaking of Stalin's "crimes." For a long time he denounced the speech as an obvious swindle by the State Department, and he canceled his subscription to the *Daily Worker* when the paper finally admitted its reality. He remained a Communist, a leader in a union unrepentently "Stalinist"; but a lot of the gaiety dribbled out of it, and as they grew he took more and more of his emotional sustenance from his children. In 1960 they drove across country instead of going to "camp" for vacation, and thereafter Sam had fewer gatherings at his house.

He went beaming to the twice-a-year performances at the

ballet school in Rockville Centre to which Martha went as her friends went to religious education, and he had a cork floor, a bar and a wall-length mirror installed in the rumpus room in the cellar. Sam kept the car an extra wheezing year— the best year he'd ever had with a car, he said; he enjoyed fixing it, teaching Oscar to be his own mechanic—so the payments could go instead to buying Oscar "a good piano." Every day, almost as much for his own pleasure as for the good he knew it would do his son, he took an hour to hear Oscar practice. Exercises, Bach, Chopin, Brahms (Sam's favorite)—it made no difference; Sam listened. He wrote admiring and grateful letters to Oscar's teacher, and sold the union locals blocks of tickets to the annual recital of the teacher's students.

At fifteen, Oscar was almost as big as his father; at seventeen, he was the powerful pulling guard on a high school team that was the best on the South Shore. Big fingers, big wrists, a great spread of shoulder, a head almost massive for an adolescent, the blond-brown hair swept high in a pompadour. Sam was intrigued that his son was in the National Honor Society, and he could not keep from telling a union meeting that no senior at the high school had so many signatures in his yearbook as Oscar; "He's going to be a leader." For all that, the pressures on Oscar were minimal: he was the first son, of course, but the second child; his lean, longheaded, busy sister had insulated him at home and at school, and allowed Oscar to be, in several senses of the word, amiable. Senior year was a triumph for Oscar, complete with a love affair his father then knew nothing (or little) about. For the first time he was on his own, Martha having gone to college—the first of her family ever to go to college, and away from home, too. Oscar followed, to the same branch of the burgeoning state university, one year later.

And found, much to his surprise, that he did not enjoy it at all. The course work, especially the introductory course in sociology, his intended major, was not interesting; and he made no friends in class. Trying out for freshman football, he discovered a disconcerting number of his fellows both bigger and faster than he was—and much more committed to making the team. In the second week of October he dislocated a shoulder in practice, which put him not only out of football but also off the piano for six weeks. The worst problem was Martha, who had become deeply involved with a loud and threatening group of radical students modeling themselves on the Free Speech Movement in Berkeley and various televised student celebrities. Infantile leftism, Sam called it when Martha brought him mimeographed broadsheets denouncing the university, academic requirements, racism in room assignments (first because black students were allowed to room together, then because they weren't), labor unions and the Old Left. Mao, Marcuse, Franz Fanon—Martha quoted them all, and Sam finally roared at her. Sam merely had to put up with the literature; Oscar, if he wanted to see his sister, had to put up with her companions. He took to coming home most weekends—in time for his piano teacher's Friday-evening musicale, and Sue Johnson. The love affair surfaced.

Sam thought it was funny (Martha did not) that Oscar was dating the daughter of not only an FBI man, but an FBI man specializing in what Sam called "political warfare." But he approved of Sue—"She's like a worker's daughter, good bones and good manners," he said—and made jokes about Romeo and Juliet and if Johnson would not be a Capulet he would not be a Montague. When he met Johnson at one of the musicale evenings, they joked about knowing a lot of the same people, and complimented the playing of each other's children. But Sue was clearly the more impressive pianist. When she came to Sam's house and played for him the Shostakovich Preludes, which he had never heard before, she had a complete conquest. "You gotta remember," Oscar said, "she don't play football so good." She kicked him. In the spring term, Oscar missed only one weekend home.

The next year, however, Sue was up north, which gave Oscar less reason to go home. He switched his major to history, and found himself fascinated by the wittiest professor on campus, whose revisionist views of the years right after the war consorted well with what Sam Riskovsky had been saying right along; Oscar thought he might become a teacher himself. He tried football again, and found that several of those bigger and faster than himself had not returned to college; he made the team, and acquired that special position reserved for the occasional football player who is also a successful student. Agreement on the hatefulness of the war brought students of unobjectionable habits into the kind of political group Martha had joined the year before, and the expansion of its strength made the group less conspiratorial, less raucously demanding, less apparently childish. Oscar's relationship with his sister resumed, and he even found himself willing to spend time with her friends. Several of them, he told his father—like them or not—were damned smart.

So when those friends decided that the time had come to take over what had been a moribund student government, they had Oscar available as a candidate. As the Front Against the War, what had been the Liberation Movement took two of the top three posts, including, for Oscar, the first-vice-presidency reserved for the next year's junior class. It would probably mean the end of any piano for a year, he wrote to Sue in one of his increasingly infrequent letters, but the student movement had become the only force against the war and he had obligations to his classmates. And, selfishly, he wanted to do anything he could to assure that he would not himself be called to die for the corrupt fascists of South Vietnam. That summer, with Sam's enthusiastic approval, Oscar went south as a volunteer to work with black sharecroppers in Alabama. He taught in a ramshackle shed converted to a summer school, with partitions that smelled fresh and bled sap, and little black children who did exactly what they were told. It was remedial reading mostly, though he had thought he would be teaching American history—and Oscar was jailed twice following demonstrations, "but they haven't tried to beat me up," he wrote Sue; "they beat up only on the little guys."

Oscar was thus perfectly placed that fall when the campus blew following the expulsion of a black football player caught stealing a hi-fi set from a white student, son of a state senator. Martha was among the group that "seized" the administration building and barricaded themselves in the president's office. The demands lay thick on the ground: amnesty, an end to racism, a university declaration against the war, bigger subsidies to Hispanic students, the abolition of grades and requirements, faculty tenure by student vote—the litany grew longer every day. Oscar was on the outside, and after he urged the football team to play the next-to-last game of the season despite the strike, the dean's office discovered that he might be useful as an intermediary.

"Negotiations" of course had been forbidden by both sides, but Oscar persuaded the dean to turn the heat back on in the buildings and for God's sake not to turn off the water, to permit not merely the delivery of sandwiches and Cokes to the nine students occupying the office, but even a change of clothing. In return he secured a pledge from the seven boys and two girls that they would not vandalize the office. As the strike dragged into a second week—three deadlines for eviction having been imposed and not enforced—the university moved some distance to satisfy demands: there would be money allocated to a Third World program, amnesty was impossible but punishment would be in the hands of a faculty-student committee without administration participation, a number of courses would be offered on a pass/fail basis. On the eighth day, Oscar sat in on a meeting with the trustees, and learned that the fourth deadline, for the next morning, would not be allowed to pass. He promised to try and persuade the revolutionists inside that they had got as much as there was to get, that much of the student support was falling away (the football team, having lost the next-to-last game, was especially disgusted), that, as one of the New York businessmen among the trustees had cynically suggested, the radicalization of the campus could be carried on by revealing the injustices of the trial-and-punishment procedures as well as by the continued occupancy of the office.

Oscar was in the office with his sister and her friends for five hours that night, sprawled on the couch for the last two of them, mostly listening to what he later told his history professor was "a foul-mouthed discussion of the metaphysics of repression." In the end, only the other girl, who had an upset stomach, went out the double doors with him. The doors locked behind them. She went through the police line undisturbed, and at Oscar's urging she phoned back from her dormitory to make the point. She said there seemed to be a lot of noise at the other end.

The dean said he would see what he could do to postpone the police raid at least one more day, but the next morning at five Oscar was shaken awake by a young instructor, leader of the most radical caucus of the faculty, who had been keeping vigil. Oscar pulled on a jump suit and ran to the building, where about twenty students and young faculty were being herded into wagons to keep them from interfering with the upcoming operations. The lawn was blue with police. Oscar ran through the lines and up the stairs, shouted through the doors and was admitted. The office was a horror—the furniture ripped open, desks splintered, secretaries' typewriters smashed, files dumped everywhere, paintings off the walls, thrown into corners, frames broken, canvas slashed. Stretches of wood paneling had been splintered. Chair legs were being held as clubs. Martha was nowhere to be seen. When Oscar shouted for her, a head jerked toward the president's bathroom, and Martha, eyes a dull red, sweater stretched shapelessly, fingers working, came to him. "No," she said. "No." He took her by the hand and ran out with her, and the police held them both at the outer doors downstairs. A stink of tear gas presently rolled down the stairs, and then the gang came down, two and three policemen handling each of the seven students, a black boy pulled down by his feet, his head bouncing on the marble steps, everyone shouting— except Martha.

At the police station, the boys were booked; Martha, at Oscar's urgent representation to the dean, was released in his custody. They sat in a corner booth at the back of the coffee shop near the police station, just opened at six o'clock, and she babbled: "Don't blame them, it wasn't something they wanted to do or decided to do, it was just that the moment you left they knew they'd lost and I was the only girl and it was the end of the world. It was like . . . Oh, no, don't think about it; they *didn't mean* what they were doing. It was just . . . Look, I'm going away for a while."

Martha left that afternoon; she did not go home, but told Oscar what to pick up for her; and later wrote him with an address in Indianapolis to which her things should be sent. Having done some service to the state, Oscar was able to arrange the dismissal of all charges against her without her reappearance. Her name was briefly in and immediately out of the newspapers, and none of the seven students who had been in the seized office with her ever spoke with Oscar about what had happened there. Sam and Raia got a letter from Martha saying she had dropped out of school for political reasons, and they believed it; they were unhappy but not distraught. Oscar was dissuaded by the dean from resigning his student government post. Almost from the moment he saw her at the bathroom door, he had known what revenge he would take. That weekend, home to pick up Martha's things, he went to Harry Johnson and offered his services. This meant that Harry alone became the repository of his confidence; he broke down and cried while giving it, and the hour that followed established a relationship with Harry Johnson unlike any other in Oscar's life.

In fact, Johnson wanted no part of Oscar's services, partly

because he did not wish such relationships with his agents, partly because he did not think the plan would work. Oscar argued he would still be trusted, they would never raise the subject with him and would assume his sister never told him. It was not impossible—not even unlikely—that the ending of the strike and the occupation would have radicalized him in their image. Yes, he would have to give up Sue; Harry, he said, trying a joke, didn't really want him to marry Sue anyway. He and Sue hadn't written to each other much this term, she was getting more and more tied into her music, and he had almost given up the piano now—it was going to go somehow. Harry was moved by the depth of the damage Oscar had suffered. Quite apart from his concern for his daughter, he did not wish to be a party to that; he told Oscar to wait and think it over, let the wounds heal.

In the event, Harry was not surprised when Oscar turned up one evening during Christmas vacation to see Sue, and picked a fight with him about the Vietnam War, a fight that quickly degenerated on Oscar's side into hurled obscenities of a kind Sue could not bear; she ran screaming from the living room, ordering Oscar to leave her house. Harry's benediction was "Don't think about it, girl; he has to do it"; that made matters marginally worse. When the university blew up again that spring, Oscar was one of the leaders, and got himself arrested in a futile attempt to storm the administration offices once more—an attempt the police were able to counter because they knew exactly what was coming and when, and they knew because Harry Johnson had told them. Harry sent Oscar a check after this episode, and Oscar returned it. But the next fall, when he was able to supply information about an arsonist group at Brooklyn College, acquired through his increasing web of acquaintances in the movement, Oscar kept the reward.

When he finished college, he accepted the draft, and he went to Vietnam, on the stated grounds—to his father, to his friends—that when workers everywhere lacked his options, he could not duck out as (face it) the middle-class son of middle-income parents. Sam spoke about Greek tragedies, about the impossibility of growing up with a consistent moral code in a capitalist society, about the terrible conflicts of loyalty that would bedevil a man fighting an unjust war—but he accepted Oscar's argument. A man had to fight in his country's army, even if it was a czarist army; Oscar could organize the ranks, for a future day. Harry, having been solemnly informed by Oscar that their deal was personal, that Oscar agreed with the people on whom he was spying that the war was "an atrocity," nevertheless arranged his introduction to counterintelligence, on the understanding that Oscar would have no part of a thought police, but would report whatever he learned that seemed designed to get Americans killed.

On the ground, Oscar found the war even more terrifying and disgusting than he had been saying it was. Because he made clear from the day he off-loaded at Danang his feeling that this war was one "no American should be asked to fight," he knew active hostility from daily acquaintances for the first time in his life—and he guaranteed what he wanted: that he would never be more than a grunt in the Army. It was only after a botched helicopter "insertion" had eliminated four noncoms that his college degree won him so much as a corporal's stripes. Word came to him from other antiwar soldiers, and he went to meetings at bars where comments cast in the tone of normal grousing had in fact a more specific meaning. Information from Oscar led to the dissolution of two fragging rings in the northern sector, and a secret commendation was put in the files, later to be very useful when a decision had to be made about the quantity of government money that would be spent to patch up the damage done to an apparent terrorist by his own bomb. Oscar served thirteen months in Vietnam, and emerged a veteran of forty-seven separate insertions—actions he described in a letter to Harry Johnson as "search and destroy raids that don't involve much search (because there's no way you're going to find anything here), but lots and lots of destroy. It's not like my father's war, and it's not like yours, either, not from anything I read. But you're not here. You're there."

When he returned to New York, Oscar was alone: his father had retired to Florida, where his mother was fighting emphysema; his sister, now married and trained as a teacher of disturbed children, was living happily and nonpolitically in Detroit. Almost his only friends in the eighteen months before he was drafted had been other students in the movement; he fell in with them again, was exhilarated by the growth of their support nourished by the spreading hatred of the war and the government, terrified by the increasing acceptance of violent games even by those who once would never have been told such things were possible. Almost the only older man living in New York with whom Oscar had a relationship of any content was Harry Johnson, whose marriage had broken up and who was at loose ends in the evenings. They took to dining together once a week in Harry's homemade safe house—the restaurant in Bay Ridge. And Harry convinced Oscar, who had begun to acquire irresistible qualities as a potential agent, that the objective situation of the antiwar movement required the frustration of violent designs, the surveillance of those who might create them. Like Oscar's father—which was not, as they both would say, an accident—Harry was always talking of "objective situations."

Oscar moved into a tenement in the East Village, studied Spanish, began to teach in an alternative school, became part of the nonleadership of the anarchist-minded Vietnam Veterans Against the War. Egged on by a press that loved them for copy and thus insisted on them as a serious social phenomenon, the crazies of the movement laid increasingly dangerous plans, which Oscar duly reported—though no longer in person, for as he became more useful, Harry became more reluctant to run even minimal risks that they would be seen together. It was a schizoid existence, knitting the web of revolution in the daytime and unraveling it at night; and still the war continued. Oscar's amiability began to fade. He drank too much, and one night in the East Village he got into a fight with a leather-jacketed motorcycle type that landed them both on the police blotter. He went to Florida for a week to see his parents, the bills paid by the FBI, and for one liberating half hour danced around the idea of laying all his uncertainties and unhappinesses at his father's feet—but then he knew that his father's oldest code, the insistence that everyone is on one side or the other, would make him an impossible receptacle for such a confession.

On return to New York, Oscar found that two young men—boys, really, college dropouts, speed freaks—had decided to include him in their cadre for an operation that involved bombing the passport office in Rockefeller Center. On the basis of explosion expertise acquired in Nam, Oscar insisted on arming the bomb himself; and as he fiddled with it, sabotaging the contacts, the thing exploded on the table.

Sue and Martha came to the hospital the same day, Martha radiating the happiness of her fulfillment behind the screen of her terror at what had happened to her brother. As she sat in the room and told him lies about what the doctors had said they could do for him, and described her work and her husband and the nephew he had never seen, he thought that he had now for sure paid in full for both his presence and his absence at the university, that when he came out—if he came out—he could do as he pleased. Coming out, however, was fourteen months away, months that saw rarely as much as a day without pain. And when he left the protected, sometimes grim yet often cheerful ward of the Veterans Hospital atop the hill in the Bronx, he found that the job his old friends had reserved for him, in the legal office with Craig Spitts, was the only job he could get.

97

The tenement where Oscar had lived was now an abandoned hulk; he found a place for sixty-five dollars a month on the third floor of a walk-up in the West Forties. Harry had been shocked; what with the pimps to one side and the Puerto Rican gangs to the other, it seemed a fearfully dangerous place. Oscar said, "We are all cripples here."

Harry had been uncomfortable with Oscar's job, too, afraid of trouble in the press and the courts if his cover was blown, and it was agreed that Oscar would do no reporting from the legal office. At least, now, the damned war was over; and Oscar was emeritus with the Veterans. But every so often one of the younger enthusiasts would look him up, and very occasionally Oscar would have a report for Harry. Two people on the FBI's wanted list had been picked up through tips from Oscar, and so far as Harry was concerned he more than earned his monthly check. Because of possible complications related to the job in the legal office, Harry was paying it himself, from the Whitmont money.

Oscar usually was depressed in the evening, and the contact with Harry did not help. Riding the subway back to Manhattan, he tried to concentrate on the book he had taken from the library, another one of those things about Watergate, which he couldn't stop reading. A policeman's life is not a happy one. He got off in the damp squalor of Eighth Avenue and Forty-third Street, and walked head down into the drizzle. In a doorway stood a black girl in a red raincoat, cheeks wet and shining under enormous granny glasses, a red beret over a head of soft curls. "Mister," she said quietly, "would you like a girl?"

Every day; every night; but this time he stopped. "You know—I would," he said.

"C'mon nex' door," she said, took his hand and began to pull him, around the corner, into a building marked Hotel—a dirty floor of broken tiles, a splintered desk manned by a grizzled drunk in a plaid wool shirt. The elevator stank, but the hall was not so bad, and the room she took him to—blond desk, blond chair, blond bedstead, piece of carpet on the floor—was the remains of a repair job, not of decay. As she opened the door, she said, "Fifty dollar for a french."

"Ain't got it," said Oscar.

"Forty," she said, then turned to look at him in the light for the first time. Her eyes found the empty sleeve sewn into the pocket of his raincoat. She winced. "I guess maybe you'd like it straight," she said.

Touched, he smiled for the first time in days.

She said, "Twenty-five, straight," and looked at him again, eyes wide, with what he thought was no small courage. "Guess you ain't no cop," she said, and threw her raincoat on the chair. She turned her back, lashed down the zipper, wriggled out of her dress and turned to face him, naked under the red satin slip that clung to her hips and her pointed breasts.

"Do people tell you how pretty you are?" Oscar said admiringly, an urgency in his gut.

"Nobody got no time for that," she said, and reached under his raincoat for his belt. "Nobody got no time for people like us." The gleam on her cheeks could have been rain, could have been tears; the urgency was gone. We're all cripples here. Oscar said, "It's all right; let's forget it." He was holding up his pants; she was pulling on them. She unzipped his fly and put her hands on his testicles. "It's all there," she said, giggling. "I make it good, I make it good for you."

Half laughing, half wretched, Oscar said, "No good. I'll pay you, but it's no good—forget it."

"Make it good!" she said hysterically, squeezing him.

"No good!" he shouted, and she fell away, crying.

He pulled up and zipped his pants, looked at her crouched on the floor, said, "I'm sorry," threw a ten-dollar bill on the bed and fled, running down the stairs, past the unconcerned deskman, out into the streets and four damp blocks back to his rooms. He flung himself onto his bed without turning on the lights or taking off the wet raincoat, and lay crouched on his side, looking out the window at the gas station sign that almost filled it. "No good," he said to himself again, then with an effort of will sat up, discarded the raincoat on the floor, pulled over the telephone and called Sue.

VI

The Greek

Nothing about their conversation or the block of identical brownstones had prepared Harry to find the elegant figure of Kaganopoulos—slim, aquiline profile, red corduroy smoking jacket, a brush mustache of glistening individual dark-gray hairs. But it was the right house. "What the fuck you want with me?" said the voice from the aristocratic figure in the half-opened door.

"That's for you to tell me," Harry said, showing the card in its glassine envelope.

"You gotta warrant?"

"I don't have a warrant, and I'm here alone," Harry said. "Let's just talk."

"I gotta license for every handgun here," said Kaganopoulos. "And you don't need no license for long guns."

"Look," said Harry, "it's nasty out here. If you're the guy we want, we're going to get you, and if you're not, you

101

can save yourself a lot of time and trouble by talking with me. Just let me in, and we'll sit down for half an hour, and that's probably it."

"Yeah, sure. You're on some fucking fishing expedition, and I oughta make you get the fucking warrant, but to hell with it. Come in."

A mousy brown female head poked around a door at the rear of the entrance hall as Harry entered, and Kaganopoulos said, "Nothing for you here, Fricka"; and the head disappeared. Kaganopoulos took a roll of keys out of his pocket and opened a door onto stairs leading down to a finished basement. This was no rumpus room. There were overstuffed leather couches on either side—the leather soft and polished, Harry noted with some surprise—but the central presence was a set of some twenty straight-backed chairs, five rows of four, facing on a display of flags and rifles on the end wall. Three of the four glass-fronted cases on the rear wall held a further collection of guns; the fourth was full of trophies. Under the crossed Greek and American flags at the front was a ribbon of Greek lettering. "You know what that says?" said Kaganopoulos.

"Not me."

"It says, 'Death to the Communist Traitors.' Now, how'dya like that?"

"All for it," said Harry casually. "May I sit down?"

"Yeah. Take a chair."

They sat in the back row, chairs turned so they were facing each other, their knees almost touching. Kaganopoulos waited. Harry waited. Finally Harry shook his head and said, "I'm here about the sniper murders."

Kaganopoulos snorted. "Shit," he said. "Why me?"

Harry waved a hand at the trophy collection. "Those you?"

"Who the fuck you think they are?"

"Well, we're looking in on everybody in this part of the country who shoots like that—because this sniper, whoever he is, he shoots like that."

Kaganopoulos began to laugh. "You think I go around shooting people just like that? Christ, I got more important things to do." He pushed back his chair, as though fearing contamination by triviality.

"I don't doubt it," said Harry. "I just want to be sure. Just tell me what you were doing on some dates I've got here—where you were, what you were doing—and so far as I'm concerned, I've got nothing more to do with you."

Kaganopoulos got up and loomed over Harry. "You think I'm some fucking child, I believe a story like that? You wanna know about my group, that's what you're here for. I'll tell you about my group—good, solid Americans, guys who served their country. Even you FBI pimps should be grateful—"

"No, no," Harry said, crossing his legs. "Mind if I smoke?"

"Yeah, I mind. There's no smoking in this room."

"Where were you Tuesday evening?"

"Here."

"Here is near enough to Hoboken. Did you have a meeting of your group?"

"Nah, I was just here with the missus."

"She'll say you were here all night?"

"Goddam right she will. She'll say whatever I tell her to say."

"Were you in Allentown October twenty-fifth?"

"How the fuck am I supposed to know? I was in Pennsylvania one day that week. I'll get my book and let you know."

"Thanks," said Harry, and watched Kaganopoulos climb the stairs. No way, he thought; this guy has other outlets. But, then, you never know. He thought of a psychiatrist friend who was forever complaining that the patients stole things from the office. The fact that they're *your* nuts doesn't make them less crazy—or less criminal. Kaganopoulos returned, carrying a Week-at-a-Glance calendar, with a new bulge in his breast pocket that was doubtless meant to be observed. It would not pay to try and take this man in tonight, whatever

103

was said. "What's the book tell you?" Harry called cheerfully before Kaganopoulos had reached the bottom stair.

"I was in Bethlehem October twenty-fifth. That's right next door. What's so fucking big about Allentown on the twenty-fifth?"

"A bum got shot there while he was bending over a garbage can. Were you in New Hampshire on the fifteenth?"

"Wait a minute. No. I was here."

"That's too bad—that's the day the Puerto Rican truckdriver got shot here."

"What are you, some fucking wise ass?"

"What is it exactly that you do when you travel?"

"I sell barber supplies—clippers, hair tonic, hot-towel machines, chairs—everything a guy needs for a barber shop. You already know that."

"Are you the muscle?"

Kaganopoulos sat down on the couch across the room. "No."

"You make arrangements for the muscle?"

"You're talking now, not me."

"Were you in Stamford, Connecticut, on the sixth?"

Kaganopoulos consulted the book. "That's a weekend."

"I know."

"Nah, I wasn't in Connecticut. I was in New Jersey; there was a sales meeting of my corporation. In Red Bank."

"Play some golf down there?"

"Yeah."

"What did you shoot?"

"I dunno—seventy-eight, seventy-nine. That's a tough course down there."

"One more. Concord, New Hampshire, September seventeen."

Kaganopoulos flipped pages. "Springfield, Mass.," he said.

"Springfield?"

Kaganopoulos rose in something like a rage, sweat on his

forehead. "You're not gonna fucking railroad me on this fucking thing," he said. "I got friends, and they got friends. I got nothing to do with this sniper, and you know it, you cocksucker."

"Fact is," said Harry conversationally, and rose to face him across the room, "I don't think you're my man. But get your friends out of your head—they won't help you on this. Seeing how upset you are, I'm going to leave now. When people get this upset, I don't like to talk with them unless they bring a lawyer. I don't think that's necessary here. You consult that book of yours, make a list of the people you saw on all those days—last Tuesday, October twenty-fifth, October fifteenth, October sixth, September seventeen. Write down the days. Especially in the evening hours. You come in with that list Monday morning, before you go out of town. You don't have to stay—just leave it, but check in with me. Johnson, ninth floor. You're not going anywhere this weekend, are you?"

"No."

"Glad to hear it. Don't."

Kaganopoulos was trembling. "I'll get you your fucking list, but if you frame me, I got friends for that, plenty friends. Now, get outa this room, get outa my house."

"You lead the way," said Harry; and after a moment's pause Kaganopoulos did so. Not until he was out of the house did Harry think, This was my government's thin red line of freedom in Greece. Jesus Christ!

And not until he was in the cab he caught under the el, heading back toward Manhattan, did he remember the other thing Oscar had talked about at dinner. Well, Harry thought, there were so many protections on that, he had no cause for worry. He grinned to himself in the back seat, realizing that was probably what Kaganopoulos was thinking, too, right now.

He was wrong; Kaganopoulos was scared.

Because too many people whose counsel was needed would be unavailable once the market opened, Coffees Monteblanco had from the days of old Julius Whitmont established a pattern of breakfast meetings for decision purposes. Tony when possible scheduled them for Fridays before weekends in the country, when he would be leaving the office early and could put in a full day only by starting early—and when he'd have the weekend to mull the results. This Friday the meeting was educational, as he told the seven men who gathered in his office for what was probably the best cup of coffee being served in New York City at that moment. "I need the education," he explained. "I'm not objecting to hitting old Ensor for another eight hundred thousand dollars, I'm not objecting to the use of my home for the purpose, but I want to know very exactly why we need it and why Charlie here can't handle it through the vice-president who made the first loan."

"Tempo," said Charlie. "Goddam building just costs more than we thought it was going to cost. We've got contracts to deliver freeze-dried out of that plant in May, and you can't get that machinery shipped down there without the letter of credit."

"Why do I hear about it this week?" Tony said. "More important, why does Ensor hear about it this week? I thought we already had that letter of credit."

The oldest man in the room—they were all older than Tony—was the operations vice-president, an American Gothic type Julius had stolen from General Foods a generation before, who still knew what General Foods was going to do a month before anyone in White Plains knew. He began to answer with Charlie, who stopped talking. "Well, we sort of used it already, Tony," he said, removing his rimless bifocals as though to look at him more directly. "Charlie got an okay from the bank, but I'm not sure they entirely understood what we were saying. The contractor down there got way over a few of the estimates, and we couldn't afford to

106

have him go belly up. It's been like that in Santos—big development projects with government interest, they get the good workers. We've been hitting their people on schedules, there were a couple of change orders, and there were some—uh—political problems associated with importing some of the electrical equipment; you'll recall we had a meeting on that, and it wound up costing money. I thought we'd had a couple of places where we'd saved something, but we didn't. I can go over all the drawings and specs and estimates and final prices with you, but frankly, it would just waste your time. It's only a ten percent overrun, Tony; that's not out of line these days."

"Do we have a good enough reason why we can't do it ourselves?"

"You know the position in the market. Would you rather fiddle with Chemical on the commodity loans, or Ensor on the building?"

"How about mortgaging some of the development property in Connecticut?"

The financial vice-president rushed to be heard: "That's an upstream loan from a subsidiary for the purpose of a subsequent downstream loan to another subsidiary. Tony, it's Penn Central stuff—after a while you don't know where you stand any more. We've got partners in Connecticut. You going to tell them about it?"

Tony looked around the office—the pickled pine walls which had been his mother's taste, the portrait of his father glowering from beyond the conference table. "Not the world's best reasons," he said. "Are you guys sure this thing makes us money at these costs?"

The operations man nodded vigorously. "The margins are very good," he said. "Everybody's running at one hundred five percent, because the fast-food chains decided they could save some dough not making the coffee. Long-term contracts; big customers; no sweat. Anybody who builds next year, it costs him more. Hank has all the figures, you don't need them. It's a good case, the only thing is we don't want to get stuck with the committees in that bank. This is a very distant loan for them and they can take a long time in Philadelphia."

"All I want you to do," said Charlie, "is make sure that loan officer is looking forward to hearing me when I show up on Wednesday."

"How soon do we need the money?" Tony asked.

"First of the month," said the comptroller, quickly.

"Guess I'll have to turn Carla loose on him," said Tony gloomily. "It's a hell of a way to run a business."

"We're in with that savings bank," said the financial v.p. reasonably, "because the fellow is a neighbor of yours."

"All right," said Tony. "All right. Anyway, it's all set, I'm seeing him tomorrow night." He turned to his chief trader. "Last week you were exercised about a feeling you had that we couldn't put a finger in the air at the exchange without somebody was already there looking for it. You still think there's someone ripping off our programs?"

"Yes. More than ever."

"What have you done about it?"

"Well, there's two of us keeping an eye on the order desks, and we've changed the access code at the computer."

"Have you thought again about hiring an agency?"

"Yes, and I'm still against it."

"Why?"

"Just makes that many more people who know our troubles."

"Which are that we owe too much money against an asset in Brazil," Tony said, sighing. "And where *do* we stand on the open position this morning . . . ?"

Oscar was in the office early because he hadn't slept well, and he killed a little time with the receptionist, going over the day's court calendar, which she kept. Shortly before nine o'clock, Adrian Francis came purposefully through the door, inquired for Spitts, whom Oscar had not known was already at work, and vanished. Oscar went to his office hoping to be called into that meeting, but he wasn't, and at ten o'clock he ambled over to Spitts's door. "Is that congressman's assistant still there?" he said to the secretary.

"No, he's alone. Shall I tell him you're waiting?"

"Un-huh."

She buzzed, spoke into the phone, and nodded, and Spitts was looking somewhat quizzically at the door when Oscar entered.

"I'd hoped you'd want me at that meeting."

"No need."

"Did you talk about the High Hills business?"

"No; he wouldn't know any more about that than I would."

"Don't you think you should alert him?"

"Just get more people in trouble. You know better than that, Oscar."

"I'd love to see somebody bury it."

"What else?" said Spitts.

"Nothing else. If I may, what *were* you talking about with Francis?"

"His boss is almost ready to move on those FBI hearings. He wanted advice on how jazzy I think the privacy issue can be."

"What did you tell him?"

"Plenty jazzy. But he doesn't quite have his case yet."

"Think I could help?"

"I don't know yet," said Craig Spitts. "I'll find out."

Harry's workday stretched out in tangles as he drank his coffee and looked over the washed rooftops, brilliant in a November sun. At eight o'clock he called the prison upstate and got through to the warden. "I don't want to panic you," Harry said after identifying himself, "and I don't want to tell you right now exactly what prompts the call. If there's something to do, I'll give you everything I know; right now,

I'm not authorized to make any requests. I want to know, what are the provisions for preventing visitors from smuggling weaponry into the prison?" It added up to the inspection of packages and a light frisking by guards—which could be a heavy frisking if there was a reason for it. "What about lawyers?" In principle, the same; the prison claimed the right to examine the contents of the briefcase. In practice . . . the voice said, and trailed off. Then picked up again with obvious questions, which Harry, rather than evading—no point in that—simply declined to answer for the moment. He assured the warden that what he had been tipped about was not scheduled to come down today, and that he would report back either way later in the day. Then Harry read the first half-dozen pages of the *News,* the front pages of two sections of the *Times,* put the newspapers aside and picked up the computer printout again, whispering the names as he read them.

At the office he went first to Adams's room rather than his own, and finding the outer door still locked, he taped a message on the frosted glass: "Must talk with you muy pronto." The call came only a few minutes after he got to his desk, without the intervention of secretaries. When Johnson finished his précis of the High Hills story, Adams said, "I was sort of hoping you wanted to talk about our sniper."

"The impossible takes a little longer," Harry said.

"Well. What do you want to do?"

"I'd like our anti-hijacking people to borrow metal-detecting equipment and personnel from FAA, and put them into High Hills tomorrow for the day. I think the warden will be happy to have them."

"All right. I'll have them call you."

"Who pays for it?"

"Oh, shit," said Adams. "I guess we do. They could never move fast enough."

"Shall I make the arrangements with the warden?"

"You made the contact. I guess you have to follow through. I hate to see you take the time."

"I do have one possibility on the sniper problem," Harry said. "I saw him last night. I rate him two, maybe three, on a scale of ten."

"You want to tell me about him?"

"Not worth your time right now."

"You want a tail on him?"

"If I did, I'd put one there. When I need more people, I'll ask. Someone in organized crime may know something about this guy, though; I'll have a talk with them."

"I had two phone calls from Washington to my home last night," Adams said. "The next time this guy hits, the pot boils over. The Bureau would find it very useful right now to put this fellow away."

No kidding, Harry thought; but what he said was, "Yes, sir."

"Check in with me this afternoon," Adams said, "so I know what to say when they call me tonight."

Less than half an hour later, the anti-hijack office called; less than an hour later, the FAA had assigned a team of three, an x-ray machine, a metal-detector doorway, and two hand-held units, all to be loaded at Kennedy and ready for an FBI driver to take them to an unannounced destination at seven the next morning. Between the two calls, Harry disposed of Druck, the second-best-chance name on the CIA list, by a quick telephone call to his office, which was entirely convincing in its statement that he had been assigned ten months ago to the California division and had not been East since. (That explained why the name had not been on the computer printout; some people's computer files, Harry thought, were more up to date than others'.) He called one of the Mafia experts, and requested a readout on Kaganopoulos at their convenience.

Then there was a long conference call with the warden

and his security chief, a complete report on what Harry feared might be planned for Saturday at the prison, and on the support he was prepared to offer. The warden first checked and found that "the gentleman in question" was indeed to receive a lawyer's visit the next midday, and that the visitor had specifically demanded a "touch" visit, with no grille between himself and his client. The warden began to grow disturbed, even excited, as he contemplated the hazards; he eagerly welcomed help from a metal-detection team; he told the security chief to see to it that this inmate was sequestered from any and all possible friends for the next twenty-four hours.

Harry stressed the importance of putting *all* of tomorrow's visitors through the procedure, to reduce the risks to his informant. The warden inquired how many FBI people would be at the prison to help, and was, to say the least, disappointed when informed there would be none. Harry suggested state troopers, but the warden wouldn't hear of it: "Alerts everybody and his family to the fact that there's something up at the prison." No, he'd go with what he had—except that he'd expect Harry himself to be there. Harry patiently explained that his presence was impossible, for the same reasons of risk to the informant, but the warden wasn't having any: Harry could stay in the warden's office, young Fitch wouldn't ever know he was there, they would need his advice. A state matter, this was, Harry murmured; that lawyer who's bringing the gun is a congressman's son, said the warden. And just because it was Harry who carried the news, it was automatically a federal matter.

In the end, there was no escaping, partly because the warden probably *would* need advice before tomorrow was over. It was agreed that Harry would get there by ten in the morning, would not meet with the FAA people or supervise their installation, would not meet with the security detail, but would be available in the warden's residence (rather than his office) until visiting hours were over. Should Fitch be arrested, it would be on a state charge, and no doubt the prosecutors would have to know something about why High Hills had begun using metal detectors on precisely this day— but all that could wait. The warden thought that perhaps a permanent x-ray and metal-detection apparatus could be installed in the future; the more he thought about the idea— and this conversation ran more than an hour—the more he liked it.

Behind this call were others, one from Vinnie Palio at New York police headquarters, thanking Harry for the computer list so far, mentioning that there were several people on it about whom they already knew a fair amount and wished to know more, and asking when the telephone company would be ready with the more extensive takeout. Another from Wu, a chief of staff's twice-daily check-in, with word that one of the agents assigned had gone down to Philadelphia the night before and had already reported back with word that the two Philadelphia names on the CIA special list were all clear, one of them being an entertainer who had worked the month of October in Acapulco, the other being a factory foreman with a time-clock record (the agent had asked not for anyone's record but for lists of absentees on specific days; due care was being exercised).

Tilly had pulled the file on young Fitch the gunrunner, and now Harry browsed it—thirty items, mostly garbage reports on student demonstrations. The congressman's son was trouble prone: three times he had been beaten up, once badly enough to be hospitalized; he'd sued a campus guard for what was apparently a vicious assault, including a deliberate kick in the testicles. It seemed unlikely that anything on that order could happen to a prison visitor, but the history gave Harry another reason for attendance on the morrow.

He went out at noon as usual and emptied the mailboxes in the post office, but he lunched at his desk, catching up with the newspapers he'd neglected at breakfast and the clips he'd pushed aside in the morning. As he read, the second channel of his mind was constantly repeating the names from the printout: Carson, Handelman, Gross, Silvano, Gilette, Harbison, Cratter. . . .

Carl Ensor showed up, unexpected and unannounced, in the Cherry Hill conference room a few minutes after lunch, looked around at the computer terminals and the men attending them, and closed the door gently behind him. It was one of his own people who heard the door, and turned. "Mr. Ensor! Sir!"

Gilette, who had been at one of the keyboards, illustrating a retrieval problem, spun around and got up. "Didn't know you were coming, Ambassador."

"Thought you might want some help selling these fellows, Nick." Ensor was a large, stout man with a benevolent expression, not much over fifty but distinctly on the other side—fringe of puffy gray hair around a tanned scalp, thick horn-rimmed glasses on a stub nose. He carried himself with easy authority, both parts being real—the ease and the authority. It was a land owning family; his father had been chairman of the bank before him, and he had resigned from the Foreign Service to take over when the doctor told his father the truth. That was five years ago, and everyone agreed he had fitted in easily at the bank. It had been his life's work—fitting in easily in new places—and this place was familiar from his childhood. By now, he thought (though he was wrong, for reasons he could not have imagined), he would probably have been assistant secretary of state for some Godforsaken region. Being the chairman of a savings bank, he often said, was not that much unlike being an ambassador. Except that in a bank he didn't get much chance to use his French, his German, or his Serbo-Croatian. "How is this stuff my friend Gilette wants to sell us?" he said to the four men from the bank, who were all standing now in variously uneasy attitudes.

"Well, sir," said the senior of them, "there are things it can do that we can't do now. And they tell me it's plug-

114

compatible with our IBMs. By the time you're done, though, it's going to cost more than we thought."

"Always does," said Ensor cheerfully. "Well, I was at lunch on this side of the river, and I decided there wasn't much point going back to the office. I thought," he said to Gilette, "that if you could get away a little early, I'd show you where we're shooting tomorrow. What is it, six, seven years since we've done this together?"

"Eight years," said Gilette, smiling.

"Won't be like Brioni," Ensor said, "but it ought to be a candidate for the second best you ever saw. And I've signed you up for dinner tomorrow. I hope you don't mind."

"Delighted," Gilette said. "And happy to be out of here now, too—my associates can do everything I can do. I'd like you to meet them."

Ensor had immediately noticed the black area sales manager, with whom he now firmly shook hands. He approved of that: he was on the board of Leon Sullivan's Opportunities Investment Corporation in Philadelphia, and gave speeches about the need for builders especially to increase their hiring of blacks. The bank was heavily involved in two federally guaranteed urban renewal ventures, but was under attack for redlining in North Philadelphia, and the sight of Gilette's area manager reminded Ensor that he had given orders for everyone to be on the alert for someone "from that community" who might be a "suitable" senior lending officer. "You're the fellow who's actually got to make this sale, eh?" he said. "Well, we'll give you your chance."

"I'm sure you will, sir," said the area manager, very enthusiastically.

"Do you do any hunting, son?"

"No, I'm afraid I don't, sir."

"Too bad. Most democratic thing in the world, hunting," Ensor said expansively. "One of your fellows has a blind in the bay—oh, maybe ten, fifteen miles from mine. Man's a good shot, it can get him accepted anywhere in the world.

Oh, I don't say immediately, but soon enough, soon enough. Look at Nick, here. Just a boy off a farm, really, with medals for shooting, and he got to eat dinner with Marshal Tito on Brioni—one of the most powerful men in the world wanted him to come and go hunting with him and even come to dinner."

"That's right," said Gilette.

"Damnedest thing," said Ensor reflectively. "Matter of fact, the Jugs knew about him before I did. I got a call asking me if this new lieutenant on the diplomatic list was the same Gilette who'd been at Leiden with some American college-champion rifle team, so I called Nick in, first time I laid eyes on him, and he said, yes, that was him, and we were off to the races. Anyway," Ensor said, returning to the area manager, "teach your son to shoot."

The area sales manager, who had heard the same advice from a very different political perspective only a few years before, said, "Yes, sir, we'll do that."

"Good!" said Ensor, and slapped him high on the shoulder. "Now, I bet you're better than Nick at showing off this equipment of yours, aren't you?"

"Not really, sir," the area sales manager said, "but I think I can do everything that's left."

"You go get yourself packed up," Ensor said to Gilette, "and I'll see how the spiel sounds from your man."

"Do you need any of this equipment with you," the area sales manager said to Gilette in a low voice, "on your Monday or Tuesday calls?"

"No; Monday's an existing installation, and Tuesday's a meeting at IBM about the software package, some proprietary problem. That's just papers. And lawyers. What we can say, what they can say—if we demonstrated, we'd take away all the fun."

Ensor said, commandingly but not impatiently, "You get yourself ready, Nick." And to the area sales manager, "You show me something with my boys here, something I haven't seen before."

Gilette nodded, and smiled, and went off. He returned about twenty minutes later—having allowed enough time for Ensor to see one of the retrieval-and-sorting tricks the equipment was especially good at—carrying a big suitcase in one hand and in the other the leather-covered, ornately tooled gun case with the hooks that hung it concealed under the dashboard of the wagon. Ensor was watching printout emerge from the fast printer. "Stow that stuff in the Caddy," he said. "I'll have the chauffeur drive your car and we can ride together. Let me take another minute and see if I can understand what your man is showing me here."

When Gilette returned from the parking lot, Ensor said, "Well, don't want to get off so late we catch the traffic. You fellows," he said to his technicians, "get a report on this to me by—what do you say—Wednesday all right? And you," he said to the area sales manager, "give me a call, oh, a week from today, just ask for me, and I'll tell you who you ought to see next. Okay?"

Gilette had already given his keys to Ensor's chauffeur, who was standing by the Cadillac now, waiting to open the doors. Gilette slid into the passenger's seat and stretched his legs onto the furry pile of the alpaca floor covering. "I don't see how a driver stays awake in all this comfort," he said.

"You've got a point, Nick," Ensor said, and backed the car out of its slot. "Sorry Maria couldn't be with us this weekend," he said. "She'd have enjoyed the party tomorrow night. We liked that girl; lovely child, *bien élevée*. Good daughter makes a good wife. Ann's been pushing on me to ask the two of you for weeks and weeks, because she got it into her head that she wanted to see Maria."

"You know how it is," Gilette said, "when there's a kid. She'd have loved to come, but she couldn't get free. And

I'm afraid she hasn't really been feeling too well recently."

"Nothing serious, I hope."

"Doctor doesn't think there's anything. It's mostly psychological—worries about her father. You haven't been getting any news from Belgrade, have you?"

"No."

"It's been five months since we've heard from her father, and they were allowing him a letter a month until now. She's sure something's happened to him."

"They never have let him out, have they?"

"No."

"Tell me again when we get to my place," Ensor said, "and I'll make a note to see what I can find out next week." He looked at his watch. "If we hustle," he said, "I can show you the territory we'll be in tomorrow, before we go to the place. We're going to have only one crack at it, I fear. Put together our presence at dawn tomorrow morning and a party with dinner served at like ten o'clock tomorrow night, I've got too old to go back for more on Sunday."

"No problems," Gilette said, watching the frieze of denuded trees move past the car. "I've got to be in Binghamton Monday morning, so the earlier I leave on Sunday, the better."

Ensor pulled the Cadillac into the fast lane, and gunned it.

Harry's afternoon featured Kaganopoulos at its beginning and, disturbingly, at its end. His friend in the organized-crime division reported in with a Bureau view that Kaganopoulos was at most a part-time and more likely only a potential soldier, a route man on an extortionist run that had been laid out by others long ago. He had come in as a friend of a friend on Corfu; his outside interests were considered freakish by his employers; the word was that someday on a difficult job he might be useful to them, especially on a rooftop job. He was reputed to have killed a couple of people in Greece.

The Mafia expert assumed Harry was interested as part of the subversives-control operation, and Harry said nothing to disillusion him.

The call at the end of the day was from Vinnie Palio. "Look," he said, "we think Kaganopoulos is a live one."

"Maybe."

"One of our guys called him," said Palio, "and asked him to come in; and he said he'd already seen you and that was enough. Is it true?"

"I saw him," Harry said.

"So far as we can find out," Palio said, "he's not got an alibi for any of the days. We've talked with his employers—"

"Oh, have you, now?" said Harry.

"—and they want to be helpful here, you know. He's in it but not of it, if you know what I mean, and even if he was one of their own, they don't like the idea of this sort of solo work. Anyway, his schedule put him within reaching distance of every one of these victims, and none of these guys was with him on any of the days."

"He told me he was at a meeting of theirs on the Saturday crime," Harry said.

"No. He was there Friday night and they shooed him. We know about that meeting; there were some bigger shots there than like to associate with the likes of Kaganopoulos."

"Interesting," Harry said.

"He's got another lady on the side," Palio continued, "and she's up in Connecticut. You'll remember that's where the shooting was that weekend."

"So," said Harry.

"We put a tail on him this afternoon, and he saw it and slipped it," said Palio. "Now he's back home. So our guy went and called him, and he told us you'd been there."

"I'd like you to leave him alone," said Harry. "He's coming in here Monday with an alibi sheet, and I'd like to have our people check it out. There are reasons."

"Look, you son of a bitch," said Palio, and it was not just bantering, "we're tired of having you cut us out on mob investigations. It's insulting."

"This isn't a mob investigation," Harry said, and decided he would have a drink tonight.

"You're damned right it's not. It's a homicide investigation, and the homicide occurred in our jurisdiction. You're in here, supposed to be helpful."

"I'm trying to be helpful."

"I don't see how it's helpful for you to go see a suspect on our turf, and tell us to leave him alone because he's bringing you an alibi sheet."

"What do you want to do?"

"The whole number. Arrest warrant, search warrant—we want to fire those guns he's got and see what the bullets look like. We've had our eyes on him for a long time: surly, unstable bastard."

"I don't deny that," Harry said. "But I don't think he's our sniper."

"Any reasons?"

"I spent an hour talking with him, and that's my judgment."

"Do you have some reason to protect him?"

"If I did, I couldn't tell you."

"Shit on that," said Palio. "Either we're partners in this thing or you can take your computer printout and tiddle with it yourself."

"He may not be that easy to pick up," Harry said. Palio said nothing. "Of course, I can't stop you," he added.

"I don't figure it," said Palio. "You and I never had any problems. One of our guys called your strike force and they told us you'd put through a sort of casual query on Kaganopoulos today; they thought it was political. If you'll tell me the game you're playing, maybe I can help. If it's just that you feel we have to accept your judgment, you're asking me for more than I can give."

"If you go ahead," Harry said mildly, "I hope to Christ he's our man, because if he isn't, there's going to be a lot of pain in this thing."

"We know we can't keep a tail on him," Palio said ruminatively. "He's got the talent, he had the opportunity, and he's a nut. We have the responsibility here, not you."

"That's true," Harry said. "I said I couldn't stop you. If you want to talk to me tomorrow," he said, "use that number I gave you."

"Will you be at your office?"

"No."

"Where will you be?"

"Can't tell you that, either."

"We're going to get those warrants tomorrow," said Palio decisively. "I'll call you before we move."

"Thanks," said Harry, and the conversation ended. Harry called Frank Wu, "to put you in the picture"; then set up a meeting of his miniature task force for early Sunday afternoon, when with luck the material from the telephone company would be in; then debated with himself putting in a call to Langley, to alert Phil, and decided there was no need, not yet. It was the first of several mistakes he would make that weekend.

VII

Our Troubles Come
Not as Single Spies . . .

Apparently built into one of the supports of the fourposter
bed, the alarm went off in Nicholas Gilette's ear like a hand
grenade in a bunker, and he was on his feet instantly, facing
the door, where Carl Ensor stood in purple velour bathrobe.
"Sleepyhead," Ensor said. "It's after four-thirty." They had
been drinking the night before, with Ann Ensor and the two
men who would join them in the hunting party that morning—the senior partner of a Philadelphia law firm and a
United States senator. Gilette felt the results from one ear
to the other, right across his forehead.

"Shave when we get back," Ensor advised. "I've got a
breakfast on the table for you, and I don't want to throw
it away."

Gilette remembered that one of the things he had envied
the FSOs in Belgrade was their capacity to forget the next
morning what they had drunk the night before. He mumbled

agreement and went to the huge bathroom with its bright-pink oversized tiles, twin marble sinks, sunken marble bath-tub. And this was only one of six guest rooms in the brick "place," probably not the most elaborate, what with a senator there and all. Gilette pulled on thermal underwear, heavy plaid shirt and thick corduroy hunting trousers. Then he took the shotgun from the long box, and wiped invisible specks of dust from the barrels with a chamois cloth, and sighted out the window to a distant tree. It was a Swiss gun, his grandfather's originally, ninety centimeters double-barreled over-and-under, sixteen gauge with a choke he had further reduced, greatly compressing the pattern of shot at the target. His grandfather had been the one who had taught him to shoot, starting with a half-sized shotgun when Nicholas was nine years old, on the farm bought through ten years' unremitting labor as lumberjack and yardman by a man who had never been known to spend an unnecessary penny. Except on his only grandson, his daughter's boy by the auto mechanic's son who had gone off to Korea and died in one of those forward hospitals the TV people found so funny. Gilette loaded his own shells; he took a handful of them from a cardboard container wedged into the end of the carrying case, and put them in the pocket of the ski jacket.

Gilette's companions of the morning were already at the six-foot-long table in the center of the large, wood-panelled kitchen. A sullen black servitor was flipping pancakes in a skillet at the huge iron stove, and shoveled four of them onto a plate for Gilette as he sat down. Greetings at five in the morning are never particularly warm or time-consuming, and Gilette applied himself to breakfast. Ensor was looking at his watch, and Gilette drank the steaming black coffee straight down, searing the back of his throat. Outside, in the light from the kitchen window, the mist lay between the great oaks like cotton. "Are we going to be able to see anything out there?" Gilette asked.

"Tide's turning," said Ensor, and he looked at his watch

again. Then he led the way out to the Land-Rover, already parked in the illuminated driveway, with the two coal-black Labradors jumping about in the back. Gilette took the senator's gun and gave him a hand to help him into the back seat. Ensor, a Philadelphia Phillies baseball cap perched incongruously over the round face, dropped the sack with the decoys into the back with the dogs, climbed into the driver's seat and hustled them away.

The dirt road ran through the woods to a gray dock where the headlights shadowed missing slats. A car was already parked to one side at the end of the road, and an unshaven leather-skinned guide was waiting in one of the two rowboats with their low-powered outboards. There was a gray brightening as the night loosened. Ensor gave the guide the decoys to set out, and put his two older guests in the guide's boat, and then he and Gilette started after them. The smell of swamp was strong in the fog, and bits of moisture congealed on their cheeks as they went off toward the rush-covered mud islands dimly outlined half a mile into the bay.

"Best duck-hunting country in the world," Ensor said approvingly. The wake of the rowboat ahead of them seemed to be moving the water enough to make the fog lift. Wooden platforms stood on piles hammered through the mud in the high rushes. Bits of sky were appearing toward the north, and the two blinds were close enough for conversation. "I think let's have Nick take the first shot," Ensor said. "Show us how to do it."

"No way," said Gilette. "The senator has rank on me. I'll pick up anything he leaves."

"Looked like a small bore on that gun of yours," the Philadelphia lawyer said invisibly from the other blind. "Is it European?"

"Started off European," Gilette said. "My grandpa did so much work on it and then I've put it through the shop so often that it's mostly American now. But it's a sixteen. The shells are my own Weatherby, basically; makes me good for fifteen or twenty yards more than you fellows are, if I shoot straight."

"Still shooting competitively?" Ensor said.

"Not so much. Don't have the time. And some of the new guns they use take a lot of the fun out of it. I don't like to *shoot* with a computer. But I keep my hand in."

"I bet you do," said Ensor.

The day had brightened considerably, and the fog was reduced to wisps. The sky had taken a pattern of high clouds and lightening blue; somehow it seemed colder without the moisture. Ensor stamped on the boards of the platform. In the boat behind the blinds, the guide said softly, "Here they come."

Off in the northern distance was a high, ragged V of ducks, pointing toward the bay. They swooped down, then up, then down again, toward the decoys bobbing a hundred feet from the blinds. "The senator first," Ensor said in a low voice, and there was a click from the adjacent blind. The pattern of ducks dropped rapidly, swerved west, then came at the hunters almost head on. Gilette slipped the two shells into their chambers, raised the gun to his shoulder and sighted the incoming birds. "So beautiful," he said in a whisper.

The senator shot, missed—too high—shot again, and the lower part of the pattern caught one of the birds on the right side of the V. It struggled to fly on with a broken wing. The flock rose noisily away, and Gilette shot once, twice, each blasting away the neck of one of the fleeing birds. The dogs splashed into the water to retrieve them. "What'd I tell you?" Ensor shouted. "What'd I tell you? If the dogs don't mark 'em you can sell 'em in a butcher shop, as though you'd raised 'em. Not a ball in the flesh, right, Nick?"

"Dunno," said Gilette. "Maybe one or two. Not a perfect shot."

"I bet you could do it with a rifle," Ensor said.

"Oh," said Gilette, beginning to clean the gun, "I imagine I could. I'm better with the rifle."

125

The gray fortress walls of High Hills Prison loomed surprisingly, some hundreds of yards off through the bare trees, as the car came to the hilltop. Big and ugly. A prosecutor had once said to Harry that he felt about prisons the way Justice Holmes felt about taxes: they were the price he paid for civilization. In his reports and in his conversation when he was careful, Harry referred to them as "penal institutions," and he thought it folly to deny that their purpose was punishment. In Harry's experience, penal institutions drew to their long-term service three types—politicos after a soft berth, sadists who enjoyed being in the presence of punishment, and masochistic optimists who thought they were operating an educational facility. High Hills, Harry had found out, was in the care of a politico; might be better or worse for the inmates, but it was an upbeat thought for Harry.

To say the least, High Hills was expecting him. At the gate, the two guards saluted, and one of them insisted on climbing into the car to ride with Harry to the warden's house, suburbia-within-the-walls, complete to garden. Here one of the warden's cars had been removed from the garage so Harry could park indoors, which would help conceal his presence. The guard insisted on toting the two stuffed briefcases Harry had brought with him, all the way in to the warden's study, which was to serve as Harry's office for the day. It was a pompously wood-paneled, dark little room, decorated almost exclusively with steel-framed black-and-white photographs of the incumbent at some affair with governors, state senators, assemblymen, judges, county executives, party chiefs. The desk had been cleared, and a television set facing it was tuned to the output of a camera in the prison visitors' area to enable Harry to follow the action.

Coffee was served, and Harry watched the FAA installers complete their assembly of the x-ray machine and the metal-detector gate while the carpenters hammered up the partitions that would screen the area. There were almost a dozen people

126

involved; fast work, Harry thought. The warden demonstrated the use of the telephone to reach the control post in the visitors' area, and was attempting to make conversation about what should be done after his people had seized Joshua Fitch's gun, when Harry urgently begged to be permitted to peruse what was in his briefcases, which was the virtually complete documentation to date of police interrogations related to the sniper killings. The warden rather stiffly acknowledged his dismissal from his own study, and went out to make personal inspection of the work in the visitors' area.

Harry was looking for a car. Everything about the maps and descriptions of the killings argued that the sniper was working from an automobile, and obviously he was escaping in an automobile. The police prowling the area after the shooting would routinely inquire about any unfamiliar vehicles seen in the neighborhood, and would note all reports. Equally routinely, this material would be screened out of everything passed upstairs, because for any one police department the descriptions of thirty different vehicles seen near the scene of the crime would be useless. But if any one of them turned up in several cities, there might be something worth knowing. Might. Harry took an oversized pad of graph paper out of one of the briefcases and notated the columns in his neat, rounded handwriting: New York, Allentown, Stamford, Concord, Hoboken—a separate page for each make of vehicle. Then he began reading through the raw reports, page after page of illiterate summary that would never have come out of notebooks without his request. He did the small cities first, and had got through Concord and Stamford when the telephone rang; it was the warden in the control room at the visitors' area.

"We're starting to process people," he said.

Harry looked up at the television screen and saw a black lady with a shopping bag depositing it on the familiar airport conveyor belt. "Very good," he said.

"Seems to be working fine," said the warden encouragingly.

"I thought it would," Harry said.

"No sign of Fitch yet," the warden said.

"Well, let me know," said Harry.

The warden seemed to be waiting for something else, which Harry could not supply. "Well," he said finally, "I'll keep in touch."

"Excellent," Harry said, and returned to the graph paper. There were, of course, dozens of cars reported, all makes and models, sizes and colors. It was remarkable how rarely they duplicated. After the first hour, Harry could no longer entirely trust his memory, and had to run down the page to make sure he wasn't missing a duplication. You saw people's prejudices at work in these lists: sinister black Cadillacs, "foreign sports cars," "dirty old cars" of various makes. The difficulty of distinguishing current brands of automobile emerged in a rash of "or" identifications. But there were duplications: a blue Plymouth hatchback, a gray four-door Olds, a white Ford station wagon, a red Volkswagen, turned up at least four identifications in at least two cities. Harry kept at it.

A little after eleven, the beeper sounded, and he called his reference number. It was Vinnie Palio in New York police headquarters. He returned the call, to be told that a warrant had been secured on Kaganopoulos, and the plans were to pick him up as he returned from church Sunday morning, seize the guns and test-fire them that afternoon.

"What about if he knows you're coming?"

"I've got good security."

"You've got judges' clerks. And as he will tell you, he has friends. What kind of car does Kaganopoulos drive, by the way? Have you checked that out?"

"You mean when he's traveling?"

"Yes."

"It's a gray Dodge panel truck."

"I'm looking over the police reports on cars seen in the neighborhood," Harry said conversationally, "and that's just about the only description I don't find in them."

"Look, we arrest a lot of guys and let 'em go."

"Sure," said Harry disgustedly. "Wish we could get warrants on our side as easy as you do on yours. So you're going to pick him up and take him to the station house and wait while he gets a lawyer on a Sunday—"

"Gives us time to fire the guns—"

"And when you're done questioning him, in the presence of a lawyer, you're going to let him go. All I can say is, I wish you wouldn't."

"And all I can say is, I wish I knew what you're fretting about. Off the top, I'd think anything we could do to get this guy out of the way would be nice and congenial to your normal operation."

"You'll keep me informed?" said Harry.

"Damn right."

"Good luck."

The next call was the warden's: "He's here! Young Fitch— he's here!"

"How long before you put him through the scanners?" Harry asked.

"Not very, not very—his client's already up here in a holding pen."

"All right; I'll keep my eye on the screen. You're all ready?" Harry inquired. "Everybody knows the procedure you're going to follow?"

"Oh, yes," said the warden. "But we've decided we want an hour or so with him here, to see if maybe he knows anything about a couple of attempted breaks last month. I figure that if we notify the county police immediately about what we've got, they'll take more or less an hour to get here."

"Sounds acceptable to me," Harry said, watching a young lady on the screen fastidiously remove a gravity knife from the handbag of one of the visitors. "Just make sure someone says to him that he's being detained under the inherent powers of the warden to preserve safety, and he is *not* under arrest.

Let the cops do those things, and get him his lawyer, too."

Another fifteen minutes elapsed before the rather fleshy visage of Joshua Fitch adorned the television screen. It was an unattractive sight: a young man with a bush of curly hair, a fake Afro, wearing lumberjacket and blue jeans, and carrying what was even in black-and-white a very expensive attaché case. Harry leaned his elbows on the desk and watched. The attendants, who had not been told there was anything special about this passenger, went about their business. When the metal detector buzzed, one of them suggested the deposit of keys and coins, and another try. Again it buzzed. At the right-hand edge of the screen, a black, uniformed prison guard began to move to the runway. The attendant took the hand-held probe, ran it as normal over Fitch's back and under his armpits when he raised his arms, and then between his legs—and the device screamed.

The prison guard said to Fitch, "You carryin' somepin down dere?"

"I got a special jockstrap I wear," Fitch said.

"Yeah, sure," said the guard. "Let's go inna next room and lemme take a look at it."

"I tell you, what's setting off that thing is this special cup I wear, it's a fiber reinforced with steel, because I had a bad experience once and I've got to be careful."

"You wanna go inna prison," said the guard, not particularly tense, "you gotta have a skin search." He put a hand on Fitch's arm.

"Let go of me!" Fitch screamed, and reached for the attaché case as though to swing it on the guard, who simply threw out an arm and knocked the case against the partition. Fitch screamed again: *"Motherfucker!"*

Harry picked up the phone, horror-struck, and dialed the number the warden had given him. Even as he dialed he thought, Twenty-six years old, ten, twelve years of activism, the fat prick still doesn't know enough not to call a colored guard a motherfucker. Some people are accident prone. But the guard had merely tightened his grip on Fitch's arm; the menace came from elsewhere, as the warden and another of the guards—this one with a drawn gun—came running into the picture. Harry heard the telephone ringing through the earpiece, through the sound from the television screen. The two guards took Fitch by the forearms and dragged him off camera, and Harry looked at the empty runway, waiting for the telephone to be picked up. It was picked up. "Did you see *that?*" the warden called into it.

"I was watching," Harry said.

"What do you make of it?"

"I think he's wearing a jockstrap with a metal-reinforced fiber cup," Harry said. "He got kicked in the balls once at a demonstration; put him in the hospital."

"What else has he got down there?" the warden crowed in anticipated triumph.

"My hunch," said Harry, "is that your question is one for him and his girlfriend, not for us."

"What do you mean?"

"I mean we come up empty," Harry said. "All you had to do was watch him. He's clean."

"Jesus!" said the warden. "Hang on."

The phone hit the table noisily as the warden dropped it, and Harry saw him run through the camera's field and disappear. Less than a minute later, he was standing in the runway, looking at the camera. "You were right," he said. "Or, you were wrong."

Harry waited patiently for the warden to realize that he could not reply through the television camera, and to return to the telephone. "What do we do now?" the warden said.

"Put an extra man watching him during the interview, just in case," Harry said. "But you come back here; we have to do some work to make sure you have the right story to tell on Monday."

"You mean I can't say it was on a tip from you?"

"Just come pick me up here," Harry said wearily, and

began to assemble his pads of graph paper. "We'll get out and have a good lunch together. There could be all sorts of reasons why this thing didn't come down. It was a good tip. He's my best agent; usually he predicts and it happens. Your people didn't beat this fellow up, did they?"

"No, no."

"All right, then it's not so serious as all that. What we've got to do now is protect my agent."

"I'll be right with you," said the warden. "I'll be right there."

Harry called the emergency number for the hijacking squad, and arranged for the FAA metal-detection team to stay at the prison for at least two or three more days. By the time the warden returned, Harry was able to tell him that the first steps had been taken to provide a soft answer to any oncoming wrath. The warden was too wrapped in his own concerns and resentments to see that the protection went much more to Johnson's tipster than to himself.

The duck-hunting party broke up after a lunch of crab soup, terrapin and Meursault; the senator went back to Washington and the lawyer to Philadelphia, both ready to accept any incredible story Ensor might tell them in the future. When they were gone, Ensor offered Gilette a choice between an immediate nap and a visit to the horse show, where Ann already was in attendance and where he could meet his hostess for the evening "on her own grounds—she rides like you shoot." Recognizing what was expected of him, Gilette pretended eagerness for the horse show.

This was half an hour away, up the peninsula in an area of low wooded hills. Almost ten minutes' drive on a private road was required to get from the highway to the timber course where the show was in progress. Station wagons all but lined the long white rail fence, their gates down, steaming stainless steel canisters of coffee and soup on some, bottles and ice buckets and glasses on others. A November day:

bright sun but low; the sky had edges and hinted darkness. Several hundred people were scattered along the grass between the tailgates and the fence, a fair proportion of them in jodhpurs and boots. Two dozen riders were in a saddling enclosure to the right of the course, some mounted, some standing beside shining horses. Four judges sat in a little house atop a twenty-foot scaffold just inside the fence, their backs motionless against the caning of their chairs.

Ensor pulled the Cadillac near the saddling enclosure and called into it to his wife, who was standing inside, stiffly erect in her tweed suit, discussing something with some mounted ladies. "Now she knows we're here," Ensor said, "let me take you around to meet some people." On the course, two men on horseback were rising in pairs to take what seemed to Gilette like impossibly high, heavy fences. Ensor watched his gaze and said, "They tell me that once you've jumped here, there's no place in America that scares you. That Goddamned water is something like fourteen feet wide."

Once one turned away from the steeplechase course, the feel of the place was that of an outdoor cocktail party: the level of the booze in the bottles was dropping much faster than the level of the coffee in the steel cans. Most of the day's events were over, and most of the conversation was about who had won them and how, and about horses. Ensor livened up his introductions of Gilette by describing him as "a friend of Marshal Tito's." Ensor was by appearance the oldest man in the group: everyone else, tweeded observers or costumed riders, seemed somehow the same age, a handsomely preserved forty. Ann Ensor, who really was a handsomely preserved forty, came striding over to where her husband and her guest were leaning against a station wagon with two women who seemed a shade younger than the others, and who were laughing at Ensor's descriptions of the morning's duck shoot. "Here you are," she said. "Cindy, Jane," she added rather reprovingly, "I thought you were riding in the last event."

"Carla is the last event all by herself," said one of the women, studying Ann with some surprise. "I'd rather watch her than ride, this late in the afternoon."

"You can do both," said Ann, and Gilette realized she was not, in fact, in authority here; but she gave orders, especially to women, wherever she went. The women looked at each other, and the smaller of them shrugged, and they walked off toward the enclosure. "Carla told me to get them," Ann explained, and then said to Gilette, "I'm so glad you came here. Otherwise you'd think the women around here are like me, good for nothing but wearing clothes and feeding the animals. *You* ride, as I remember?"

"Where I was brought up," Gilette said, "every farm had horses. But not like these."

"Maria rides, too, doesn't she?"

"I guess she did when she was a girl," Gilette said, "but never with me. You knew her before I did."

"I *can,* you know," Ann said. "But I don't. I'm awfully sorry Maria didn't come."

Gilette smiled. "Carl told me you were really inviting her when you asked me."

"Well, *I* was," she said, laughing, "but not Carl. With those other important guests of his last night, I didn't even have a chance to ask you about her."

Gilette looked down at the tire-scarred turf. "It's not easy for her," he said. "And, I told Carl, she's worried about her father."

"Of course, she's right to be worried," Ann said in rather a flat voice. "What she probably needs is some companionship from the old country."

"She has some of that," Gilette said. "There's this church in White Plains. Of course, Maria is very American now. She speaks to Jack only in English. That's the way we both want it."

"But she can't forget," Ann suggested.

"It's her father. If we could hear her father was all right,

I think we could work out everything else."

"Can't her Croatian friends find out?"

"No. I hoped the Ambassador could."

"I'll tell Carl he *must,*" said Ann.

Gilette was conscious of the fact that the distant buzz of conversation had stopped, and there was a charge in the cold afternoon air. Ann had looked away, into the track. Following her gaze, he saw a solitary rider, a woman on a large dark horse, start off around the track. There was a smoothness, almost a laziness, about the way horse and rider gathered speed going for the first, light rail fence, and seemed to come too near it before they rose, one animal, front legs tucked under with the same effortlessly smooth pacing, and easily cleared the barricade. There was no break of pace as the horse landed, and the neck stretched, the rider bent slightly forward, heading for the next jump, a timbered brute. Again they rose, like a centaur, at least a half step closer to the fence than anyone else had attempted, disappeared behind the hedge and emerged still smooth, now speeding up again for the water jump. Gilette watched the undulating motions of horse and rider, feeling the mathematics of it in his mind's eye, as though he were leading it with a gunsight.

"Marvelous," he said. "That's—"

"Carla Whitmont," said Carl Ensor. "Your hostess to-night."

"Beautiful," said Gilette.

"Extraordinary," said Ann Ensor, herself leaning forward, as though imagining some participation in her friend's accomplishment.

Now horse and rider were on the far side of the field, and the rhythm of their motion was more perceptible. Nicholas Gilette found himself trembling. "Thank you," he said to the Ensors. "My God," he said. "So beautiful."

From the landing Sue Johnson watched Oscar climb the stairs to her apartment, and having thought through the situation, she welcomed him with a no-nonsense bear hug and a peck on the cheek. She did not help him with his coat, which he shrugged off onto a chair and then hung up with practiced if awkward speed in her closet. She was awkward herself—awkwardly dressed in a high-collar, tight pullover top that stretched over her bony shoulders and heavy breasts; awkward pouring the drinks that she brought back and placed on the polished floor next to the huge overstuffed cushions that substituted for a couch.

They sat side by side and Oscar admired Sue's collection of abstract paintings and lithographs, shiny aluminum-foil and other *objets* that hung rather incongruously from the patterned moldings of the high walls. The room was dominated by a piano almost nine feet long. Behind its bench stood a high white plastic bookcase in which each shelf was mounded with a litter of music that appeared to be and in fact was almost unorganized. There was a pause in the identification of objects in the room, and Sue asked Oscar about the paralegal business. After he had explained a little, she said, "Funny. You're sort of an investigator, like Daddy."

"Maybe so," Oscar said, and his mouth opened crookedly in part of a laugh. "And you," he growled. "Say something funny about yourself."

Sue told him about takeovers and mergers and accounting practices, and the fun of confronting corporate treasurers with worked-up information and projections not their own, finally provoking from him a faintly weary, "We're all investigators. Like the women of the Hebrides, we make a living by taking in each other's dirty wash. Why don't you play something for me, instead?"

Sue finished her drink, went to the bookcase and rummaged, and took something to the piano. Her long face assumed that specially serious expression Oscar remembered from years before, and with an equally familiar gesture, the slow descent of her left hand, she began to play. It was a

Satie *Gnossienne,* with stumbling rhythms and white-key harmonies and falling cadences, the music of a lonely and regretful man. In the small room, even the soft tone of the big piano filled the crannies, crept under the cushions, probed for response. Sue's eyes were on the music, her head nodding just a little from side to side, the regularity of its motion emphasizing the rubato of her performance. She nodded briskly as she lifted her hand from the final chord, letting the pedal carry the dying conclusion, and turned to Oscar smiling broadly; and found him crying. He blew his nose into a handkerchief and turned his body away from her to stuff the handkerchief back into his pocket.

"My God, I'm sorry," she said.

"No, did me good," Oscar said, his voice trembling, and added, irrelevantly, "I never played that."

"It's a lovely piece. But really it's something to play for yourself, alone."

"Pfah," said Oscar, releasing. "Someday you'll play it for me again."

"Soon." She ran her fingers over the keys in the opening bars of a Haydn rondo and said, "What good times we did have, Oscar."

"I know."

"It was best the year before you went to college. When we really were chasing each other, except I wasn't supposed to be chasing you. And we'd meet after the football games; you'd be the first out of the dressing room. Your parents thought it always took an hour to get out of the dressing room and they wouldn't wait."

"I remember."

"And days like today, we'd just go and sit and look at all the gray water in the bay. Then we'd come back and go to my house and we'd play duets. We got good at that Mozart andante, remember?"

"How's your mother?" said Oscar.

"Oh, for Christ sake!" said Sue. "Look, if I'm going to play the piano for you, this outfit is really silly—let me change into something that leaves my shoulders free. You just sit here—I'll not be a minute."

"I ought to hear the seven o'clock news," Oscar said. "There's something that may have happened today and I ought to know about it if it did."

She brought in a portable radio and departed. Oscar turned it on and listened as the woes of the world paraded mellifluously through the loudspeaker. He got up and walked to the window overlooking the now gray and barren garden behind the brownstone, and thought it must be pretty in the spring. There was nothing in the radio news about Fitch or any incident at High Hills. Oscar wondered whether they had called it off, or whether the police were holding the story for some purpose—or whether Johnson had decided not to move on the tip. Whatever had happened was over now. He turned off the radio, went to the white bookcase and began to look at the music: Brahms, Chopin, Rachmaninoff, Schumann, Weber. She was taking her time in the bedroom. He heard the door open, and said, "Your tastes have been getting very romantic, haven't they?"

"Yes, indeed," she said, and he turned to face her. She was wearing a golden robe gathered at the waist with a golden cord, the lapels clinging to the inner outlines of her breasts. Her blond hair was luminous from the brushing she had given it. She lifted her eyebrows and made her blue eyes big. "I'll fix you another drink," she said. "Sit down."

She sat beside him on his left side and took his hand. "I've got a good dinner for you," she said, "but unless you're awfully hungry, it's really better before you eat."

"Ah, Sue. I don't know."

"And one of the nice things about these big cushions," she said, "is that you don't have to go into the bedroom, all that respectability in the bedroom." She reached up and turned a knob that dimmed the lights.

Oscar looked away. "I think of the way it was," he said. He shook his head. "I don't like the idea of what you'd see when you look at me while we're doing it."

She took his hand and raised it to her breast. "If that's what's worrying you," she said, "there are several known solutions. I can turn off the lights entirely and pull the drapes, or I can close my eyes, which I guess you never noticed I used to do anyway. And I know all sorts of perfectly lovely things we can do where there's no way I can be looking at you while we do them. . . ."

The Whitmonts' Maryland mansion was just that—a truly enormous house, antebellum, a portico of six fluted columns, a center hall large enough for all three dozen of the evening's guests to stand and drink if they had wished to stay by the bar; most drifted into the fifty-foot parlor, and stood in some relation to the roaring fire. Ann Ensor had warned Gilette as they approached up the great curve of the driveway: "Every time you drink a cup of coffee, that Jew-boy makes a couple of pennies." Her husband disliked the comment. "Nonsense," he said. "There are lots of good companies in this business, many of them bigger than Tony's. But his people know what they're doing; the day old Julius Whitmont bought a house down here was a damned good day for the bank." Ann said grumpily, "You know perfectly well what a hard time Julius had, and if it wasn't for Carla, two-thirds of the people you'll see tonight wouldn't touch the Whitmonts with a pole. They just like to know somebody they read about on the sports pages, which is the only part of the paper any of them do read." Leaving the car in the hands of one of the young men the Whitmonts had hired to do the parking, Carl closed the conversation: "As Nick is about to see, there are more reasons than that for wanting to visit Carla Whitmont."

She was dressed in a strapless gown as black as her long hair, with a patterned Japanese silk stole over her shoulders as she greeted guests in the drafty center hall. Strings of diamonds hung from her ears and flashed as she moved her head; a silver sunburst of platinum and diamonds held together the front of the dress. "Ann, Carl," she said, flashing a smile, "and you must be Nicholas Gilette. I understand I must go someday and watch you shoot."

"I have already watched *you* ride," Gilette said, and the nervous smile disappeared as he gazed at her. Her skin was a barely perceptible pink under its cream surface; her rounded arms were a demonstration that for riding, as for shooting, muscles were not required.

"Oh, I thought you were here just for the ducks."

Carl said, "I brought him over for the end of the meeting, so he could find out what he was up against."

"How kind of you," said Carla, but the next guests were arriving. Tony picked up the Ensors and their guest as they gave their drinks order to a waiter, and walked them over to meet the Brazilian ambassador, a florid, pudgy man with a white mustache and bulging eyes. "Here," he said, "is the only man you can talk to in this room who won't tell you what mare is in foal to what sire."

"Yes, but you know," the ambassador said in an English accent, "I don't wish to talk about coffee, either."

"Not even freeze-dried coffee?" Carl inquired as Ann drifted off in the direction of friends.

"For that subject, I could perhaps make an exception. Are you connected with the coffee business, too, Mr. Gilette?"

"No, my work is in computers."

"Ah, yes. You know, as recently as seven or eight years ago, when I was assigned to Washington as a first secretary, one never *met* anyone who worked in computers; they existed, but one did not meet them. Now, it seems I am never at a party without someone who says he is in computers."

Carl and Tony had moved off toward the corner by the stairs, and were in earnest converse. The ambassador said, "Have you ever been in Brazil, Mr. Gilette?"

"No, I have not," Gilette said, smiling again, bored again.

"I did meet some of your compatriots, though, when I was representing my country in international rifle competitions."

"Did you win?"

"I'm afraid I did." They had turned around each other as they talked, and Gilette was now facing toward Carla, who was still near the door. "And when I was on station in Yugoslavia," Gilette continued, looking at Carla, speaking without much interest in what he was saying, "I knew one of the men in your embassy—Captain Madeiros, I believe it was."

"Oh, yes, I know who you mean. He has moved into the civil service now; he has a responsible position in the northeast. You know, *she* was there once, in Recife."

"Is that so?"

"She was still a student; she was then considered a dangerous radical. Of course, she never was a radical really, but it was thought that she was."

"I've just met her tonight. What do you know about her?"

The ambassador had watched Gilette rub his mustache while studying Carla, seen the tongue working through the thin lips. "Ah, she is a woman of mystery," he said. "Doesn't she look like a spy?"

Gilette said nothing.

"Or perhaps a film star. I think she is a great actress. Perhaps someday you will know her better."

"I hope so," Gilette said.

Over by the stairs, Carl Ensor was making a face and shrugging his shoulders; and Tony with a sudden bright smile and a wave of his left hand was brushing away the subject. They returned to Gilette and the Brazilian ambassador, and the conversation turned away from Carla.

But Gilette was seated beside her at dinner—it was a mark of how seriously Tony took the cultivation of Ensor that his houseguest was given this place. Carl was with the Brazilian ambassador's elegant little wife, Ann at the table with Tony. Gilette had been too well trained in attaché duty to

141

seek to monopolize his hostess, but it was hard for him not to look at her. "I *must* see you ride again," he said finally. "Tell me where I can go to watch you."

Carla was feeling the pressure of his slate-blue eyes, a pressure quite new in her experience. Soldiers, she thought; but it was more than that. The sensation was not entirely displeasing; meeting Gilette's gaze, she remembered the attractions of danger, and realized with some surprise that she missed them. "I almost always enter the horse show," she said. "You can see me at Madison Square Garden."

"That's months away."

"Or tomorrow—I will find you a horse and you can join our hunt for the day."

"But the Ensors are not part of your hunt, are they?"

"I am afraid not."

"And I would just make a fool of myself." He shook his head. "There must be someplace near New York."

"Of course there is. In my park—the state park. But there I cannot invite you."

"There must be another place, too."

"Not for a public."

But later in the evening, just before they left the tables for coffee and liqueurs, Carla said to him, "You know, I teach an equestrian class for a girls' school, on Tuesdays and Thursdays, and we have two more sessions before Thanksgiving. You could see how many girls there are who ride well."

"Where is it?" he said quickly.

"Not far from Peekskill; do you know where that is?"

"I drive past it when I go to Poughkeepsie for IBM meetings."

"All right, I'll tell you where it is. Listen carefully, for I will not give you a map, I will just tell you once. Then, if you can find the place, you will see me ride there. At this season, we start at three in the afternoon."

Having bought the warden the best lunch Putnam County had to offer, and sat drinking with him much of the afternoon while he waited for an anticipated and feared call from the governor (which never came), Harry had no particular need for dinner. He picked up a sandwich at a deli and went to the office, where the first sheets of AT&T reports had arrived. But after half an hour of looking at them in the eerie stillness of the deserted ninth floor, he said to hell with it and went off to the Mayfair to play backgammon. He won $375, most of it from a hotshot twenty-year-old, who was beside himself. "To what do you credit your success?" the kid asked sourly as they rose from the table, and the knowledgeable internationalists who had backed him in the side bets were irritatedly paying off something considerably more than $375.

"I'm unlucky in love," Harry Johnson said. "Sometimes in other things, too."

VIII

... But in Battalions

"Do you call your father on Sunday mornings?" Oscar asked as Sue emerged from the bathroom, brushing her blond hair.

"What a hell of a question at such a moment."

"No, I'm serious. Do you call him?"

"Very rarely, but it can happen."

"I'd like to talk to him."

"You can call him yourself."

"No, I can't. Not directly. I'm not permitted."

"What does that mean?"

"There's a special number, then he calls me back. I can't believe you don't know."

"Believe," she said. "But I guessed." She came and sat beside him on the bed. "Did he do this to you?"

Oscar laughed. "He thinks so, sometimes. But it isn't true."

She bent to kiss him; he put his arm around her and pulled

her down to him. "I'm not unhappy now," he said.

"I should hope not," said Sue. "Lord!" She sat up. "I'll call my father."

Harry picked up the phone on the first ring. "Johnson here."

"How come you never say, 'Hello'? Don't you think you could say 'Hello' on Sunday morning?"

"Hello, Sue. I didn't know you were up at nine o'clock on Sunday mornings."

"I've got company."

"I didn't know you called me when you had company."

"Well, it's Oscar."

"Oh," said Harry. "I'm glad."

"He wants to talk to you."

After a brief delay: "Hell, I guess it's safe enough. Put him on."

"You're not very friendly this morning."

"Sue, if I started to tell you all the things that are waiting in line this morning, it would take us all day. But I do want to talk with Oscar."

She passed him the telephone. "What happened?" Oscar asked; and Harry told him.

"I guess Spitts did stop them," Oscar said.

"Maybe."

"I mean, I'm sorry it worked out to be so much trouble for nothing, but—"

"We don't yet know how much trouble it works out to be," Harry said. "From your point of view, it's the same as if we'd found a gun. The fact that they searched him means somebody leaked. You be careful."

"Careful how?"

"You'll have to play it as you find it. Would have been better without this call, I guess; except maybe you'd have been too curious. Seems to me you'll have to ask Spitts if he knows what happened, and then you'll have to be appropriately shocked, and pleased it came out all right, and worried about whether one of those Wall Street lawyers is a stoolie—but you'll have to decide on the spot."

"Going to be interesting, tomorrow morning?" Oscar said.

"Yeah. With a little luck, it's only the one morning. We're keeping the metal detectors in place, so it's plausible that Fitch simply stumbled into a penal security experiment. They know he's a guy who makes his own trouble."

"I'll let you know," said Oscar.

"I'd appreciate it if you don't," Harry said. "I'll know soon enough if there are problems."

"Whatever you say, sir."

"Good," said Harry, and hung up.

"And what was that about?" said Sue, taking the phone.

"I'll think about telling you at breakfast," said Oscar. Sue nodded briskly and went off to the kitchen; she had expected Oscar to want her gone while he got out of bed. But when he came to breakfast what he said was, "Some days the worst of this thing is that you have to wear a bow tie, because they don't make a long tie you can clip on. The second worst is trying to read the Goddamned newspaper."

"Someday I'll tell you the worst thing about being a woman," said Sue, serving eggs from a frying pan.

"That's the day I'll tell you about your father and me."

"I have to go to Denver tomorrow morning," said Sue. "Johns Manville. And there's a cattle outfit the firm has an interest in. I get back on Thursday."

"We'll have dinner Thursday," Oscar said firmly. "I buy."

Fricka Kaganopoulos knew something important was happening. Her husband had been on the telephone nearly all of Saturday night, in the basement, with the door locked. He gave her money to stock up the refrigerator "because I may have to feed some people here." And he sent her out for that purpose at night—something he never did; if there was an errand to run at night he usually insisted on doing it himself, or at least coming along with her. So she was not surprised, though she was unhappy, when he told her there was a meeting of the Society that morning, she would have to go to church alone, and she should go to her cousin's for lunch.

The men arrived at the row house in Bay Ridge only a few minutes after her departure—four of them, carrying suitcases and grocery bags. Except for a neighbor looking out the window and two children playing in the street, they were unobserved: Sunday morning, this community was at church. Four police officers had been assigned to the Kaganopoulos case that morning: two patrolmen from the precinct to pick him up and bring him to headquarters, a detective and a detective second class to secure the house, to take possession of all papers and guns, to deliver the former to the lieutenant in charge, the latter to the lab. ETA from church was eleven-thirty; the detectives, who lived near each other and not far from Kaganopoulos, had taken advantage of the schedule to sleep late and make a ten o'clock mass, and the patrolmen were simply operating to a time sheet. No one from the police department was on the street to see the gathering of the clan.

When all four of the men who had volunteered were present in the basement room, Kaganopoulos took the lectern at the front and after the usual pledge of allegiance, outlined the situation and his plans. Everyone would remember that during the visit of the traitor Papandreou he had been seized and held so that he could not participate in their patriotic protest. Now something more sinister was to be done. They were framing him on a murder charge. If they could get away with this, no one would be safe. The men grumbled.

As they all knew, Kaganopoulos continued, he had powerful friends. But with the political situation as it was, his friends would not move until forced. Right now, in fact, it would be most convenient for them if he simply fell into the hands of the authorities and disappeared. Not just for his own sake, but for the sake of the movement, this must not be permitted. His powerful friends must be made to remember that they were not all-powerful, they still needed Kaganopoulos. These four plus himself—we are the cadre who can make them remember.

His plan was to be like a hostage. The Society would not let the police take him. The storm of publicity would then be their protection. He would demand a safe-conduct and a plane to Greece for himself, and for them a guarantee that no charges would be brought. After all, no one would be hurt—they would not have committed any crime. And he could preserve the organization in exile until the time came, he thought very soon, to return. Now, as was traditional with them—theirs was the inheritance of true democracy— he would put his plan to the vote. .

Soft-skinned, sheepish, peddlers by trade—their wives would keep operating the hot-dog carts if they had to remain with Kaganopoulos—the four men rose to their feet and welcomed the plan with applause. Kaganopoulos had already boarded up the three windows that opened onto the top of the basement walls. Now the men moved through the house, pulling drapes and shades, barricading doors with furniture, preparing for the confrontation when the police came to take away their leader.

His luggage augmented by a styrofoam box containing four dressed ducks quick-frozen in dry ice by Ensor's guide, Nicholas Gilette left the Ensors' a little after ten o'clock on a gray morning, with cold wisps of cloud chasing angrily after each other just above the treetops. Ann had not showed up for breakfast—her husband explained that it was probably the crab casserole of the night before, but whatever it was had kept her awake much of the night—and after a few minutes of conversation about the people who had been at the Whitmonts' affair, Carl and Gilette found they had nothing much to talk about this morning. Gilette's recollection of the party was heavily concentrated on Carla, about whom he did not wish to speak; Ensor's was haunted by his early conversation with Tony, and the need to decide about the collateral he would require—for clearly the freeze-dried plant in Brazil was mortgaged as far as he wanted to go—before the bank could advance another four-fifths of a million dollars to Monteblanco. Both men felt a mix of gratitude for the morning's sleep and regret for the missed opportunities at the bay.

The result was that Gilette had something more than an hour of time beyond what he had budgeted for the drive to the Binghamton area. Ensor had given him a Xeroxed map to direct him to the main road, and looking at it, Gilette guessed that a somewhat more indirect route would take him where he was going by way of the horse country he had seen the day before. With a notion that he might find Carla jumping fences and bushes as he drove by, Gilette took the back roads. Whenever the road neared water, the fog was heavy enough to dispel the last regrets about the loss of the morning's hunting: you'd have had to get near enough to the ducks to club them before you could see anything on the water on a day like this.

He was driving slowly, looking for the entrance to the horse-show grounds, when a reddish animal slipped under the fence just ahead of him, running fast, and he had to swerve to avoid killing it. The fox swerved, too, back into the stubble of the cornfield whence he had come, and in the far distance Gilette heard the baying of the hounds on the trail. The highway bent just ahead, and a dirt road went off it and over a ditch to a closed gate. Gilette turned the car onto the dirt road, and noted that between the bushes at the bend his car window framed the spot on the fence from which the fox had emerged.

Gilette rolled down the window, slipped the catch on the leather-covered gun box, and without looking down, removed the .22 from its case. His left hand at the same time took a cartridge and slipped it in the chamber. He locked the bolt and sighted to the fence, and only then looked around him to be sure there was no farmhouse with an easy view. Suddenly the cornfield was alive with beagles, the lead dog bounding on with superbly muscular stride, bobbing and weaving, head up to look, down to track, purposeful and delighted. Gilette let him get under the fence, full blast, and stop, and turn, once in a circle at the road, then off again full speed toward the opening where the fox had returned to the field, shouting to himself or to the pack, you can't tell with dogs; and Gilette pulled the trigger. The dog was stopped instantly; his feet left the ground, and he lay on his side in the mud. Red coats were visible in the far distance, rising and falling, brown horses under them. Gilette skillfully, bent low over the wheel and using his left hand alone, backed the station wagon not too far out onto the road, just enough to turn. His right hand slotted the gun by feel back into its cradle in the box, and snapped the box closed; and he was away on his interrupted journey, feeling really quite exhilarated, at least for a while.

The plainclothesmen were already parked across the street from the Kaganopoulos home when the patrolmen drove up in their squad car. Looking down the street to the Greek Orthodox church four blocks away, they passed the time of day, casually prepared for the morning's work. Presently a crowd formed at the head of the stone stairs to the church, and began to disperse. The policemen eyed the passers-by with slight interest. The senior of the two detectives knew Kaganopoulos by sight; anyway, they were to pick him up at the door of his house, all but eliminating any identification problems.

For fifteen minutes the churchgoers passed along the street, and nobody came to the Kaganopoulos house. The mood in the two cars began to tighten. Finally one of the patrolmen came back to the unmarked car and said to the detectives, "I guess he ain't coming home."

"Or maybe he never left," said the junior of the detectives.

"What yo-yo thought up this plan anyway?" said the patrolman.

The older detective said, "The rackets guys who know him well said he *always* takes his wife to church. It's what he does for her; he never gave her no children."

"Well, not today."

"No."

The older detective heaved out of the driver's seat of his car and said, "Let's see if he's home. If he isn't, we've got the search warrant, and we'll do our job, and you guys can go chasing. But I agree with Morris—I think he's inside."

All four men went to the house, and one of the patrolmen rang the bell. No response. Again. And again. The senior detective had stepped back out to the sidewalk and was examining the building. "There are people in this house," he said. He looked up at a tall second-floor window deep-set in the brownstone, and saw nothing but the lining of a drape. He called out, "We're coming in." A shot sounded and echoed on the street; the bullet splattered asphalt in the roadway not far from where the detective was standing. "Holy Mother of God," he breathed. "He shot at me!"

All four officers, crouching and weaving, ran back to their cars and got behind them. One of the patrolmen reached out the microphone and called the precinct for reinforcements, using the code for "under attack." Within three minutes, the air was heavy with sirens, seven patrol cars were blocking off the street, and a good fraction of the population of this and neighboring blocks were ringing the invading force, trying to figure out what was happening. Even worse was in store, for Kaganopoulos had called the newspapers, and before the officers from Manhattan who had ordered the arrest could arrive in Bay Ridge, there were three reporters and two photographers plying their trade with the bewildered policemen, neighbors, and members of the growing crowd that pressed toward the Kaganopoulos home—from which,

151

since the shot, there had emerged no sign of life.

Harry got the call at home, just as he was about to leave for the office and the meeting with his team of agents. It came from his friend Vinnie Palio, who was in Brooklyn. "We seem to be having some trouble here."

"What trouble?"

"Bad trouble." Ringed by reporters, who could not be kept outside the perimeter, Palio was limited in what he could say. He was also limited in what he knew. The reporters had been on the telephone with Kaganopoulos, who had refused to speak with the police. "Can you get out here?"

"Right away." Harry called Frank Wu, told him as much as he knew, and asked him to run the meeting as best he could. Sunday midday, the taxi got Johnson to Bay Ridge in about twenty minutes. He found a score of policemen, high officers, detectives, reporters, clustered behind two large police department wagons pulled up across the street from the Kaganopoulos house, and people hanging out the windows on both sides of the block. All the curtains were drawn *chez* Kaganopoulos, but otherwise the scene was lively; hot-dog sellers, some of whom knew more than the police, were clustered at both ends of the block to serve the gathering throngs. There was a fair amount of pedestrian traffic on the street itself, because police were admitting people who could prove they lived here, and some were bringing friends, supposedly for Sunday dinner. Harry went into the paddy wagon with the seniors, looking for a little privacy.

A neighbor had told the police that Kaganopoulos was not alone in the house. How many men were there, and for what purpose, was still obscure. Palio had called Leone, the Mafia lawyer, to see what help he could give, and Leone, after making a phone call of his own, reported back that Kaganopoulos had talked about an airplane ticket and a safe-conduct to Greece—and (Palio suspected this had arisen from Leone's attempt to reason with the man) an agreement never to seek extradition from Greece. Leone said he had urged Kaganopoulos to give himself up, and had been cursed out for it. The lawyer was unwilling to become further involved in the matter, at least until after the man was in custody.

For Palio, all this, if true, was tantamount to a confession of Kaganopoulos's guilt; for Harry, who said it rather forcefully, it was not "sniper behavior" by any stretch of the imagination. The police psychologist who specialized in public nuttiness—exhibitionists, suicides, hostage takers—had gone to the Meadowlands in New Jersey for the football game and was being pulled back to Brooklyn.

"Anybody talk to the wife?" Harry asked.

"No. When you call and say it's the police, they just hang up in there."

"What makes you so sure his wife is in there?" Harry said. "This is dangerous; I don't think a man like Kaganopoulos subjects his wife to dangers. Let's nose about for that wife—she probably doesn't know what's going on."

Palio nodded, and made a note.

"And what have you told the press?"

"Just that we want him for questioning on the sniper murders."

"Great," said Harry. "That brings us like a hundred more reporters in the next hour or two. Couldn't you have tried some other reason?"

"Never occurred to me. They find out somehow, you know."

"Sure," Harry said. "Got a cigarette? Thanks." He lit up and took a deep, irritating pull. "Did you mention the Bureau to the reporters?"

"Oh, yeah. I told them we had Kaganopoulos's name from you."

"Better and better," Harry said. "We're always looking for publicity, aren't we? Well, let me go see if I can talk to Mr. K."

"Jesus, you might get shot," Inspector Palio said.

"That's what I want to do," Harry said, leaving the wagon. "I want to bare my breast."

He walked slowly, firmly to the house and rang the doorbell. A window opened a crack directly above the entrance, and a familiar voice shouted, "So you're here, you fucking FBI stool. Not gonna get me so easy as you thought, are you?"

"Why don't I come in and we'll have another talk about it," Harry said. "I've got no arrest warrant—I'll keep the cops out. No gun, no buddies. Just want to talk."

"One cocksucker never gonna be in this house again, it's you," the voice said, but the window stayed open.

"I'll send them away," Harry said. "All the cops. Once you let me in."

"Aah, they'd come back."

"But you'd have me," Harry said reasonably.

"Whaddaya think I am, some fucking radical freak?" the voice said. "I don't take no hostages. *I'm* the hostage. That's what people gotta understand." The window slammed, and Harry, eyes narrowed, returned to the wagon to await the psychologist, or the wife, or both. The population around the police vehicles had increased; another half-dozen reporters had already arrived.

Taking charge, Harry told Palio to commandeer the house directly across from Kaganopoulos's as a temporary police post. It would give them a place to talk, and a telephone line not constantly monitored by the press and perhaps others. Flanked by two sergeants, the inspector went off; Harry noticed that at the end of the block, other policemen were arguing with a television truck. It would be a great day for the football game, Harry thought; a little cold, but a great day for football.

Carl Ensor had gone off to deliver the Labradors to their kennel for the week, leaving Ann free to get her letter off her mind immediately. The letter was to a young man in the Yugoslav Embassy, who (she was reliably informed) had come into possession of some disgusting pictures of her with a blond ballerina in Zagreb almost ten years ago. He had called her at home in Philadelphia two months before, and then more urgently three weeks ago, demanding information "you can get" about the marksman-officer who had been a military attaché at the embassy. Now she could make her reply:

> Nicholas Gilette was here as our houseguest this weekend. I had opportunity to speak with him about his wife, her information about her father, and her contacts with the Croatian émigré community.
>
> I see no reason to believe that she actually knows her father is dead. She is suspicious that something has happened to him because she has not received any letters recently. Mr. Gilette requested my husband to find out anything he can from Belgrade about the present situation of Mr. Mandragora.
>
> Mr. Gilette says his wife has not been well, and he attributes her condition to concern over her father. He made no secret of her contacts with the Caffra group. If she has been conspiring with them in furtherance of some criminal plan, her husband does not know about it. As your concern is with him, I cannot see that it is well founded.
>
> I do not see any convenient way that I can make direct contact with Mrs. Gilette. She would not come to my house for the weekend, though invited.
>
> I hope this will be satisfactory.

She did not sign the letter.

The police psychologist was a young man with a long, straggly light-brown beard and a head of ample hair to match, the whole topped with a crocheted yarmulke. He wore a rumpled, mud-brown overcoat that came down below his knees. He moved in small, rather tentative gestures. "Al Goldberg," he said, putting a hand halfway out. "Dr. Goldberg."

The police had appropriated the front room of the house across the street, pushing an excited but not entirely unhappy elderly Italian couple into their kitchen and upstairs bedrooms. The front room had a splendid collection of furniture from the old country—couches and chairs with carved mahogany legs and frames, and a prickly red surface, lace antimacassars, lace curtains. Dr. Goldberg waved the inspector and the FBI agent to the couch with a short gesture, and sat in one of the chairs, head thrust forward between his shoulders, studying them.

Looking at the psychologist, Harry could not imagine anyone less likely to make contact with Kaganopoulos, but he was wrong. Having taken a sketch of the suspect's career and attitudes from Harry and Palio, the psychologist abruptly left the room. On the street, he appropriated a bullhorn from the wagon and called through it to the house, identifying himself as a doctor and announcing that he was about to telephone to find out exactly what Kaganopoulos would like him to do. And this call, made from the hall of the house, the door open to the front room for the view across the street, Kaganopoulos accepted, stating his demands—slowly, the psychologist requested, so he could write them down. They were as Leone had reported.

At the end, Dr. Goldberg said, "I don't know how much I can do for you, but I'll see. I'll call you back. If you want to reach me, I have a number for you. Now, do you have a pencil and paper so you can write it?"

What he said to Harry and the inspector was, "Long siege. The fact that he's got company in there won't make it any shorter. He obviously expects something to happen that will help him—I can't think what. There's no danger here, by the way—he obviously does want to get out, and he knows that can't possibly happen if he shoots someone."

"But he's been shooting people. Killing them," Palio said.

Dr. Goldberg turned to Harry. "Do you believe that, too?"

"No."

"Of course, anything's possible," said the psychologist. "Anything . . . is . . . always . . . *possible.*" He took a deep breath, and turned meek again. "We are certainly dealing with a man who considers himself a victim, not an offender."

"But he's crazy," said the inspector.

"Obviously." Dr. Goldberg waved a hand aimlessly toward the street. "There's a bar and grill on the corner," he said. "I'm going in there to watch the Giants game. If your man calls, or you find his wife, come and get me."

Harry and the inspector then returned to the street and held a brief joint session with the assembled press behind the wagon, Harry attempting without much success to emphasize that Kaganopoulos was merely wanted for questioning, that there was no hard evidence to link him with the sniper murders. Palio stressed the fact that there was known to be an arsenal in the Kaganopoulos home, including several guns similar to that used in the killings. Harry professed total ignorance of the politics of Kaganopoulos's "Society," thereby outraging a reporter from the *Daily News,* who had put an assistant to work in the morgue and already knew better. All the reporters now had their own telephone lines at work, having purchased from houses along the block the assistance the police department had requisitioned. The inspector had to take half an hour to work out new tours of duty for uniformed men; it was clear to all that there would be no quick conclusion to this story.

Wu checked in through Harry's beeper, and conveyed the good news that the second batch of telco printout had contained an unusually large dossier on Kaganopoulos, his long-distance calls (including calls to or from all the murder sites), his travel habits, mob connections and presumed violent proclivities; it looked, Wu said cheerfully, as though the New York police had struck it lucky. In any event, he was adjourning the meeting, and giving the men some time on Sunday. Would his presence be useful in Bay Ridge? Harry objected firmly: the purpose of the meeting was everybody but Kagano-

poulos, and he wanted it to continue until each agent had
a rank order of jobs to do on other possible suspects; when
they had those ducks in line, Wu should call back.

Fricka Kaganopoulos, having been called at her cousin's,
came running onto the block and was captured, not without
difficulty, by a policeman, who led her to the post across
the street from her house. This was observed by Kaganopoulos, who called the number Dr. Goldberg had given him,
and demanded to talk with his wife. It was a quick conversation: he would not hear her at all, and ordered her, she reported, to return to her cousin's, stay the night, and await
his instructions. It might be several days, she should borrow
clothes, he was not going to allow her in her house. The
psychologist, summoned from the bar, arrived while this conversation was in progress, but made no effort to interfere.
When Kaganopoulos hung up, leaving his wife looking at
the telephone and crying, Dr. Goldberg took her away to
the kitchen, forbidding Johnson or Palio to follow. Here the
solicitous mistress of the house, who liked Fricka and had
been a repository of her laments about her husband, made
cups of bitter coffee. Dr. Goldberg conducted a rambling
conversation with Fricka and the old lady, and solidified his
views of what the police were up against.

Time passed quickly; the November afternoon darkened
and lights went on in the Kaganopoulos house. Other television trucks arrived, complete with floodlights and young
women to pose on the street and speak into a microphone
about how this was the house where the sniper suspect was
holed up with his friends, and the police were calmly prepared
to wait him out. Dr. Goldberg permitted himself to be interviewed on camera for the purpose of saying he was in touch
with Mr. Kaganopoulos and hoped to have everything
straightened out soon. But he warned that it would not be
correct to describe his conversations with Mr. Kaganopoulos
as "negotiations." There were no "negotiations." Palio was
interviewed also, but no broadcaster aired the section of the

interview in which he stressed that the man under siege was merely a suspect and should not under any circumstances be described as "the sniper."

Harry had a call at the police post from Adams, who was irritated but not upset—indeed, almost jocular. "What the Christ have you been doing?" he said.

"Tell you tomorrow. It would take too long to explain."

"All I know," Adams said, "is that people are mad as hell at you. Langley keeps pissing in my right ear, and Congressman Fitch *himself* has been pissing in my left ear. All day. I gather his boy was not running guns into High Hills yesterday."

"That's right. Why the hell has he been calling you?"

"Somehow he found out it was the FBI that tipped the prison."

"Shit," said Harry. "It's the damned warden; he got in trouble and laid it off on us."

"Congressman Fitch didn't say where he got his information, but he's strongly insistent. I've made an appointment for you to talk with the guy he says you have to see—name of Craig Spitts, radical lawyer of some sort. Tomorrow at two-thirty in the afternoon, in your office. Have an explanation ready for him, Harry."

"How can you do that?" Harry said, almost frantic. "I'm not going to have any loose time tomorrow."

"C'mon, Harry," Adams said. "It's a congressman. I can't see why they'll need you tomorrow in Bay Ridge. Anyway, the important thing is that we've got the sniper. The President will be pleased."

"No way," said Harry.

"What do you mean, 'No way'?"

"Even the city's getting doubtful," Harry said. "If I may coin a phrase, Kaganopoulos is part of the problem, not part of the solution."

Adams was crushed. "Then I'm afraid we may have a *lot* of trouble with Langley."

Harry could not think of a comment.

Adams snorted a short laugh. "Hasn't been your finest hour, this weekend, has it, Harry?"

"No, sir," said Harry Johnson. "It hasn't."

IX

The Dead Dog Barks

Harry Johnson rolled out of bed in response to the alarm clock, and looked out at what was still a black sky: six-thirty of an overcast November morning. Though he was sure he would have heard if there had been any news—nobody hesitates to wake up an agent—he put through a call to Bay Ridge even before he relieved his bladder. As expected: no change. A light had been on all night in the window right above the doorway to the Kaganopoulos house. No special problems. The old couple housing the police post had been rather pleased than otherwise to have a couple of cops in the parlor all night long.

It took some small effort of will to open the door and collect the newspapers. The story was, of course, on the front pages, though only on the bottom half of the *Times*. In the *News,* it led the parade. Big picture, apparently taken from the roof of one of the houses near the corner, showing the mob of police, residents, reporters, television trucks on the street, with a white circle marking the Kaganopoulos house itself:

CORNERED

IN B'KLYN

POLICE TRAP SNIPER SUSPECT

Harry read the *Times* story first. It was dull, thank God, and suitably cautious—a statement that Kaganopoulos had been sought only "for questioning" was in the second paragraph. Reading on, Harry kept thinking that the reporter was about to refer to an "alleged suspect." Good, for once. Though the FBI was credited institutionally for having located Kaganopoulos, there was no mention of Harry Johnson.

The *News,* unfortunately, gave the siege more than twice as much space (it was, after all, the *News* that was read in Bay Ridge), in a story that left a strong impression the search for the sniper had ended, though all the contemporary pieties were observed. What caveat there was, Johnson noted, had been placed in his mouth, which might be helpful, though he had no recollection of uttering the words between the quotation marks. A sidebar featured a recent photograph of Kaganopoulos, taken from the program of an annual Orthodox Church Charity Picnic, where the events included a skeet-shooting competition that Kaganopoulos had won the year before. Not a bad picture. Harry read carefully what the *News* had dug out about Kaganopoulos, and noted with considerable relief that the emphasis was more on current Mafia contacts than on Greek politics, and not at all on American politics. There was no hint that CIA might know the answer to any question about Theophilus Kaganopoulos.

Neither cheered nor further discomfited, Harry returned to his conventional pattern of newspaper reading. Directly below the Kaganopoulos vignette, he found on returning to that page, was a headline: *10*G REWARD FOR DOG-KILLER.

A Maryland millionaire fox hunter had offered a prize that size "for information leading to the identification of" whoever it was that had shot his beagle Freddie that morning. He was sure it wasn't the farmer over whose land they had been hunting, for all permissions had been arranged. He didn't want to accuse anyone. Everybody knew that the Hunt Club had been sued the month before by some other farmers, and that there was bad blood over the quick, contemptuous dismissal of the case by a judge whose daughter was a member of the club. But he couldn't believe any of these farmers would have done such a thing to his dog, a wonderful animal, absolutely lovable, a house pet when not hunting, the children were devastated. It couldn't even be one of these damned hippy kids around the countryside; it was some sort of monster, who took target practice on a dog.

A monster, who took target practice . . . When he was involved with training new agents, which happened every three years or so, Johnson always told them that the important thing was to *know*—to trust that moment of insight that provided something more than information. Later you might find out that what you knew was wrong: *knowing* could never be a substitute for verification even in daily work, let alone a court of law. But while the spirit was on you, you were required to give it employment. This was one of those moments. A corner of the veil had been lifted; for the first time, Harry Johnson saw something he could grip.

He called the night duty officer in Baltimore, and got telephone numbers for the man whose dog was dead, and at eight o'clock he called to start a process in motion. He identified himself, said he thought he might be able to help, asked what had been done to the corpse. *Mirabile dictu,* this was a family that kept a pet cemetery in a corner of its spacious lawn, and the poor beast had been given a decent burial. Was the bullet still in the animal? No reason not. Would an exhumation be permitted for the purpose of removing that bullet and testing it? After the children went to school—

163

and what did you say your name was? Clearly, Johnson said, he couldn't do it himself; he'd have the Baltimore office send a veterinarian with an agent. It would be that morning, as close to ten o'clock as possible.

The special agent in charge in Baltimore was an old acquaintance with a reputation for early arrival at his desk. Harry dialed his third call to Maryland, and explained his situation.

"I thought this one was under control," said the special agent in charge.

"Negative."

"What's this story out of Brooklyn?"

"You don't have time to hear it. Someday."

"All this is a little far out, Harry, isn't it?"

"It's pretty far out that I'm assigned to this case, to begin with."

"All right. We'll do it."

"You'll get the photo of the rifling to me on the telefax machine as soon as you've got it, right?"

"Right."

"And if it's what I think it is, you'll stand ready to lend me some people for a search down there?"

"I'll stand ready for a request. If you're talking about a whole lot of manpower, I'd prefer to get it from Washington."

"Good man. I'll have the request ready to roll."

In the Vermont valley where Nicholas Gilette grew up, television reception was virtually nil and radio reception was poor; and Gilette never acquired the dependence on broadcasters common in his generation. The radio in the station wagon had gone blooey more than a year before, and he'd never troubled to have it repaired. Checking into his motel room in Endicott after ten on Sunday night, he called Maria and then read over the letter file on the shoe factory he would be visiting the next day, and left the television set alone. So when he came down to breakfast in the morning he knew nothing of the siege in Brooklyn, the "solution" to the sniper murders hinted by the New York police and eagerly adopted by the press. He learned about it when he saw the headline on the paper in the machine beside the elevator; and he broke up in a fit of laughter.

The fit concluded—the girl at the desk and several men entering the elevator looking strangely at him—Gilette put coins in the box for the paper; but on his way to the dining room he read the headline and subheads and first paragraph again, and hysteria returned. He had it down to a shaking giggle when he sat at the breakfast table, and read through the entire report. On consideration, it saddened him a little— that poor bastard trapped in his own home by those fools. Gilette felt a kind of obligation to free him, and felt also a touch of resentment that the police could believe what seemed in the reading like a rather ordinary man to be capable of what he had done.

He had time to read the story yet again, shaking his head and chuckling subaudibly, before the kitchen managed to generate his eggs. But when the food arrived he put the matter out of his head and considered the shoe company he was about to visit, the peripherals and the software package they had bought. One thing at a time.

On arrival at the office, Oscar heard from the receptionist that Mr. Spitts wanted to see him immediately. Spitts's secretary reinforced the message as Oscar walked past on the way to his own cubbyhole, to which he proceeded nonetheless, hanging his coat on the tree and glancing quickly at the in basket, as though something there might offer sustenance. Then he went to do his duty. He found Spitts looking out the window at the morning crowds emerging from the subway. Spitts gave him a glance, told him to sit down, and resumed his study of Union Square. "We've gotta have a talk," he said in a low voice.

"What about?" said Oscar heartily.

"Lotta things. I imagine you know what happened this weekend."

"I didn't see anything in the paper, so I assume nothing happened."

"Not quite. They put a metal detector in the entrance to the visitors' area at High Hills. Young Fitch was stopped and skin-searched when he triggered the detector."

"Was he holding?"

"You said you didn't see anything in the paper. I assure you, if he'd been holding, you'd have seen nothing else."

"It's good news, though, that he wasn't carrying that gun," Oscar said, leaning forward earnestly on the couch, though Spitts still was not looking at him.

"Uh—huh," Spitts said.

"What do you think triggered the machine?"

"He wears a jockstrap with a metallic cup," Spitts said, "ever since he got kicked in the balls at Cornell. But they were looking for him, Oscar. They were looking for him."

"Are you sure?"

Spitts finally swiveled around and looked at Oscar through his thick lenses; Oscar instinctively turned slightly away, to show the side of his face that was as nature had planned it. "Yes," Spitts said. "I'm sure."

"You think somebody tipped them?"

"Yes, I do."

"What makes you think so?" Oscar said, pleased with himself for not squirming. It was not going to be so hard as he—and probably Johnson, too—had feared.

"The warden told Congressman Fitch. FBI, he said. He didn't give a name, or Fitch didn't remember it, but I think it has to be our old friend Harry Johnson."

Oscar made a bitter face—overdid it a little, maybe, he thought as he relaxed his mouth. "How many people knew about that meeting?" he said. "Got any ideas? Want me to look into it?"

"No ideas, Oscar," Spitts said, and looked away again.

"Information. Knowledge. Proof. It's you."

"Me?" Oscar gave Spitts what he hoped was a look of amused disbelief. "You can't *mean* that."

"There never was any discussion at any meeting of Fitch being used to smuggle a gun to High Hills," Spitts said.

Oscar felt himself falling through the couch, into space, as though the fuse were about to detonate again on the kitchen table. He was silent. Spitts got up, walked around his desk and sat on the corner of it near the couch. He looked at his wounded employee—colleague, he had thought—and nodded his head several times, quickly.

"Why?" Oscar managed finally.

"Dunno," said Spitts. "I'd been a little upset about the way you pushed me when I told you a couple of the Weatherman types had been in touch. 'Upset' is too strong; you did it well, nothing surprising, just subconsciously . . . So I gave you a test. You failed. Or maybe you passed. Anyway, I now know something about you, something I wish, I really do wish," he said, walking back around the desk and resuming his chair, the authority position, "I wish I didn't know. But I do. You've got a second job, Oscar, don't you? You're not just a paralegal in this office. You're an agent."

Oscar's left hand was massaging the empty sleeve of his jacket. He shrugged his shoulders.

"How long? How long have you been an agent for Harry Johnson?"

Oscar took three deep breaths, and looked Spitts in the eye. "Long time," he said softly.

"Tell me about it," said Craig Spitts. "I don't want to put you through a cross-examination. It's more than a year now you've worked in my office; I think I know you. I have decisions to make, not only about you—about a lot of cases that passed through your hands at one time or another. What have you reported from this office to the FBI?"

"Three things," Oscar said, his voice still soft, looking down at the metal knobs on the feet of Spitts's desk. "The Fitch business. The Weatherman contacts. And the time that fellow from NASA came in and said he was in trouble, he'd been passing secret material to the Czech attaché and he thought they'd caught up with him, he had to get out of the country."

Spitts laughed harshly. "He was an agent himself, that fellow."

"I . . . gathered so," said Oscar. "But those are the only times; nothing about a case. Look, Craig," he said. "You've got me. I can't deny what you know. I can't try. The truth is that Johnson didn't put me here—you know that. He wasn't happy about my taking this job, said it could make trouble for him someday—"

"Yessirree—"

"And he's never asked me for information from this office. What he wanted from me was Vietnam Vets stuff."

"Were you working for him when you blew yourself up?"

"Yes."

"I never figured you that way," Spitts said, and rubbed his eyes under his glasses. "Jesus! You were talking people into bombing things—you were the big man in that cadre, for Christ sake—and then . . . I guess it was pretty stupid of me to feel sorry for you, wasn't it?"

"I never asked you to feel sorry for me."

"All right," Spitts said, and sighed. He hesitated, then said, "Of course, I can't believe you now."

"But you know damn well," Oscar said, feeling the unfairness—feeling new strength, he thought, rather encouraged—"you know damn well I never talked people into bombing things. I never pushed for anything of that sort around here, either. *I* didn't say Fitch should smuggle in any gun. You know that."

Spitts considered, frowning. "What got you started on this line of work?" he said finally.

"That I can't tell you."

"Years and years ago?"

"Yes."

"Well," Spitts said, shaking his head decisively, "I can't make any quick decisions about this. Too many people's lives are involved in this one. I don't know what I ought to do, and I don't know how I ought to do it. I may be able to get a lot of convictions overturned with this; I don't know. I'm seeing your friend Johnson this afternoon. Don't look at me that way—I haven't talked to him yet. I made the appointment through his boss—or, rather, I had the congressman make the appointment for me. I don't want you talking to him before I do."

Oscar said nothing. Spitts continued, now thinking aloud. "I can't arrest you. Maybe as the first step toward your rehabilitation, as we say in the courts, you could agree that you will not try to get in touch with Harry Johnson today."

Oscar smiled sourly. "That's reasonable," he said.

Spitts slammed his hand on his desk; it made a loud noise. "How much does that son of a bitch know about this office, thanks to you?"

"I've told you," Oscar said. "I've spoken to him about three things, none of them the work I was doing for you."

"I wonder who else he's got on his payroll around here. It's like my home's been burgled," Craig Spitts said, near tears. "I'll never feel the same walking in in the morning. And here I was, turning soft, too. Well. Fuck it. I've got a bankruptcy thing down the Lower East Side, the guy owns the broken-down building where the store is and he lives in it, and I want to know whether we can get anything at all out of the homestead exemption. Most of the work's going to have to be done at the County Lawyers, but there's a full morning's worth of stuff in our library here. Do you feel up to working this morning?"

"Sure."

"I want you in that library until two-thirty," Spitts said. "I don't want you near a telephone. I'm sorry, but that's the way it has to be. If you've got to go to the bathroom, raise your hand and I'll take you there. Tell the girls what you want for lunch; they'll order it for you. Leave the door open while you're talking to the delivery boy when it comes."

"I've told you the truth," Oscar said.

"The hell of it is," Spitts said, looking out the window again, "that I'll never know whether you have or not. Never. Come on, we both have work to do. I'll take you over to the library and get you started."

For Harry Johnson, as for most people who need their memory in their work, the computer was magic. It was of course a tool, "only a tool," but the same could be said of fingerprint analysis. Garbage in did not mean garbage out: miraculously, as in the human mind, an input of waste paper, mere lists, might generate information, even circumstantial evidence of considerable power. The machine could sort and order and compare, force analogies—in short, memorize, as an active verb—infinitely faster and more effectively than the best-trained and most conscientious agent. Faster than Harry Johnson.

To feed it, no doubt, required slave labor, the apotheosis of the routine, endless asking of simple questions to which any individual answer was meaningless. The promise was often illusory: hotel registration records in Allentown or Concord were most unlikely to match up with the marksman list in a way that would pinpoint a suspect, because the suspect almost certainly did not bed down where he committed his crime—though if Harry's guess was right about the dog, there was reason for higher hopes about the Maryland query. The crime had occurred in the morning and its site was between Baltimore and nowhere: probably, the sniper had spent the previous night in one of the little towns of the Eastern Shore; plausibly, his name was on a register. Meanwhile, the obvious garbage about the cars seen near the site was being implanted into the machine: it would be worthwhile—not vital, but worthwhile—to know whether a suspect owned a car like one that had been "identified."

Harry went over all this at the nine o'clock meeting of what Frank Wu called "the attack team." The entire telco printout was now available, and was being distributed to the police departments. More than three hundred names of men with four points or more on the original marksman search had been put through Bell's machinery. For perhaps a quarter of the list, AT&T had little information; among the others were seventeen salesmen or sales executives, a dozen or so accountants and lawyers, five truckdrivers, a magazine writer, a stock-car racing driver, an OSHA supervising inspector, a bank examiner, a pollution control consultant, and a minor-league nightclub musician who did thirty to forty weekend or one-week gigs a year. Some were long-term employees of one company; several were self-employed; some were job-hoppers. Some had credit cards for long-distance calls, and had used them from the following cities on the following days. . . .

There were three cases of possible suspects who had charged to home phones calls to or from one of the sniper cities on the day of the killing, the day before or the day after. Kaganopoulos (it was an obvious defect of the system) had called everywhere; he seemed to do a lot of his business on the telephone.

Of the three dozen "best" names on the merged lists, four had already been looked at and labeled unlikely; the remainder were parceled out, with special attention to places where there had been no killings and the local police were not at work. The job to be done was delicate. Given enough time, Harry's crew could have worked from a cover role as travel consultants checking with people's employers to see who went where in different companies, but that would mean days, in some cases weeks, of playing charades in many offices. The purpose now was elimination, not investigation; there was no reason not to be entirely straightforward. Harry handed out copies of a question form he had drafted for use with personnel officers at corporations and government bureaus, or with the heads of smaller companies.

There was some discussion of this approach, centered on the inescapable fact that it left the team little to do with its Monday but wait for returning telephone calls; but in fact there wasn't much else to do, and Harry, who had to go back to Bay Ridge, pointed out also that this was not the best day for the FBI to give an appearance of frantic activity. Harry choked off a burgeoning discussion of the weaknesses of the local police departments, and the group dispersed. He then called Adams, reported what little there was to report, and was reminded of his afternoon appointment with Spitts: "I've no doubt you can handle it," Adams said, and Harry murmured gratitude for the confidence.

"When do you expect to hear about the dog?" Adams inquired.

"Maybe by noon; maybe this afternoon."

"Washington has okayed the assignment of Baltimore manpower."

"Thanks."

"*Only* if the bullet is right."

"No point in it otherwise."

"No more flights of fancy, Harry."

Or cakes and ale, Johnson thought; but swallowed it. In Brooklyn, he found a new cast of characters, police union rules having made it finally too expensive to keep the same team on duty. Dr. Goldberg had gone off to teach a class, leaving word that he did not expect any significant negotiations to be possible for at least twenty-four hours. Residents of the block had been issued passes, and the police line was more effective than it had been on Sunday in keeping mere neighbors off the street. The television trucks were gone, but all three newspapers still had reporters manning telephones in brownstones across the street from the Kaganopoulos house. Word had gone around that agent Johnson was doubtful about the Greek nut as a "perpetrator."

Kaganopoulos had seen Harry arrive, and made indirect

contact with him by calling the newspapers to tell them that the real villain of the piece was again on the scene. Harry told the reporter from the *News* that the Bureau was following other leads and not "placing all our eggs in this basket," hoping that when word of that got to Kaganopoulos it might produce some movement. But the *News* reporter came back a few minutes later to say that when told of Johnson's statement, Kaganopoulos had responded with the simple comment, "Fucking liar."

The early edition of the *Post* was delivered to the site; its screamer headline was SIEGE CONTINUES, with a blown-up picture of the doorway of the house, and another of the perfectly ordinary window from which, the paper said, "shots" had been fired at the police. It made the officers on the scene, who had been moving about freely, more conscious of the supposed need to remain crouched behind cars. Harry, whose pleasure with Dr. Goldberg had grown steadily in retrospect, now openly admired his suggestion that nothing significant would happen for twenty-four hours. He decided to make his own contribution to the creation of calm by disappearing from the scene. The *News* reporter having identified himself as a former student radical from a group the FBI was believed—correctly—to have infiltrated, Harry invited the fellow to lunch with him, and they went off, appropriately to a Greek restaurant, where they argued about the propriety of using informers in "political organizations." It was, Harry thought, a good warm-up for the afternoon conversation with Spitts. But Spitts might want to talk about Lincoln Continentals, too.

Gilette enjoyed the morning at the shoe factory, where he made a routine inspection of the company's equipment, all of which was functioning to specifications, admired the computer-controlled machines that cut lasts to a new variety of sizes, discussed with the technical staff certain additional uses that could be made of the electronics and the coming development of improved sensors. It was a pleasure to be in an expanding end of the business: much more fun than banks. No selling; he was there at the company's request, to consult. There were questions to which Gilette didn't know the answers, and arrangements were made for a future visit to which he would bring one of the design staff from Pleasantville. They invited him to lunch with them, and he followed the shoe company car through the ragged industrial valley to the new hotel beside the new civic center in Binghamton. Gilette nursed a single drink, explaining that he was kowtowing to the government because his company did so much government business; their company, they said, defiantly reactionary, insisted they put in chits for a three-martini lunch.

More perceptive men—men who had taken only two drinks—might have noticed that Gilette's conversation was almost mechanical. The story in the newspaper once again had jumped to his sight from the newsstand in the hotel. It disturbed his balance; it was a kind of insult: he had done things since September that no other marksman *could* do. It was demeaning that "the sniper" had been located in the home of some kook in Brooklyn.

Fortunately, the subject did not come up at lunch. This was a contact Gilette had inherited from one of the founders of his company, with no military component whatever: none of his companions knew about him as a sportsman, the possibility, now squelched, that he might be part of an Olympic team.

At the end of the lunch, the four men from the shoe company went straight back to the office, parting from Gilette at the door to the men's room, where he wanted to wash up before resuming his travels. Their car was gone when he emerged into the bright November sun. He walked to the end of the long parking lot, now mostly empty, and as he settled in behind the wheel he noted across the distant roadway, in the empty area behind the civic center, a solitary jogger in a sweat suit. He sat and watched as the man turned and circled back, his head bouncing in faintly irregular elliptical patterns. Just within range.

Risky? Not much. His companions at lunch could not imagine anything of this sort. The shoe company had reserved the table and paid for the lunch. All life was risky; you had to take chances. It was an interesting shot. Difficult. He looked around: there was no one in the parking lot. He could exit without passing in front of the hotel. It would show the police how stupid they were about that Greek in Brooklyn. He started the car and turned it to where he would have the best angle on the distant jogger. He unsnapped the latch on the box, lifted out the gun with a single smooth motion, laid it on the seat and felt out a cartridge from the container. He looked around again at the parking lot: not a soul. He cradled the gun against his shoulder, and as the jogger turned for yet another round, he pulled the trigger. The noise seemed to him a little louder than usual. He grimaced, then smiled as he saw the jogger fall, a different, fuller smile than was his habit. Unhurried now, he swept the gun back into its carrying case, and drove out, around the turn to the easy access to the highway.

"Your appointment is waiting," said Tilly as Harry came into his office, a few minutes after two-thirty. "And there are calls from the lab and from Maryland."

"Get me the lab first. Then Maryland. Then we'll let the lion tamer make his entrance."

The lab said that tentatively—hell, surely, but what's the point?—the bullet taken from the dog had been fired from the same gun that fired the bullets taken from the people. Hollow and high-powered, with killing capacity far beyond that of normal .22 ammunition; the rifling "not inconsistent with."

Maryland office already knew, and the requests were out to the state police, the chiefs of all the little towns, to get the hotel registers for Saturday night.

It was adrenaline. Harry felt his search snapping into place, piece by piece; he wanted Kaganopoulos off his back, and Craig Spitts, and everything that might keep him from entire concentration on the maneuvers he was directing, the armies rising now to do his bidding. But nowt to do about it, as his mother used to say, and he told Tilly to make the caller welcome.

Spitts came in, frowning, shoulders squared, eyes cold behind the big glasses. He wore for the occasion a three-piece gray suit with a striped tie: the model of the successful young lawyer. Harry took it in quickly, rose from his desk and shook hands, rather to his visitor's surprise; waved Spitts to the couch and took the chair beside it. "I'd offer you a cigarette, but I don't smoke. Coffee?"

"No, thanks."

"Sorry I'm late," Harry said, continuing the ritual. "We're in the middle of a murder investigation, as you probably know. And I do have to get back to that as quickly as possible. Meanwhile, what can I do for you, fast?"

"You can avoid trying to run me over, to begin with."

"I beg your pardon," said Harry.

"Forget I said it. But you were driving a car that almost hit me, the other day downtown."

"I have no recollection of that whatever," said Harry amiably. "Perhaps it was some other FBI agent."

Spitts swallowed an expression of distaste. "Look, we have a problem," he said. "A very *serious* problem."

"Yes?"

"You've had an agent in my office."

"Mr. Spitts! Whatever makes you think that?"

"Don't think it. I know it. The guards at High Hills went after Joshua Fitch Saturday because they thought he was smuggling a gun to a client."

"Yes, I heard about that."

"The warden says it was at your suggestion that he ordered the search."

Harry said nothing.

"There never was any plan to smuggle a gun into that prison through Fitch. I told Oscar Riskovsky there was, but it wasn't so."

"Then why did you say it?"

"What made me suspect Oscar? I don't know. What makes you suspect anybody? Of anything?"

"You can write books about that question," Harry said. It was unfortunate, all this; like all inevitable surprises, it came at the wrong time. On any day, any agent could be blown. The question was, what happened then? And, always, why now? "You've talked to Oscar, I assume," Harry said conversationally.

"Of course. This morning."

"What did he say?"

Spitts shook his head. He removed his glasses and wiped a lens on a gray sleeve. "No," he said. "This is . . . We can't have this sort of conversation. I have to know the extent to which my cases have been compromised by reports to the government about our strategy. There are criminal convictions here that perhaps should be overturned. I'm not talking about publicity, or congressional investigations, or any of the other things I might talk about. Later, maybe, but not now. First I have to know exactly what you stole from me, so I can recover it."

Harry crossed his legs, leaned back against the leather-covered cushion, and smiled; there was admiration in the smile. "I'm afraid I can't help you," he said. "I haven't stolen anything. Under the circumstances, I'm not going to be such a fool as to deny that Oscar Riskovsky has done some work for me over the years. But the work he did for you was no part of the work he did for me.

"Then why was Fitch searched?"

"There have, I think, been three occasions when Oscar has reported to me on something he learned while working for you. Fitch was one. Another was an incident when Oscar thought your people might be helping to secrete—or even to export—two fugitives from justice, bail-jumpers following conviction on charges of assault with a deadly weapon."

"They had approached me with the thought of turning themselves in."

"Oscar didn't know that. Maybe didn't believe it. They didn't turn themselves in, did they?"

"No."

"The third was a suspected espionage situation—"

"That was a setup," Spitts said bitterly. "You were trying to trap me."

"I wasn't," Harry said, and brushed something from a creased knee. "Maybe somebody else was." His gaze fixed on Spitts. "You seem to have done better at trapping than whoever it was that tried to trap you."

"All right, so you and Oscar agree," Spitts said, returning the stare; but you can't win these things in another man's office, and he looked away first. "What really kills me," he said, "is that I'll never have any way to find out whether that's because it's true or because the two of you cooked it up. Mr. Johnson, I have a *right* to defend people accused of crimes. They have a *right* to my services."

"How could I possibly quarrel with that?"

"I have a *right* to conduct meetings with my associates without somebody eavesdropping or bugging and passing along to the Justice Department everything I say."

"I agree."

"Then why did you plant one of your men in my office?"

"I didn't plant him. You recruited him. It was by no means the job I would have chosen for him."

"Why'd he take it?"

"You'll have to ask him. I think it was because he liked you, liked the work you were doing, liked the idea of working in a law office. As I'm sure you know, Oscar is an idealist."

"Yeah, sure. That's why he spies."

"Yes."

Spitts shuddered. "I don't see how we can live this way," he said. "Chilling effect! My God, it's a freezing effect. Don't you think three people have a right to get together without each of them worrying that one of the other two is a spy?"

"That's the age we live in," Harry said, not uncomfortable. The circumstances of this encounter—the incident that had occasioned it, the blunderbuss of congressional intervention, the Big Surprise—had created at the beginning even for the two participants a false notion of who had reason to be afraid of whom. However clean Spitts was, there were of course things that had happened in his office that would not bear exposure. How could he be sure of what Johnson did or did not know? Any such weaponry would not be wasted in preliminary discussions.

And what would Spitts gain by going to court? A U.S. attorney, Johnson, Riskovsky, all swearing that no information about defense plans had been solicited, gathered, communicated. A judge might be furious; the newspapers surely would be furious; but new trials for his clients? Not bloody likely.

"*You* make it the age we live in."

"No, I don't," said Harry Johnson. "I'm not so big and bold as that. You ask me a good question, and I want to give you an honest answer. When three people meet to discuss dropping LSD in a water system, or robbing a bank, or blowing up a computer center—yes, you can bet your life I want each of them to think one of his companions is a spy. That's my job. You guys in law offices come into these things late. You think the purpose of the criminal justice system is to punish people, so you feel sorry for them, you look to help them, make sure all their rights, real or concocted, are carefully preserved like mummies. My job is different. My job is to protect society. I'm perfectly willing to have some criminals and some nuts paranoid about the FBI—I'm willing to have college kids and newspapermen and lawyers who aren't criminals paranoid about the FBI, provided there aren't

179

just too many of them—so I can keep ordinary people from being paranoid. I think the purpose of the criminal justice system is to prevent crime, and nothing does that like giving people the feeling they're being watched."

" 'Big Brother Is Watching You.' That's what you mean."

"Nonsense."

"It's not nonsense that you've been watching me."

"Inadvertently," said Harry.

"Systematically," said Craig Spitts.

"We seem to have a disagreement," Harry said briskly, and rose from the chair. "Right now, I have to see what I can do to protect someone from a sniper. All I can say to you is that I hope you won't embarrass my office—or Oscar— by seeking to make a lot more of this than is here. I honestly do not believe you will do yourself or your clients any good by exploiting this situation, but certainly it's yours to decide."

Craig Spitts smiled to himself and looked up at the apparently confident man—the *official*—who had succeeded in controlling their time together. He struggled to his feet—it was (deliberately?) a low couch, hard to get off gracefully—saying, "You haven't told me everything"—grunt—"everything I'd wish to know. Everything I ought to know."

"How *could* I have done that?" Harry said with a slightly condescending nod.

"And I think we'll be talking about some of these things again."

"I'm sure we will. Irresistible subjects. It will be a pleasure to discuss them with you." Harry held out his right hand, which was, after a perceptible pause, taken. He opened the door for his guest. "Tilly, will you accompany Mr. Spitts to the elevator? Thank you."

X

The Learning Curve Rises

Oscar was in the corridor chatting with Spitts's secretary when the lawyer returned to his office. Spitts nodded, asked his secretary about messages and which of them seemed important. She suggested that Adrian Francis had seemed especially importunate, and Spitts, telling Oscar to wait while he talked with Francis, disappeared into his office and firmly closed the door.

Francis's story was a strange one. Early that afternoon he had received a call from a CIA official who had been perhaps the most secretive and devious of the whole crew of witnesses in the executive hearings. Surprisingly, even astonishingly, this informant was now suggesting to Francis that—entirely off the record; he would of course deny ever making such a telephone call if he had to deny it—he thought he might possibly be of some help in the committee's ongoing FBI investigation. The committee, he thought, would find it especially rewarding to look into an old and still unsolved kidnapping, the Whitmont case, and agent Harry Johnson's involvement. Perhaps the committee would come to believe that the case had remained unsolved because of steps Johnson could have taken but did not; perhaps the committee might even find interesting reasons *why* Johnson had not taken those steps. In any case, he was—on this wholly personal basis only, of course—happy to be of service.

"When thieves fall out," Spitts said cheerfully.

"Does look that way, doesn't it?"

"Does your grapevine bear any reasons why CIA might wish to put a knife in agent Johnson?"

"No. I haven't talked about it with the committee staff. I've learned that you don't just throw out suggestions around here. Either your idea gets buried in the mounds of paper or somebody senior clutches it and locks you out. I can't go to the congressman and talk with him. The first thing he told me when he hired me was that I wasn't in college any more, and he didn't want any bull sessions. I have to bring him something sewed up like a baseball, so he can pick it up and throw it himself."

"You can have bull sessions with me," said Spitts.

"Well, if you really want to know what I think, I've had this sense that these guys develop an extra-fine sense of territoriality. The size of the job, the size of the budget, depends on the size of the turf. So they get very upset when somebody starts putting his feet on their side of the line. If you understand what I mean."

"Oh, I think I do," said Spitts.

"Johnson must wander into CIA territory all the time. I've never met the man. You told me you were going to see him today."

"I did."

"How'd that go? Anything the committee should know?"

Spitts told him. They agreed that right now there was probably more to lose than to gain by pushing the Johnson-Riskovsky link to public attention. But if the tip from CIA led somewhere . . . perhaps. Francis had already looked up the clippings on the Whitmont kidnapping; now he proposed that he would personally speak with Tony Whitmont. Meanwhile, Spitts suggested, they should see what use they could make of Riskovsky—at the least, ask him to return to the matter of the Lincoln Continental, and follow up.

"What if he won't?" Francis inquired.

"Oh, he will, you know," said Spitts.

"Will he let Johnson know?"

"I'm sure."

Francis whistled into the mouthpiece. "Hey!" he said. "We might even get the bastard's wind up."

"That I doubt," said Spitts. "But I don't mind trying it."

With Oscar, Spitts was quick and rough. "I don't have much to tell you," he said. "Johnson pretty much admitted you've been spying for him. He backed up your story on when and why you transmitted information about things learned in this office. I haven't decided what to do about it, and I haven't decided what to do about you. Do you want to continue working here?"

"I don't know," Oscar said, standing in the middle of the room and looking away. "Do you want me to?"

"Mebbe," Spitts said briskly. "Would you be willing to work on Johnson material?"

"Such as?"

"The business with the Continental."

"Oh, yes. He said if you wanted it I should do it."

"So you talked with him about that little investigation you did for me, eh?"

Oscar swallowed.

"Makes four times you told him about things in this office," Spitts noted mildly. "If I had you guys under oath, I could make you squirm. Did he admit he'd been driving that car?"

"He didn't *deny* it," Oscar said.

"But he said he didn't care about your investigating it."

"He said you were my boss and that was my job. To do what you told me to do."

"All right," said Spitts. "You're on. Go back and finish tracing that car. We'll do the bankruptcy stuff later in the week."

"Yessir," said Oscar. "It will probably take a trip to Connecticut."

"Do that tomorrow."

"Am I still under ban against talking to Johnson?"

"No, no," Spitts said. "Entirely up to you. I don't know what you'll want to say to him, of course." He swiveled his chair to the window, then back, almost with a kind of glee. "Going to be hard work being a double agent when everybody knows you're a double agent, eh?"

"Maybe I ought to just quit."

"That's one solution," said Spitts, and made a gesture of dismissal. "Let me know."

Oscar stood. "I'd like to know," he said in a tight voice, "what's right for me to do."

Spitts now looked at him, the eyes still cold behind the glasses. "Do you think you've been doing what's right?"

"Yes, I've always thought so."

"Have you taken money from him?"

"Yes."

Spitts shrugged his shoulders. "I've got a lot to do today," he said, and went back to the desk.

Harry reported to Adams that he thought the Fitch problem was contained—but it was a real problem: an agent was blown. It was admittedly a bad time for that to happen, with the House hearings on the horizon. "But the only things he knows are things that might hurt *them*. I don't think they can make much of it."

"Is he on a payroll?"

"Not recently."

"Special funds?"

"My control. Incidentally, as you probably know from Maryland, we have a positive on the dog."

"Yes, I've heard. Good work. Have you told Palio and the New York people?"

"Not yet."

"How are you going to do that?"

"I wish I knew."

Tilly poked her head around the doorway. "Man on the other phone says it's absolutely essential he talk to you at once."

"Somebody says he has to talk to me," Harry said into the telephone. "Call you later if anything interesting happens." He hit the button: "Johnson here."

It was the chief of police in Binghamton, New York. "You're coordinating the sniper case? . . ."

They'd sent the bullet to their labs; they'd telefax the microphotos. Assistant manager of the arts center; jogged there every day in lieu of lunch. Probably shot from the hotel parking lot: they'd already acquired the register for the night before, all the reservations and credit card diners at the restaurant at lunch. Names would go off on the teletype. No press announcement yet—they hadn't found the fellow's wife and would have to inform her first. Yes, if Harry wanted it, they could hold the announcement for some hours, probably all night: the body had been found by a policeman, no witnesses, no public curiosity. Just as soon wait for a report from the FBI lab on the bullet photographs anyway. Yes, he'd be happy to come down and join the detectives and chiefs from the other cities at a meeting tomorrow afternoon at five o'clock especially if his bills were paid.

First call to Wu: tell him, and set up the meeting. Everybody but the New York people—Harry would invite them himself.

Second call to Dr. Goldberg. "Are you alone?"

"Yes."

"Off the record."

"Yes."

"We've got another sniping, up in Binghamton. Killed a man again. We're waiting on the bullet, but I don't think there's any doubt."

"Yes."

"Have to get Kaganopoulos out of there safely. Palio, too."

"Yes."

"He has to hear he's safe from somebody he trusts more than he trusts either of us."

"Yes."

"But if we wait until it's in the newspapers, we have a hell of a mess."

"Yes."

"I guess I know someone he would believe. It's worth my taking some trouble to bring them together, isn't it?"

"Yes."

"Can you come out there and help oil the thing once it's on the rails?"

"Yes."

Harry looked at his watch: four-thirty. "About seven o'clock tonight?"

"Yes."

"You've been very helpful, Doctor. Thank you."

"Yes."

Third call Harry made from the communications room, on the secure line to Langley. He got the young lady: very cold. Doubtful if he could speak with Phil. But after some delay Phil was on the line. "What do you want this time, Johnson? The antimissile laser?"

Harry told him about the Binghamton murder, and the need to get Kaganopoulos to surrender and vamoose before the story was out. "Look. He's got to accept arrest. If nothing else, for resisting arrest. Quid pro quo: we give up the search. His home is his castle. Then there should be no problem about getting him released immediately. On recognizance, pending the day when it blows over. Neither you nor I wants him out there pissing on the street with the reporters. His employers won't want that, either. We can give him a nice vacation—not to Greece, I guess, but somewhere, maybe Florida; it's getting cold here. To get us out, he has to believe it's his friends who protected him. That means you."

"There's a key phrase buried in that disquisition," said Phil. " 'Should be no problem.' There should never have been a problem. How are you going to control the city? Six gets you ten those clowns will say that this guy in Binghamton is a different sniper."

"We'll have word on the bullet in an hour. We already know it's the same kind of bullet. I assume you *can* reach Kaganopoulos?"

"He has a code."

"Phil, just do it, will you? Get word to him he's safe, you've intervened. It'll make him feel good all over. Stress to him that he's under orders, and is to make no statement to the press. Then I've got somebody who I think can work out the details with him. Smart psychologist."

"When?"

"About seven o'clock. I know I can keep Binghamton under wraps till after eight. If we play it right we can tip up the whole episode in Tuesday's papers."

"I'll call him."

"Right. Thanks. We've got almost two hours. If there's the slightest indication that I may have trouble with my friends in the city police, I will be back to you. But I can't imagine it."

"My worry about you," Phil said, "is that you seem somewhat deficient in imagination."

Johnson found himself nodding at the telephone. "Some other time," he said. "When we're both retired."

Then back to the office for the call to Palio, who was out at the observation post opposite the Kaganopoulos home. For a wonder, there was no objection: it was all too obvious that the siege in Bay Ridge had to end before the papers got wind of the murder in Binghamton. Palio restrained his curiosity about the identity of the father figure whose word would be law for Kaganopoulos. He awaited instructions.

"We'll want Mrs.," Harry said.

"She's here. Living here with the neighbors. After you left this morning she tried to get home again for a change of clothing, and he told her to wait. She's a wreck."

"There's a lot to organize," Harry said. "We have to get those friends of his out of the house very quietly. And I'd love to see him and his wife on an airplane tonight. We'll want Leone to talk to the press. Every man needs a lawyer."

"I'm sorry we did this to you," Palio said.

"You didn't do it. He did. I wish he was our guy, myself— but he's not, and never was. We're not going to have any fights, you and I. We've still got a sniper out there. I'll see you as soon as the traffic permits."

For this one, Harry would want a driver; Wu volunteered to take the job himself. Finally, the report to Adams, who was depressed. "Do you have any objection," Adams asked, "if I let Washington know immediately about the Binghamton business, so they have time to prepare some sort of statement?"

"Can we trust them to keep their mouths shut until Binghamton announces?"

"Oh, yeah. There's no credit to be got here."

"That's for sure."

The lab called as Harry was packing his papers: the telefax from Binghamton had arrived, and there was just no question it was the same gun, the same sniper. Harry asked them to hold off sending the information to Binghamton until eight o'clock, just in case. This gave the lab both a how-to-do-it problem and an *amour propre* problem, which Harry solved with the suggestion that in half an hour or so they could call Binghamton with a regretful statement that the telefax was not quite good enough for certainty, and a request for another run through the machine.

Then it was seventy minutes through the loathsome traffic to Bay Ridge. The siege was an item at the tail end of the six o'clock national radio news; wise of Adams to give Washington a reason to be glad the Bureau had a New York office. We are on the ball.

Harry's beeper went as they crawled along the expressway. He picked up the message through the car telephone: Oscar. "You'll excuse me," he said to Wu, and squelched the car speaker. Then he called the number, and got a rather thick voice on the other side. "Can't talk to you," Johnson said; "I'm in an official car heading to the Kaganopoulos mess. There are receivers that can monitor me."

"But we've got to talk," Oscar said.

"Just possibly tomorrow. Try me then."

"I need—"

"Impossible," Harry said. "Just impossible." And hung up. Wu was looking straight ahead at the lines of cars. "I have an agent under cover who seems to have been exposed," Harry explained.

"Can't do much for him, can you?" Wu said.

"Never can," said Harry, and closed his eyes.

But in Brooklyn everything ran like a watch. At seven o'clock the tap on the Kaganopoulos telephone went haywire: electronically defeated, a technician reported, very sophisticated stuff. Johnson told Palio not to worry, and presently Dr. Goldberg called to sell the luxuries of Florida in November. Kaganopoulos still wanted Greece, but could be persuaded that he had to stay in the country. There was some backing and filling before Goldberg offered Hawaii, which was accepted.

Palio alerted the reporters that there was about to be a development, and they trooped into the windowless wagon to hear about it while the four soldiers left the Kaganopoulos house observed only by the police and the neighbors, and Mrs. Kaganopoulos returned, tearful with joy, to pack their bags. Courteously, Palio gave the reporters time to call their papers and stations with the headline before he organized the performance of the act of surrender. Mr. and Mrs. K. emerged shining from their home. The suspect kissed his wife for the cameras. A sergeant took him deferentially by the elbow and guided him to a squad car. No handcuffs.

The police abandoned the block, and a procession moved off to the precinct: the two vans, the squad cars, the unmarked detectives' cars, the reporters' cars. Like a wedding, Harry thought, riding with Dr. Goldberg (who would also be returning to Manhattan: Harry sent Wu back to the office to prepare for tomorrow morning's meeting like a good chief of staff). Or a funeral. Lawyer Leone, a Mustache Pete with a waxed one, dressed in a tuxedo—a fine old-fashioned touch—was waiting at the precinct house, and disappeared with Kaganopoulos and Palio into the interrogation room. The reporters were given the use of desks and telephones in the dusty squad room, all green metal desks and armless secretaries' swivel chairs; they called in what they had, then assembled at the reception desk, which was as near the interrogators as they could come.

Harry and Dr. Goldberg sat it out in the captain's office, where whiskey and ice were laid out for their entertainment while the captain absented himself on affairs of state. Both men took a drink, Harry abstracted with thoughts of the names arriving from Baltimore and Binghamton, the off chance, the devout hope, that somewhere in the bowels of the machinery the answers were even now emerging. Dr. Goldberg talked, developing his own ideas aloud, conscious that Harry was mostly elsewhere, but serenely undisturbed. Suddenly, Harry heard him, and came to attention.

"What was that?"

"What was what?"

"Need for increasing risk? Why?"

"Simplifying—"

"Thank you—"

"You're welcome. He has no one to talk to. In a sense, to be dramatic, he has a dialogue with danger. Not at the beginning. At the beginning it is all an accomplishment, but then the context changes. And of course there is a level at which, like everyone who kills, he knows he is doing something wrong. To be wild—"

"Let's be wild," said Harry Johnson.

"You interest me, too," said Dr. Goldberg.

"I'm glad."

"The proper study of mankind is man," Dr. Goldberg said smoothly. "Maimonides should have said it, but unfortunately he did not. We speculate. The man you are seeking is a repressed homosexual, sublimated to the exercise of a skill interestingly chosen, in this situation. There is a male model problem somewhere in his childhood, a father who absconded, something of the sort. He will suddenly have come under some severe pressure, which has snapped one corner of the web of restraints by which he has hedged his behavior. The need to restore the restraints will draw him increasingly to the commission of crimes that are more likely to lead to his capture. Because he kills so cleanly and at a distance, he will not scrawl messages on mirrors with a victim's lipstick, and he will not send letters to the police. But the need to be caught will increase within him."

Dr. Goldberg patted his skullcap, wiped his glasses, looked challengingly at Harry, who waited. "Good," he said. "Think of the crime today, the one they"—gesturing toward the door—"don't know about yet. It was clearly more hazardous for the sniper than the earlier killings. If, as seems likely from what you tell me, he shot from the hotel parking lot, he ran an obvious risk that a car would turn into the lot and its driver would see something. Or someone would come around the corner looking for his own car. I am impressed that he killed on the day when the newspapers were telling everyone that the case was closed. He could not wait to tell the world that the case is *not* closed. Soon I think he will do something even more reckless. And then, of course, normal police procedures will yield a result."

Harry nodded. "Doesn't give us much to do until more people get killed."

Dr. Goldberg shrugged.

"I am operating," Harry said, "on the theory that if you keep panning the dirt you find some gold."

"Fools' gold," said Goldberg, nodding in the direction of the interrogation room.

"Fools find fools' gold," Harry said. "I have this man's name already. I just don't know which name it is."

"You are a fanatic for competence," Dr. Goldberg said. "That often produces disappointments."

"Even disasters," Harry said helpfully. "But consider the alternatives. Doctor, I have a meeting tomorrow at five o'clock with the local police departments from all the places where people have been killed. They will be unhappy. Someone at the first meeting asked if I would lay on a psychologist for them. You arrive in my life like manna from heaven. May I count on you tomorrow?"

"You think I'm right?"

Harry considered the question. "That's extreme," he said. "I think you're helpful. It will be particularly helpful if you can persuade the cops that, at some point, what you have called normal police procedure will solve this case. But also, they want ideas; you can give them ideas. I would appreciate it."

"My pleasure," said Dr. Goldberg.

The captain poked his head into his office to see how his guests were faring, and to fill them in on developments. All was proceeding smoothly. A courier had brought a make-up kit for Kaganopoulos: beard, heavier eyebrows, dark glasses. He had refused profanely to have his mustache shaved. Another courier had gone off for Kaganopoulos's house, to pick up Mrs. Kaganopoulos and the luggage, and convey them to the hotel at Kennedy Airport, where they would spend the night. The make-up job was almost done, and Kaganopoulos would be leaving presently, through a back door. Leone had put the fear of God into him, and he would lie low. There was about to be a press briefing in the conference room adjoining the captain's office. Would Johnson and Dr. Goldberg care to attend? Certainly.

Palio ran the briefing: "Mr. Kaganopoulos has been booked on charges of resisting arrest and conspiracy to resist arrest. The charges are misdemeanors. Following our usual practice in processing second-degree misdemeanors, we have summonsed Mr. Kaganopoulos to appear for arraignment on a date certain, in this case four weeks from tomorrow. On the basis of our interrogation, we do not now consider Mr. Kaganopoulos an active suspect in the sniper cases. On the recommendation of his attorney, Mr. Leone, whom you see here, Mr. Kaganopoulos has decided that he does not wish to speak with the press, and he has already left this building. He has been given permission to leave the state"—Palio looked up with a sweet smile at the rustle of protest—"and indeed may already have done so. Because of the unusual interest in this case and the cold weather, I have invited Mr. Leone to join me in this room, and we are both prepared to answer any questions you may wish to ask."

"Is there anyone you do consider an active suspect?" asked the *News* reporter.

"We are following up a number of leads. At this moment, none of them would fall into the category of active suspect."

"Do you feel the FBI gave you a bum steer?"

"Oh, no," Palio said, almost shuddering. "In a case such as this one, as I'm sure you understand, we must cast a very wide net. Unfortunately, an individual in the area where the net is cast may not realize that our reasons for wishing to question him may be more general than usual, and need not imply any belief on our part that he is the perpetrator. The press, too, may be confused on these matters."

"Mr. Leone," said one of the reporters, "do you agree with that assessment? Do you believe the police had adequate grounds for staging this spectacular?"

Leone looked graciously to Palio for permission to speak, which was given with a short nod. "No, of course not," he said. "My client, as I understand it, was cooperating with the FBI without compulsion."

The reporters now turned toward Harry, who was sitting in a corner with Dr. Goldberg, observing; and Harry firmly shook his head.

"Mr. Johnson—"

"I'm not here to be questioned."

Telephones were ringing ardently in the next room. "Do you expect to bring a suit for false arrest?" one of the reporters inquired, while another went off in response to a summons from the door behind Palio and Leone.

"I think everything's going to work out peaceably," Leone said.

"What about the men with Kaganopoulos?"

"We don't know who they were," Palio said with a straight face. "He wouldn't tell us."

"And it's not something you checked up on while—"

The reporter who had left the room reappeared in the doorway. "Forget it, gang," he said. "There's calls for all of us. The sniper shot again today, in Binghamton. One more dead."

There was a great scraping of chairs, and the room emptied out.

Gilette got to Poughkeepsie barely in time to keep a dinner date with one of the IBM engineers who would be on the other side of the table the next day. Two years before, the two of them had cooled their heels in the same waiting rooms going after an airline contract on which they had been more or less allies—for awhile IBM was prepared to do the whole job, it had no serious objection to Gilette's proposals, which gave the giant ninety percent of the hardware contract, claiming only more flexible peripherals and a more efficient software package. Control Data had won that competition, in partnership with a San Jose company, and Gilette and the IBM man had drowned their sorrows together.

Now Gilette's bosses were puzzled and disturbed by the IBM request for a meeting to explore "ways in which we can compete without your infringing our patents." The decision to send Gilette to the meeting, alone and without lawyers, was a move in a game, an attempted expression of unconcern. Carrying a watching brief, really, Gilette was authorized to find out unofficially as much as he could by private contacts. Hence the dinner, which turned out to be at a quiet country inn known as a place much favored by IBM brass. The two men sat alone at a corner table, but the statement made by the choice of restaurant was clear enough: there were no secrets here. The IBM man bought the meal; Gilette gave him in recompense the box of frozen ducks he had shot on the Chesapeake. Maria, he knew, would throw them out.

The problem, it soon developed, was with a piece of the microprocessor, and IBM's worry that by failing to enforce a patent against this bug on the wall it might lose its rights as against more potent rivals. Tomorrow's meeting with lawyers present was part of the abundant caution enforced on the corporation by the Justice Department. A memo would be presented, which Gilette was to take home with him; there would be other meetings. Patience. In other words, the morrow would be dull, but with any luck at all, brief. After a while, the two men found other things to talk about.

It was not yet ten o'clock when Gilette returned to his hotel room, and he called home on the company credit card. The telephone was picked up during the first ring, and Gilette found Maria in a state of great disturbance—near panic. Her English deteriorated at these times; slowly piecing together what she was saying, Gilette finally understood that she had the idea the house was being watched—by men of the kind who used to watch her father's house. A black Mercedes had driven by several times, and once had parked for almost half an hour across the street. Would it be safe to send John to school? She had shopping to do tomorrow and she was afraid to leave the house.

Gilette calmed her down as best he could, reassured her that he would be home for dinner and would take care of the men in the Mercedes tomorrow night. These things didn't happen in America—really, they didn't. The edge went off her voice, and he even teased her a little: if she'd learned to use his guns, the way she'd promised when they were married, she wouldn't have to worry so much about men in a Mercedes. This proved a mistake—almost everything he did with her these days was a mistake, Gilette thought, and picked at his mustache—provoking renewed statements that she wouldn't feel safe until he was home, and what time would that be? He promised to be back before six, to spend some time with the boy, and she promised to take a sleeping pill and try to forget about Mercedes cars and the secret police.

A church bell struck as Gilette hung up, and he thought of watching a news program. It began with an announcement that the siege in Brooklyn was over: Kaganopoulos had surrendered to the police. And from what the police were saying now, it seemed they'd been going after the wrong man anyway. Gilette was pleased to hear it; sense was returning to the disorderly world. As he went to turn off the set, however, there was some disturbance off camera: the anchor man excused himself and turned away to accept a piece of blue paper from a disembodied hand. His voice rose in pitch as he read it: there had been *another* murder by the sniper, this one upstate. . . . Gilette smiled at the machine, and flicked it off.

Harry found a figure in a raincoat huddled on the step just outside his apartment house, and was thinking the usual

196

thoughts about the decline of the neighborhood when the figure looked up and he saw it was Oscar. Sodden drunk. "Waiting for you," Oscar explained.

"Good God."

"No worry. They know. Everybody knows."

"Come on in out of the cold."

"Yeah. Wanna talk."

"I'll give you a cup of coffee."

" 'S all right. Just keep me awake."

Harry held out a hand and Oscar grabbed it, pulling himself to his feet. "Maybe I just go home," Oscar said.

"You'd get rolled before you got both feet out of the cab; you'd better come upstairs with me."

Oscar was morosely silent in the elevator and to the door. Inside, Harry said, "Let me take your coat. I'll make you some coffee. Strong coffee."

Oscar allowed Harry to take the coat and staggered over to the couch, really a loveseat, standard convertible-furniture goods covered with a blue tweed fabric; it dawned on him fuzzily that this apartment was not a great deal larger than his own.

"I guess that's one of the big changes today," Harry said soothingly from the kitchen. "You can visit now."

"What'm I gonna *do?*" Oscar called out from his sprawled position.

Harry emerged from the kitchen, went into the hall and procured two table mats to place on the card table before the living room window, permanently implanted there and available for dining use on the rare occasions when Harry had reason to eat outside the kitchen. He called Oscar's attention to the Picasso reproduction on the wall across from the couch—the lady with the two heads and the belly of circles. "Sue gave me that," he said. "Very conservative, for Sue."

"What *am* I gonna do?" Oscar said, and rubbed his eyes. "I'm no use to you any more. Spitts won't trust me; he can't.

If this gets to be something in the papers, my father sees it, it'll kill him. Just kill him. Jesus!"

"I guess what you're going to do tonight," Harry said, turning back to the kitchen, "is stay here. I've got a clean toothbrush somewhere. You'd never fit into my pajamas, but I've got a bathrobe you can sleep in. That couch you're on folds out to a bed. Just a minute—you need the coffee, and it won't keep you awake, not tonight." He came out with a tray and two espresso machines. "Better take a shower, too. Get off your tail and come over to the table."

Oscar lurched up and to the table, and sat down heavily.

"That's good," Harry said encouragingly. "You're functioning."

"What'm I gonna do for *money?*" Oscar wailed. "You can't pay me any more. Nobody wants to hire a one-arm man, it turns your stomach to look him in the face. How'm I gonna make a *living?*"

Harry sniffed. "Lots of jobs for college graduates," he said. "You stink of booze. We can worry about money tomorrow—we can worry about everything tomorrow."

"What'm I gonna do about Sue?"

"Ah," Harry said, removing the cups from beneath the filters and serving his guest. "Now you've gone beyond me. But Sue, I assume on the basis of yesterday's phone call, was the one person in the world other than you or me who already knew this story."

Oscar looked at him narrowly, then took a sip of the bitter coffee and widened his gaze. "You're not very . . . upset, are you?"

"The world's a dangerous place," said Harry Johnson, enjoying the coffee. "For me, Oscar, it's all like crossing the street. When they want you, they get you. I can take care of myself, and I suspect we'll be able to take care of you. We'll talk about it," he added, finishing the cup, "tomorrow. Tomorrow's going to be a big day."

XI

Opportunities Knock

Harry Johnson awoke the next morning remembering that Oscar Riskovsky was in his living room, then immediately thought of the rest of the day, the possibility that the printouts would begin to point decisively at someone, the stronger possibility that the afternoon meeting with the police departments would have to be handled on an inspirational basis. He shaved, showered and dressed, walked quietly through the living room, not disturbing the snoring figure on the converted couch, and took the papers to the kitchen as usual. Now the front-page story was the Binghamton murder. Harry noted with respect that the Binghamton police had refrained from pinpointing the hotel parking lot as the likely place from which the shot had been fired, or the list of diners and guests as a possible source of suspects. There would be enough kooky witnesses floating up, without deliberately stirring the bottoms. Good police practice.

Both the *Times* and the *News* referred readers to a box on an inside page for the conclusion of the Kaganopoulos story. The *News* took care of it in five very short paragraphs, the *Times* in four longer ones; with no Kaganopoulos to interview, there wasn't a great deal of news. It had become a complicated story, and the complications were not news. An embarrassment to the police, no doubt; but also an embarrassment to the press—and to Washington, whence came an announcement that the FBI had increased the manpower assigned to the search. It was the first Johnson knew about that—and then he thought, They're counting my friends in Baltimore. Well, all hail the embarrassment to the press, and to Washington.

Harry went to the foot of Oscar's bed. "This is worse than being married," he said. "Get up, and I'll make you a breakfast. If you've got a head, there's Alka-Seltzer in the cabinet."

"I got a head."

"All right. Wash up. Come clean to table."

Over breakfast, Oscar went immediately to his problem with the Lincoln Continental, and Spitts's request for information.

"You find out what you can," Harry said, flipping the pages of the paper as they talked.

"You're not concerned about what I might find?"

"Oscar," Harry said patiently, regretfully laying aside the newspapers, "I can't think of a single reason why I should have been driving a Lincoln Continental on William Street last Wednesday. If you find who owns it, I'm sure he won't be able to think of any reason, either. Your friend Spitts thinks he saw me at the wheel of that car—what the hell kind of evidence is that?"

"You don't want to tell me anything about the car?"

"Not on your life. My position is that I don't know what you or Spitts or anybody else is talking about with me and that car."

"But suppose there's something that can tie you to it?"

Harry shrugged.

"Would you rather I laid off? "

Harry shook his head. "More coffee? No? Oscar, sometime yesterday you moved into the statistical world. Up to yesterday, you were unique: you knew things nobody else knew who was talking to me. If you didn't give me a piece of information, chances were I couldn't get it anywhere.

"Now," Harry continued, warming to his work, "that's in a sense a dangerous position for a man to be in, because it gives him notions. I won't deny I have them myself sometimes. But in the great scheme of things, it really doesn't make much difference whether it's Harry Johnson or John Harrison sitting behind my desk. Somebody else would try to do the same job I'm doing; he might do it worse, he might do it better. The margin of difference very likely isn't great.

"What you did for me, tipping me about a plan—a bombing, a robbery, a Day of Rage or whatever they called it, an attempt to smuggle a gun into a prison—that was something nobody else could have done. What Spitts has asked you to do for him with that car . . . well, if you don't do it, somebody else will. It's a straightforward investigation. I wouldn't be much surprised if he already has somebody else doing it, just in case. So you do it, and do it well, earn your keep, and I'll worry about the consequences."

"I feel dirty."

"Go home and change your clothes. I guess I'd better talk openly with you about the one thing that does have to worry me, a little. You're still unique, or nearly unique, for *them.* You can get up and testify and make what you've done for me sound like the awfulest thing that ever happened. Everyone would love you."

Oscar was looking at Harry and shaking his head almost frantically. Harry smiled. "You wouldn't have a cigarette on you, would you, Oscar? I know you don't smoke, but—no. Oh, well. I don't expect that sort of problem, but this is a slippery slope, and once they start using you as a witness, your feet are well on it. The only thing I want to say is that I honestly don't believe you have a single reason to be ashamed of the work you did for me."

"No, sir," Oscar said. "I can swear to that. Nor do you. It was my idea."

"I wondered if you remembered that."

"Anybody who went to jail because of me deserved to go to jail. The movement itself was better off, stronger, more realistic, more . . . true to itself, without them."

Harry really did like Oscar: big wounded mastodon of a little boy. We've done him harm, all of us, he thought. "Well," he said, "don't cast yourself as the scourge of God, either. If it were my job to pin the tail on the donkey, I bet I could find some meetings where you spoke on the activist side, used inflammatory language and all the rest." Harry held up a hand to forestall complaint. "You had a credibility requirement, no way you could avoid it; I've been there myself. And they may very well find out you were getting paid."

"I've told them that."

"Slippery slope."

"You want me not to talk to them about what I did for you?"

"Beyond what you've already told them, and what I've told them, I think, yes. Stay out of the war stuff especially; you could still get killed for that. Lay off the Pilate questions—you don't know what is truth, can't find out, ought to keep cool about it if you possibly can. Oscar, after this sniper business is done—and I really can't give much time to anything else today—I think I can find a way to take care of you. That's not an offer, and it's not a bribe, but if you get neurotic in the next couple of days it's going to be a nuisance for me. Now, you go about your business, and find out about that car for Spitts, and when you see in the newspapers that we've closed the case on the sniper, you get in touch." Harry looked at his watch. "I have to get to my office, and you have to get to yours."

"I'm going to Connecticut, on the Continental thing."

"Then you're later than I am."

On his way to the office, balancing risks—but also getting out of his mind something that had to stay out—Harry stopped off at a telephone booth and called Coffees Monteblanco to warn Tony Whitmont that somebody from a public-interest law firm or a congressional committee might come around inquiring about why he had given an FBI agent the use of his car.

"What happened?" Whitmont breathed, deeply concerned. Johnson had never called him before.

"Nothing's *happened*. Somebody thinks he saw me in the car, and there are always knives out for me."

"I'm bewildered—"

"That's the ticket. Stay bewildered. You have a monthly parking deal, nobody keeps stubs with time stamps. I don't stop to pass the time of day with attendants. There's absolutely no way for them to get any proof of anything. Your story is that you don't know what they're talking about. Period. I don't know what they're talking about, either."

"Right."

"You can do that?"

"No sweat."

Wu had already started the meeting with the task force, intelligently moving the group to the tenth-floor conference room, where everyone would have room on the table for his own copy of the printouts and of the photographs that had been procured for about thirty of the names high on the list. It was a gloomy meeting, necessarily so. Names had been pouring out of the Baltimore FBI office and the Binghamton police all the previous afternoon and evening, and the girls on the night shift had plugged them into the computer—for absolutely zero return. There is a parlor game in which the people at the party compare birthdays, and it always turns out that two of them have the same birthday. But when it counts, Harry thought, accepting the news from the machines, overlaps of identity are scarce. Which cuts both ways: it's better evidence than outsiders think when an identity emerges.

Not surprisingly, none of the agents at the meeting was hot enough about anyone on his assignment list to request the expense of surveillance. But the purpose of the meeting, as Harry somewhat testily reminded the others, was less to find the one than to eliminate the many. When he went to the massed police departments that afternoon, he wanted to reduce the burden on them sufficiently to keep their spirits up. From the beginning, Harry had been conscious that he had never worked with any of these men before. They were criminal, he was counterintelligence; oil and water. And it was his own fault; he hated to train people, hated the attitudinizing about politics that filled the conversation of the candidates who wished to work with him. Meanwhile, there were—face it—the budget reductions in his division, as the radical and student groups grew more docile and the Attorney General got scared of the press. We shall return, he thought grimly, when the wave of terrorists sweeps in from overseas. For the time being, his division—the whole Bureau—was bound by the great rule that unites politics and bureaucracy. CYA—Cover Your Ass. Harry Johnson let no one else consult, meet, speak with his undercover people—when Harry took a vacation, this part of security intelligence simply went to sleep until his return. On his normal rounds, he had no colleagues; assistants, yes, and superiors, for sure; but no colleagues.

"We set up three categories," Harry Johnson said firmly. "A great and mystical trinity. We need names; I divide them into 'interesting' names, 'unlikely' names, and 'impossible' names. What I want this morning is the impossibles, because I don't wish to distribute photographs of anyone who can't be a suspect, and I do wish to improve the efficiency of the computer search as we add data. By common consent, I imagine, I begin with the name of Kaganopoulos. He's out. All right. We cut from the bottom—each one picks one."

Pointing a finger, Harry made circuit after circuit around the table, probing, asking the opinions of others but not necessarily accepting them. "I run a guided democracy," he explained at one point. "You do what I tell you." The telco material had been useful: without alerting suspects or frightening neighbors, Johnson's team had been able to find out in one day's telephoning that more than three-quarters of the people whose privacy had been multiply invaded by computer had not been where the crimes were committed at the time of the commission. Eight times around the table produced forty definite dismissals from the list, only one of which Harry restored. Then they moved on to the "unlikelies." What would be left in the "interesting" category, of course—as Wu pointed out when one of the men became too enthusiastic for the game—was mostly people about whom they had not yet acquired any great amount of information.

The state motor vehicle bureaus were being slow about supplying information about cars to go with the names; Harry asked Wu to see what strings could be pulled to speed them up. The AT&T printout had included information about T&E and gasoline company cards; for the names that remained on the list, Harry asked his men to find out from the oil companies and American Express and its friends where and when those cards had been used since September.

"And I used to think it was boring to be out on the street," one of the agents grumbled.

Harry gave him a prolonged stare. "The man who told you police work was interesting in itself," he said, "was someone you should never have trusted."

The task force meeting ran well beyond the hour when normal people eat lunch, and when it broke up Harry wandered over alone to the local McDonald's, stopping en route at the post office to check the boxes. He would have only a little more than an hour at his desk before the police departments trooped in for the afternoon seminar. Well, between them, Dr. Goldberg and the new boy on the block, the Binghamton deputy chief, would probably give reason enough for them to be pleased they had come. Some of them at least would be happy also to have some photographs; give the men on the street something new to do. Harry opened the outer door to his office, to hear Tilly saying, "Oh, here he is now." She put the call on hold and said, "It's a Mr. Whitmont. He's very insistent—he's called every ten minutes for the last hour."

"Put him through; I'll pick it up." He did so. "Harry Johnson here."

"I'm trying to keep my thoughts straight, Mr. Johnson," said the faintly high-pitched voice at the other end. "It wasn't anything about the car; they wanted to know about the kidnapping."

"Just tell me what happened. Who did you talk to?"

"A very young man named Adrian Francis. He's on the staff of some House committee, says they're investigating the efficiency of the FBI."

"He called?" Harry said suggestively.

"Oh, yes, and then he came in—he insisted he had to come in. He told me the committee was investigating unsolved crimes where the FBI could maybe have done a better job, and one of them was the kidnapping."

"Pretty far back."

"I thought so, too, but of course I didn't say that. I told him that my father always said the FBI had done their best— I didn't know much about what the FBI was doing, because I was being held by the kidnappers."

"Very good and proper."

"Then he wanted to know about my contacts with you."

"He did."

"Yes. I told him I really don't remember much about any of the people I met in those days after my release, it was all so frantic and I was so tired. I thought your name was familiar."

"You seem to have done very well."

"But that didn't stop him. He said he had reason to believe—"

"Reason to believe—"

"That there was something fishy about the kidnapping, and that you'd been involved in protecting it. Mr. Johnson, I'm not ashamed to tell you I'm scared."

Harry Johnson found his grip on the sniper case loosening. "God damn it," he said softly. "I seem to have an enemy." But there was surely no point in adding to Tony Whitmont's worries. "I don't think it's anything for us to be frightened about. You know, that's how these fellows work—committee investigators. We sometimes, I must tell you, work that way ourselves. You pretend to know a lot more than you do, hoping for a lucky shot; if nothing develops, you haven't lost anything. Just hang on, and he'll go away."

"I can't figure out how he came around to begin with," Whitmont said miserably.

"I can," said Harry Johnson. "But what I know is sort of encouraging, because that boil's been lanced; they won't feel it any more in a day or two."

"He said he was coming back, he might want me to testify before his committee."

"He'll be back for sure," Harry said. "At least once—with the car—and very pleased with himself. You just hang on. Just tell him again what you said today."

"And what do we do about the money?"

"Money, Mr. Whitmont?"

"The monthly payments—"

"What telephone are you calling from, Mr. Whitmont?"

"My telephone, of course—my office phone."

"Don't do that again," Harry said. "I don't want to cut

207

you off now, but I have a heavy schedule today. I'm going to turn you over to my secretary, and she will give you a number to call, and a number by which you identify yourself. If you wish to get in touch with me, go to a telephone booth, call that number, and identify yourself by number. They will reach me, and I guarantee to be back to you, in that booth, day or night, within ten minutes. More likely three. Mr. Whitmont, you have pulled a brass ring. For the next week or so, it is possible you will have the status of an FBI informant. Anyway, I will treat you so."

"But—"

"Don't be concerned. I'm going to give you to my secretary now." He pushed the button, told Tilly what he needed, and began to look over the raw interview reports from the Binghamton police, teletyped to him that morning. He found them, he noted gratefully, absorbing.

Gilette was late. It had been a typical meeting with lawyers, who wanted to talk language although of course it was too soon to put anything in writing. The memo they were giving him was, they stressed, without legal effect; like conversation. What made the slow pace particularly infuriating was that the substance of what they were saying was good news. Gilette's people had quite inadvertently turned a flank: IBM, ever tidy, wished to straighten its lines, with the least possible battle. Thus the smaller company was being offered, in effect, a short but sweet alliance. This was why his buddy had bought him dinner the night before, and why the informal route was being followed. Only it had to be done just right, their way, in their language, and to draw up the language, the lawyers had to know precisely what Gilette's machine was doing on certain jobs his company had won. Sales pitches were not trade secrets, and Gilette felt he could safely be forthcoming—except, perhaps, in one corner of capability that meant most to the IBM people. So they sparred, and lunched on sandwiches at the table; and it was after two o'clock when Gilette got back on the road.

The instructions Carla had given him were for New York out, and rather than try to work out a route from Poughkeepsie, he went a few miles past where he thought the place was, got over to the road on her instructions, and followed the remembered turns. Three times he drove until he was clearly wrong, and three times he turned back. The fourth time he noticed a fork in the road she had—accidentally? deliberately?—neglected to mention, and on that fork the guide to the maze seemed accurate. Except that it didn't get him to the gateway she had described. Having gone clearly too far, he turned back, and on a road more like one than two lanes wide he caught a glimpse through the trees of the riding enclosure, the white rail fence, the track, the barn, the woman and the girls on their horses. In the summertime, he thought, with leaves on these trees, he never would have found the place.

He stopped the car and watched as the horses appeared and disappeared around the tree trunks and branches. She was riding a black horse, and wearing a black costume. The horse seemed bigger than those the girls were riding. Gilette waited and watched at his distance, while she demonstrated the art of stopping a horse very quickly without making him rear. The girls' horses all went to their hind feet. Carla demonstrated again. In this kind of light, Gilette thought unexpectedly, at this kind of distance, one would need a scope. He would have to use the scope.

Then he backed the station wagon out to the county road, turned down it, and found the gate. The driveway ended in a packed-dirt turnaround, with four sporty little foreign cars ranged around it, and a white fence gate. Leaving the car, Gilette went and hung on the gate. She had, of course, seen him arrive in the parking area, and if she hadn't, one of the girls had pointed him out almost immediately; but she left him in place for almost fifteen minutes before she put all seven of the girls to work and came cantering over to greet him. "You found us, I see," she said.

"I said I would."

"And you did. What would you like to see?"

"You."

"Watch the girls, and you will see at least one of tomorrow's champions."

"I'd rather watch someone who's already a champion."

"We'll see."

When she came back, ten minutes later, she had three of the girls with her, and they had chosen this vantage point to watch the other four ride in pairs. She had been debating introducing Gilette to the girls, one of whom had asked whether he was her husband, and she had decided against it. She dismounted and came to stand beside him, the fence between them. "How much do you know about these things?" she asked.

"Not much."

"Of those girls—which would you say is the best?"

He told her and he was right. "Do you know why?"

"Not so I could say it."

She called to the girls to go around once more, and explained some of the points. "It is in the seat, the posture, the knees," she said. "All from the legs; if they let three days go by without doing their leg exercises, I can *see* it."

"Do you do the exercises?"

"Oh, yes. Religiously. Every morning, before my family gets up. There is much work in this."

"In everything."

Men had always looked at Carla; she could remember back to when she was six years old and the men looked at her. Consciousness of the weight of their gaze had never been entirely free from either pleasure or fear. She knew that the man at the gate was watching her back, her neck; not the girls on the course. She turned to look at him, found him smiling but somehow coldly, felt in his blue eyes a pressure against her, felt herself both increasingly excited and increasingly afraid. Was she becoming one of those people who did things because they were bored? Nicholas Gilette was, as the girls might say, something *else*.

"How long have you had that mustache?" she said.

"About four years."

"It's very attractive."

"You have to pay attention to it when you drink."

"Do you drink a lot?"

"Not a lot. Sometimes. Would you have a drink with me after you finish up this afternoon?"

"No, I have to hurry home. My husband and I are going tonight to the opera."

"Do you like the opera?"

Carla shrugged. "My husband's people have had a box on Tuesdays since the family lived in Philadelphia. My father-in-law used to say the opera had followed him to New York. I like it. I like the parties at the Opera Club, everyone dresses so well."

The girls were looking at them. Carla said, "I have to get back to work."

"If I came Thursday, would you have a drink with me afterwards?"

"Why would you come Thursday?"

"To watch you ride—"

"It is the last class of the year here—"

"And to have a drink with you."

"I don't promise," she said.

"I'll be here."

"You know the way."

He stayed until the lesson was over, saw she would not return to the gate while he was there, waved a hand, and drove off. To the girls, Carla explained that Gilette was a man considering the school for a niece, next year; and she had explained to him the requirements—especially for lower-school girls—to start the equestrian class. She said casually, "He may be back Thursday."

"I didn't like his looks *at all,*" said one of the senior girls, blond hair escaping in wisps under her cap.

"I think he's a rather handsome man," Carla said.

"Oh, he's good-looking," the girl said. "But the way he holds himself—like a tin soldier, almost. God knows what's going on in his mind."

"Lechery," said another girl.

"Or *worse,*" said a third.

The deputy chief from Binghamton, a pudgy little gray-haired man in a shiny blue suit, up from a long time in the ranks, came in by prearrangement half an hour before the meeting. He was pleased to find how much Johnson had read, unhappy to learn that the names his people had passed through had all gone into the machines and out again, unrecognized. He had come, he said, mostly to listen, hoping that Johnson or someone from one of the other police departments would give him an idea his people could follow—but he was prepared to report what little they knew.

Harry passed him on to Frank Wu and looked over his notes from the morning meeting. He took five minutes more with the printout, reading it like a man looking for his keys in a place where has already, fruitlessly, searched. Then he went up one flight to the conference room, where he found the same cast of characters as the previous Wednesday, with Dr. Goldberg and the deputy chief from Binghamton added, and a substitute sent at the last minute for Vinnie Palio, who was indisposed. It was a far plainer room than the one at police headquarters—big GI table with a glass top, green leather lumpy chairs, glass-doored bookcases with trophies the FBI teams had won in softball, bowling, tennis, in the federal leagues. But it also had a federal amenity: on a side table in the corner stood a stainless steel restaurant-size coffeemaker, the brown liquid high in the visible tube, with styrofoam cups, plastic spoons, a box of sugar dots and an immense jar of powdered artificial cream. Compliments of the taxpayer.

Several of the detectives had already helped themselves.

"Our function in this investigation," Harry said, after he had introduced the newcomer from Binghamton and permitted Palio's replacement to introduce himself, "is essentially to be the nerve center for all of you—the relay point, distributing the information we are all constantly acquiring. But every nerve center imposes its own schedule of priorities on the information it processes, and I think we should all meet together at regular intervals for as long as this special process continues—not, I think, much longer, fortunately.

"Then, there are a few things we know here in the Bureau simply because we aggregate the information, which I think we should all discuss together. For example, though we are all agreed that the killer probably shot from a car, none of us expects much from neighborhood descriptions of unfamiliar cars seen near the site. But when the data are assembled from all your departments, several vehicle descriptions recur. Given the manpower you have devoted to this case, this is not statistically unlikely—I had our math department run up a probability number this morning, out of curiosity—but it gives us something we in our poor gumshoe ways can look for and find out about each of the individuals we are studying.

"I've just updated the list with the reports from Binghamton, and copies will be here as soon as my secretary has typed it. There are seven makes-types of vehicles reported at three of the sites; none at more than three. Of the seven, three are small cars, which seem to me unlikely as shooting platforms, which leaves four. A larger number, of course, were seen at two sites.

"As you have already noted, the envelope at your place contains six photographs of men who have the qualifications to be considered suspects, though I must stress to you that this means nothing more than the absence of disqualifying information—we have no positive evidence against anybody. Still, under proper precautions, you may wish to show these

213

photographs to possible witnesses, and see if any of them provokes a response.

"I can also give you a genuine goody—a refinement of our friend's itinerary. He was on the Eastern Shore of Maryland Sunday; shot a dog there. As a normal matter, this is the kind of information we would gladly publicize, but because of the media emphasis on Kaganopoulos on Monday I thought it best not to overload the circuits. Our people in Baltimore are conducting this investigation themselves, without any special secrecy precautions, and I expect the information to rise osmotically and surface later this week. For your records, however, please note now that any suspect not in Maryland on Sunday can be eliminated from consideration.

"We have a long agenda. Nevertheless, I have taken the liberty of adding to it Dr. Goldberg of the New York police, who is their hostage expert—"

"I do suicides, too," Dr. Goldberg said encouragingly from the corner, acknowledging Harry's wave in his direction and the eyes of the group.

"—and who," Harry continued smoothly, "has given me many interesting ideas during the time we were together observing the Kaganopoulos comedy. Mr. Kaganopoulos, by the way, for your private information, is now in Hawaii, enjoying a well-earned rest from his contacts with the press.

"Now. All of you have a printout of the merged file of marksmen with Bell System descriptors. I should like to begin by going over with you the names my colleagues and I have already eliminated. If you think any should *not* be scrubbed, of course, I would like to know about it. Then I shall ask each of you to add your eliminations. By the end of the meeting"—insistently; somehow, dammit, he would force on them some minimal sense of accomplishment—"we should have a workable cohort for visitations. I'm going to call on you by size order. Concord first . . ."

But the fact is that it was not a cheerful meeting. In the Kaganopoulos flap, the other police sided with New York, believing that Palio had been misled by the FBI. Palio himself was Banquo's ghost. The dog business was a carved ornament in what should by rights be a plain world. Everybody had been working hard, not only for no result, but increasingly—most of them believed—for no purpose. Now they had the further make-work of the photographs—pictures of men who didn't do it, said a detective from Hoboken, to be shown to people who hadn't seen it.

"How do we *know,*" the one woman detective in the group finally asked angrily, "that the name of the man we want is even on this damned paper?"

She was the one who had asked about the help of a psychologist at the first meeting. Harry took the comment as a signal to introduce Dr. Goldberg.

"Yes," said the psychologist, accepting the attention of the room. "Thank you." He patted the crocheted skullcap on his head, then leaned forward and looked around. "To deal first with the specific question left in the air before my participation was requested," he said, "I agree completely with Mr. Johnson that when the murderer is found we will see his name on the lists before you. The person you are seeking is essentially a sportsman. He is a technician of uncommon skill. That level of skill is rarely found in modern societies among illiterates. If he is literate, he will wish to read about his skill—about, if you will, himself; thus, he will be a subscriber to the publications whose readership forms the base of the computer list. And he will almost certainly be a participant in contests that reward that skill.

"Your search is for a hunter. What made him a manhunter rather than a duck hunter or a deer hunter is a question that will be of great interest to me and to others after he is identified. We cannot, I think, speculate too deeply on that subject without the information we do not now have. But I agree with Mr. Johnson again that we are nearing the end of our search."

With slight elaboration for purposes of elegance, Dr. Goldberg repeated the sketch he had drawn for Harry at the Brooklyn police precinct. In the twenty hours since, he had acquired even stronger views of the significance of the Binghamton murder. "This time," he said, "the man knew he was at risk, welcomed it. I would expect that a complete list of people who ate at the hotel that lunchtime would turn up a name on the papers before you."

"We've been trying that," said the deputy chief from Binghamton, spreading his hands on the table. "It's near impossible, you know. People pay cash, walk in without reservations, have guests they can't imagine are snipers—and don't want to get involved anyway."

Dr. Goldberg shrugged expressively. "The next step," he said, surveying the conference room slowly, "may even be a return to the scene of a previous killing. Before this happens, the man, who probably seems quite normal to his friends and associates, will very likely exhibit aberrant behavior. If your resources were unlimited, you could probably save a life simply by assigning an observer to every name on"—he reached across to a sheaf of printout at the next place at the table, lifted it and dropped it thuddingly to the glass top—"that list." Then he raised his hands palm outward in a self-deprecatory gesture. "Of course, no guarantees; we are dealing, obviously, with a very unusual man."

"How soon do you think he will strike again?" said one of the detectives from Allentown.

"Quite soon. Less than a week elapsed between the two most recent incidents. Counting the dog, we have three shootings in less than a week. That is a much more rapid pace than before, and is one of the reasons I believe we are dealing with a need to find exposure and capture."

The woman detective was more than mollified: she believed in this sort of thing. It was what had turned her footsteps toward police work when she got her master's in psychology. "Precisely what did you *mean,* Doctor," she said, settling in for a long chat, "when you told us that the sniper is a very unusual man."

"I said, 'obviously,' " Dr. Goldberg replied, leaning back in his chair. Harry scented danger but could do nothing about it. "He shoots people."

"But surely he must be unusual in other ways, too."

"Yes," Dr. Goldberg said. " 'Surely.' " He seemed to think for a moment, then brightened. "One thing: he doesn't put his pants on one leg at a time. He jumps into them with both legs. If the neighbors knew, they would flock to observe him, but he's shy about it. Even his wife has seen him do it only a few times."

That tore it. The deputy chief from Hoboken launched into an infuriated statement about the waste of time at meetings, the waste of time assembling dossiers on local residents who were *not* the sniper—nobody believed the man was working his own neighborhood. What was the FBI doing, aside from this mumbo-jumbo with computers? And telling jokes with doctors?

"My street agents are looking at people in some of the places you don't cover," Johnson said mildly.

"The only suspect you seem to have looked at *personally*," said one of the New York delegation resentfully, "is a man in our jurisdiction."

Dr. Goldberg intervened. "Where would you be without that list?" he said. "You would be blind men."

At the head of the table, Harry Johnson was grinning. He said, "Thank you, Doctor. I think your time is up. I must keep my agenda, and *next* on that agenda is a practical question for the representatives from the two New York State locations. What do we do with this fellow when we catch him? Who gets to try the first case?"

"Does your agenda item imply an expectation that the FBI will be the apprehending agency?" asked one of the senior men from New York City.

Harry flashed a false smile, then killed it. "Yes," he said finally. "I guess it does."

"Perhaps that's what bothers us," said a detective from Stamford, a sloucher in his chair who had previously made no contribution. "We're doing all that work, and when the time comes, whaddaya know, the feds will get the credit."

Harry looked at his watch. "When there is credit," he said, "there will be enough for everyone. Right now, we've got nothing but blame. And the heat you feel now is nothing to what we'll have next week, if we're no further ahead than we are today."

But the complaints went on, until at seven o'clock Harry called a halt. "Any of you who must, or wish to, stay overnight in the city," he added, "may charge your accommodations to the Bureau."

"Where are the expense voucher forms for this meeting?" called the deputy from Hoboken.

"Damned LEAA grant," Harry said. "I'll put them in the mail tomorrow; I'm sorry I forgot them today."

"Let's get 'em now."

"Well, we can go down to my office," Harry said, not displeased at the new tone of the conversation, "and anything I can find you can have—if I can get in my secretary's files with my keys. Those of you who would rather do it that way can come down with me. Is there anything else?"

"When do we meet again?"

"In the nature of things, I'll have to take responsibility for that. I'll call you. If we're lucky, we won't need another meeting—just a party. For now, with your consent, we're adjourned."

About half the group followed Harry to his office, where to his astonishment he found Tilly waiting for him. He looked at her sharply: her eye make-up was streaked and her cheeks glistened. She quickly provided the government forms for the detectives, typing in the name of each recipient on the top line. They all waited, silently standing around her desk, until everyone had been served. Harry had gone into his office alone, to look on the now clean desk, where he found a single telephone message sheet: Anthony Whitmont had called. He returned to the outer office to shake hands with his departing guests; only Dr. Goldberg remained.

"You didn't mind my pushing the button?" the psychologist inquired, slightly shamefaced.

"I wouldn't have done it myself. Probably not a bad idea. Why did you want to do it?"

A seraphic smile spread over the doctor's face. "I enjoyed it," he said.

"It's a pleasure to have you on my side," Harry said.

"Yes, that's what I thought, too."

"If we have another meeting, shall I invite you?"

"Why not?" said Dr. Goldberg, and stuck out a fat hand; then he nodded briskly to Tilly and left.

"I'm sorry you stayed so late," Harry said to her.

"Oh, Mr. Johnson," she said, and she was trembling; she had held it in while there were others. "I'm afraid something is terribly wrong."

Harry nodded. "Well," he said, "if nothing were wrong, you and I couldn't make a living."

"That man, when he called—he told me to tell you they'd found out who owns the car."

Harry nodded.

"Isn't he the same man I told to call you only at the special number?"

"Yes."

"The way he sounded, Mr. Johnson—I tried to tell him I didn't take messages for you from people who were supposed to call the special number. But he wouldn't listen."

"What did he say?"

Tilly squared her shoulders against a sob. "He just said something about what difference could it make since they know already."

"Sure," said Harry. "Well, it's not so bad. He'll see his

219

wife tonight, and she'll put him together."

He came around to her side of the desk and put a hand on the squared shoulder. "It'll come out all right," he said. She rose toward him.

"I tell you what," he said as she buried her tightly coifed head on his shoulder. "Let's the two of us go have a drink together, for old time's sake."

"Also," she said, pulling away and shaking herself, "I stayed to remind you to come in early tomorrow morning. You've got that meeting with the Yugoslav ambassador at eight-thirty."

For Nicholas Gilette, each homecoming now was harder than the one before. The house itself—not a suburban house, but a small-city house on a small-city lot—seemed to shrink with the passage of years. It was three-quarters of a century old, tall and thin, unbalanced: the horizontal white clapboards and squat windows exaggerated the height. One of a row of fourteen, all the same, it had been built into a hillside so steep that a four-story structure from the street side—the fourth story the one-room "folly" that Gilette had appropriated from the beginning as his gunshop—became two and a half stories in the rear. But Maria had loved it at sight; the trees were high in the old neighborhood, not like the new tracts, and the hillside was like home.

Back in Belgrade, responding to Maria's dazzling suggestion that he ask to marry her, Gilette had warned her that in America she would have to be American, "entirely American," and if God blessed them with children—it had quickly become a solemn conversation—the children would be American. But to him she already was the all-American girl of the movies he had seen in his boyhood in Vermont; she just happened to speak another language and come from another place. He blocked the colors in her country costumes when she wore them; he saw her, as it were, in black and white. The thought of taking her to bed, taking off that country costume and touching the girl beneath it, was unbearably, sharply sweet. It was a commitment he wanted from her, not action; he did not understand that action was needed.

In the first six months of their marriage, while they lived in Belgrade in an apartment beside the embassy compound, Maria had found it impossible to figure out what being an American might mean. There were so many Americans—Nico; the blond political officer who played show tunes on the piano and teased her; the fat, fast-talking economic attaché, whom she could not understand at all; Ann Ensor, who was so aristocratic but caressed her cheeks and fondled her shoulders like one of the nuns she remembered, while advising her on what would be expected of a local wife of a member of an embassy. Once she came "home"—Gilette insisted on the word, though he knew it was not one they could truthfully share—being entirely American was like playing with toys: the kitchen with its wonders, the vacuum cleaner, shopping in the supermarket, television in the morning.

Though her English took her less far with the neighbors than with Nico, she felt a friendliness, first at Quantico, where she was the youngest of the officers' wives and something of a pet, then in Croton, where a Welcome Wagon marked instant acceptance. It was no more bewildering than the plunge from school to the head of her father's table, and in some ways it was less frightening. And she bought herself what were called French nightgowns in the stores, fantasized, luxuriated—a little frighteningly for Gilette; she learned not to scare him—in her discovered sexuality. Games.

Then John was born, a hard birth, twenty hours, painful for her and terrifying for Gilette. Almost from the moment he first saw his child, Nicholas was conscious that he had never known a father himself. Maria's games changed, became exclusive female games, from which Nicholas felt himself subtly excluded. Maria was now in a foreign country for real: there was nobody to tell her what she should do, her new-found neighborly friends answered questions by looking things up in a book. Soon after the birth of her child, Mandragora fell from grace in Belgrade; and his daughter began the long slide to a belief that she had caused his agony and then abandoned him. Even after the birth of John, she had still been a girl, her baby was her doll; now she quickly aged without growing up.

She seemed to shrink at the edges. She was ragged thin, a whine came into her voice, she took refuge in an obsessive and unending cleanliness; she bathed at least twice a day, her windows shone, the nap of velvet on the couch was always just so, the kitchen floor was waxed and the utensils polished daily. Gilette's own neatness, reinforced by constant contact with the ever-neat computers, kept him from seeing how unhealthy the sterile surfaces were. She resented his traveling, and then, because he might make a mess, resented his return. The boy had fights at school because he came so clean and overdressed, and it was a long time before Maria Gilette would let him climb the hillside in old clothes to play with the neighbors' children.

This year had been the worst. Though there were flashes of good cheer that made the house bright as well as clean, Gilette normally could expect to find on each return a list of worries and terrors and grievances. He had locked the folly room, to protect her almost as much as to protect the guns; he escaped there, read through the descriptions and conditions of coming competitions printed in the magazines, planned a campaign of victories—and then, the campaign itself defeated, he dreamed. Only for a while, Maria said; until she heard from her father. And when that happened, she promised, she would give up Father Caffra and his League; she would be entirely American for him.

She tried. Sometimes he was grateful for it, sometimes angry. On nights when he arrived home from a trip, an old nightgown might come out from the dresser, and she would seize him as she had those early playing months, but the coin was counterfeit; it bought sadness. This was to be one

222

of those nights. She had made turkey with stuffing and apple pie, from recipes in a magazine picked up at the supermarket. Guilty with thoughts of Carla Whitmont, Gilette paid court to her, admired John, told her about the dinner party but not the ducks, gave her his dishonest reassurances, supposedly from Ensor, that with a new American President so stuck on human rights, Tito would not dare.

She did not begin crying until after John went to bed, and even then she took the blame on herself. She bravely asked about the hunting in Maryland, the fingers of one hand scratching at the palm of the other as she listened to his answers. He yearned to be upstairs, but he waited, and they told each other everything would be all right. Except—what could they do with the secret service in the car outside?

She had reported accurately; Gilette saw two men in a Mercedes, surely a surveillance team, parked down the street. Why in God's name would they be watching Maria? That's the problem with these damned countries, Gilette thought— each one is more scared than the other. But he told her she was imagining things; one of the neighbors at the other end of the block must have bought himself a fancy new car, and just loved to be in it. Later, up in the folly room, he became fascinated by the patterns of light into the car from the street lamps shining through the almost bare trees. At any one moment, one of the men was a possible target, the other was not. But that would solve nothing.

XII

The Name Appears

They must have needed two limousines, Harry thought as he watched the six beefy men from the Yugoslav mission settle themselves uneasily on his green couch and armchairs, and the two side chairs Jerry had hastily commandeered from another office when he saw how large a group had come. Maybe fourteen hundred pounds on the hoof, Harry thought. Very crowded. Tilly was at her station outside, early in case she might be needed. The ambassador, who had round red cheeks and a bulb nose and a mane of glistening brown hair, demanded that the door be closed, and when Jerry went to do so, one of the large men brushed him aside and closed it himself.

Harry leaned back in the swivel chair. "You asked to see me," he said rather coldly. His only previous contact with the Yugoslav Embassy had been when he had to speak with this ambassador's predecessor about a member of the mission who was being expelled after exposure as paymaster to a violence-prone Third World group at City College.

"There should be no secrets between us," said the ambassador, almost blurting the words. He had a slight but hard accent in his English.

"Of course," said Harry, setting his jaw for solemnity.

"Good. I tell you everything."

"Good."

"You are of course aware that the foreign minister of my country is coming to New York for the Special Session of the United Nations on the Neo-Colonialist Conspiracy to Maintain the Old International Economic Order. It was on a motion made by my country that the consensus of the General Assembly determined to hold this Special Session. The foreign minister of my country may well become the president of the Special Session."

"It has been in the newspapers," Harry observed.

"Good. Now I must recur to the painful subject of the outrages committed upon our representatives, on various occasions, by Croatian Nazi terrorists who have been accepted in this country as so-called refugees and permitted to organize their fascistic criminal activities in this city."

"As you know," Harry said, measuring the response, "we've created a special unit in this Bureau to monitor and control the activities of these Croatian groups. Pursuant to the Attorney General's orders, we have abandoned the surveillance of groups as such. But the agents and informers are still on our payroll. We're doing everything we can, consistent with our laws, to prevent any recurrence of the attacks on your mission and your consulate. I'm confident our precautions will be effective."

"I must tell you *officially*," said the ambassador, pig eyes fixed on Harry from above the fat cheeks, "that my government does *not* believe that everything has been done that could be done to fulfill this vital obligation of the United States as the host country of the United Nations, or that the American laws to which you refer must be interpreted to prohibit the elimination of international criminal conspiracies. My government is especially concerned at this moment with the possibility of threats to the life of the foreign minister. At this moment, I must tell you with regret, I am not prepared to inform my government that security procedures in New York are sufficient to safeguard the foreign minister. The ambassador of my country in Washington has made representations to your State Department on the matter."

"So I have been informed," Harry said, falling into the rhythm of the presentation.

"Surely your office must be unwilling to experience the scandal that would result from the cancellation of a trip to the United Nations by the foreign minister of Yugoslavia because the host country of the United Nations was unable to assure his safety."

The beefy companions stirred in their seats, and two of them shook their heads sadly. Harry said, "I'm sure your fears are unwarranted. We monitor the activities of every individual in the Croatian movement who might be engaged in a plot to harm your foreign minister."

"There is one situation we find especially disturbing," the ambassador continued, and put a finger beside his nose. Harry waited; the purpose of the meeting was about to be revealed. "It is understood," the ambassador resumed, "that everything I am about to say will be held confidential within this office."

"Of course."

"Some years ago," the ambassador said slowly, "there was in my country a deputy foreign minister and member of the Politburo, a comrade in arms to Marshal Tito from the glorious days of the resistance to Nazism, who had been a leader in the Croatian region. His name was Mandragora."

"I believe I have heard the name," Harry said.

"He became a traitor to the union of my country."

Harry said nothing.

"Six, seven years ago, he was exposed and arrested and

convicted. With great mercy, Marshal Tito spared his life."

Harry continued silent.

"But it was necessary to imprison him. I tell you now in confidence that three months ago—of peaceful causes, I assure you, a stroke—Mr. Mandragora died. His death has not been announced."

"Yes, Mr. Ambassador. I'm sorry to hear it. I shall keep your confidence."

"Mr. Mandragora had a daughter, Maria. A year before his activities with the Croatian separatists were exposed, that daughter married a young military attaché from your embassy in Belgrade. They are now living here, in a place called Croton-on-Hudson."

Harry pursed his lips. "I know nothing of this," he said. "Tell me her married name, and I'll find out precisely what contacts she has had with the Croatian groups."

"We know her contacts. She meets with people at a church in White Plains. Sometimes the so-called priest comes to her home."

Harry raised an eyebrow. "So?"

"Rumors of the death of Mr. Mandragora have been dishonestly circulated among the Croatian criminal exiles residing in this city. It may well be that these rumors have reached his daughter. The American husband would be a catch of immense value to these fascist criminals. He is no longer in the military; he is now some sort of salesman for a computer company. During his time in my country, he was considered the greatest marksman with a rifle that our sporting associations had ever seen. In three contests he entered as the guest of the Yugoslav Army, he achieved a perfect score."

"What *is* his name?" Harry said quietly.

"Nicholas Gilette. He made such a reputation in our contests that Marshal Tito invited him to join a hunt at the residence of the chief of state in Brioni, and invited him to dinner. It was at that dinner, in fact, that he met Maria Mandragora."

"In quite another context," said Harry, and the look on his face was one that surprised the ambassador, "I have had occasion to note that name. Are you sure the man is a salesman? We have him noted in a different capacity."

The ambassador looked over to the chair nearest the door, where one of the heavies spoke in a language Harry did not understand. "He functions as a salesman," the ambassador said. "Or so we are informed."

"What do you wish me to do?" Harry asked.

"We wish him in custody through the time the foreign minister is in New York; perhaps two weeks."

Harry shook his head. "I just don't know if I can do that."

"It has been done before, for others."

"Not for a period as long as two weeks. I think I can arrange to have him under surveillance, however, if your people in Washington can get a request for that from the State Department."

The ambassador grunted. "No. One day he escapes from your surveillance, and the foreign minister is dead. Shot from a window in the hotel across the street, or from a car. I cannot risk it, Mr. Johnson. *You* cannot risk it."

"From a car," Harry said thoughtfully. He leaned back in his chair, elbows on the armrests, and touched together the fingers of his hands. "I'll try," he said. "I'll try."

"The Special Session begins a week from next Monday. The foreign minister plans to visit Washington and meet with your Secretary of State the Friday before. *If* state security forces—if I—give our approval. I must have in my possession by the beginning of next week, for evaluation by my people, the complete plan for the control of Mr. Gilette during the visit."

"I'll try," Harry said again, and rose from behind his desk. This was indeed a serious request: ambassadors did not casually concede that they were part of the state security apparatus. "I'll try. And now, if you can excuse me . . ." He endured a ritual round of rather soft handshakes; the meeting ended and the whales departed.

A quick cycle of phone calls. First to the street agent listed for Gilette. "My notes show me you put him in 'unlikely' shading toward 'impossible,' " Harry said. "Why?"

The agent reviewed the reasons: an executive, not a salesman; no criminal record (not even a moving violation); no telco credit card; one T&E card (Diners) almost never used more than forty or so miles from home; military records absolutely clean.

"What kind of car does he drive?"

"I haven't checked."

"Do. What about a photo?"

"No."

"Get one. DOD, rifle magazines, college yearbook—get a picture. Mr. Gilette is your number one assignment for today."

"May I ask why?" the agent said, obviously irritated.

"Since you ask, I'll tell you," Johnson said. "I have a good reason to want to hold this guy behind bars for a week or so, if we've got an excuse."

"With all respect," said a cold voice on the other end, "I've never worked in counterintelligence, and this may be the way you do business there. In the criminal division, we don't hold people just because it's convenient."

"Somebody here just said he *is* a salesman," Harry said, ignoring the outburst. "Why do you think he's not?"

"He's listed as assistant vice-president for development," the agent said in a bored, confident way.

"To me," Harry said rather carefully, "that would mean he *is* a salesman. Development is a nice word for sales department in the computer business. Just check him out for me. That company of his does a lot of business with DOD. Call them, get half a dozen names of employees and officers; call the company, tell them you're checking clearances on a sample of their people, and give them the DOD names plus Gilette's: you'd like to know how much traveling these fellows do, where they go, who they see. Get anything and everything from the cops in Croton-on-Hudson. Find out from the Bell people and American Express whether that company has multiple credit cards its officers can use; and if so, see if you can put your hands on the use records of those cards in and around the sniper sites the day or two before and after."

"What about the other names I'm supposed to be following?"

"I'll tell Wu you're on special assignment, and he'll parcel them out."

"I still don't like it."

"You're an ex-marine, too, aren't you?" Harry inquired.

"Yes."

"When you put Gilette's name on the 'unlikely' list, was it in your mind that marine officers don't do this sort of thing?"

"I'll do what you say," said the agent.

"Damn right," said Harry.

Next, the call to the Croatian-speaking spooks, with a request for anything they had on Maria Mandragora Gilette. Or Nicholas Gilette.

And now, Harry decided, cradling the phone, blank it out. He needed time for routine. Among the professional questions that most interested him, years back, was the control of attention. This interest had first arisen, violently, in the Korean War days, when he was a commander in the field, the safety of his men (not to mention his own life) dependent on his capacity to receive, process and interpret random and minimal perceptions while holding firmly at the center the purpose of what he was doing. He'd enjoyed it—through the fearful cold (always the first thing to mind); through the weariness beyond understanding, where every year you were younger helped the odds; through the daily horrors. He'd centered on his individual mission, his own performance, he'd done well, he'd enjoyed it. He had become a detective because he thought that in no other activity could he develop and use so often this triumph of self-control—the continuing pursuit of a single knowable target coupled with a constant refining and broadening of receptors.

Exclusion was the heart of the work, and Johnson knew himself too well to believe that he could ever eliminate entirely the daydreaming, the useless but deceptively satisfying stimuli that intruded on the thinking process; but he could restrain them, he believed, within a channel that was in effect nonoperational, where distractions were labeled and discarded as distractions before they could seriously interfere. He felt a moment's gall that the exercise of these powers, now so finely honed, could be jeopardized by a casual error in the conversation of the likes of Tony Whitmont. And no one to blame, ultimately, but himself: he had been stupid. And he had to face it: he had been greedy. From the outside, it would be a classic, simple story. And from the inside, Harry thought, there are always explanations and excuses. Routine venality. Too bad.

Then that flash of bitterness, too, was discarded: even now, confronted with a personal threat more devastating than any he had known for a quarter of a century, Harry could exclude from his consciousness any thoughts or even perceptions that could not produce a useful activity.

He was a puzzle solver. It had driven his wife and his daughter crazy on occasion. Neither could come completely to terms with the fact that Harry's physical presence and apparent attention did not keep him from being in essence somewhere else; the puzzle came first.

As he knew from Korea, fatigue could sabotage the process, and fatigue was a subtle enemy. It could result not only from physical weariness but also from concentration grown fanatical beyond utility. At those moments, the sole effective resort was to routine, the established chore that had to be performed alertly. Work was its own restorative. Casting aside, then, all thoughts of snipers and Croatians, Whitmont, bribes, Spitts and Oscar, Harry reached for the clipping file, now two days delinquent, and began to read.

But how can any man tell what causes his perceptions? They are, after all, unwilled; they happen. Had he not felt his life again bound up with that of the Whitmonts, he would not have read through the clipping from the social page of a trivial Eastern Shore weekly, about a hunt meeting that closed a season, and a Saturday-night party at the Whitmont "estate." Had he not just been through that session with the Yugoslav ambassador, his eye would not have caught the mention that also among the guests, in addition to the members of the hunt and such distinguished neighbors as Ambassador and Mrs. Carl Ensor, had been a visitor from Croton-on-Hudson, New York, a computer executive and sportsman named Nicholas Gilette, who had once been the guest of Marshal Tito in a shooting brake.

"Tilly, get me the road map of Maryland." She brought it in; he found first the place where the dog had been shot, then, about half an inch away, the town where the Whitmonts had their house. "Start a file for me with the name Nicholas Gilette. Put the map in it for now."

First, to Langley. From his own desk, *en clair*—screw them. He got the young lady who had given him the names, said he had to speak with Phil immediately, and got the brush-off: impossible, unavailable, nothing to say to Mr. Johnson anyway. She was instructed to tell him so. "Listen," Harry said. "Tell him I need the complete file on somebody named Nicholas Gilette. That poor bastard in Binghamton may have died yesterday because you people held one out on me. Tell your friend who doesn't want to talk to me that so help me God I will blow him out of the water. Soon. Like this afternoon. I want to hear from him. *Schnell.*"

Back to the agent with the Gilette file: "Any news?"

"Jesus, Johnson, it's only about ninety minutes since I talked to you."

"Do you have the DOD names?"

"Yes."

"But you haven't called the computer company yet?"

"No."

"All right. I'll put my secretary on, you give her the names, I'll do that one myself. All of a sudden, I am very seriously interested in Mr. Gilette. You do Motor Vehicle and the Croton end; and I'll have Wu do AmEx and telco credit card himself. This is absolutely top priority; you don't lunch, you don't sleep, until you have all you can get. Call me every time you learn something."

He warned Tilly, called Wu, told him "a piece of the machinery" had placed previously "unlikely" suspect Nicholas Gilette at the scene of the dog sniping, and gave instructions for Wu's part of the follow-up.

Then Harry called the computer company himself and went through his story. They were not particularly surprised: clearances were always being checked. And they were used to being told in that connection that the information had to be ready yesterday.

In Pleasantville, in a room full of Lucite furniture, Nicholas Gilette was being debriefed on his trip, to general satisfaction: good week's work. It was a free-form, floating meeting of a kind not uncommon in high-technology companies, where time is put aside for thinking and people are therefore available to drop around as needed. A report would have to be put in writing during the next few days, and people from the design department, from manufacturing and from legal came by seriatim to tell Gilette exactly what could be most useful to them in the memos he would send. Toward the end of the morning's session there was a visit by the number two man in the company, the man who had recruited Gilette originally—Bob Russell, go-getter, foursquare, still crew-cut, button-down shirts. An appointment had just fallen through, he said; and he suggested lunch for two.

It turned out that Russell had more on his mind than the week's business, of which he would hear, he said, in due time. He was hard put to get started, asked in some detail how things were at home, and finally, having received evasive answers, approached directly. "You know," he said, "Frankie and your Maria got really close a couple of years ago, I think closer than we realized, when your John was so sick. Then during this last summer they barely saw each other at all, except for that one night when the four of us had dinner at the country club, and Frankie's been worried about her. While you were gone, she had a couple of phone calls from Maria, said she sounded really distraught."

Gilette gave his nervous smile and mumbled.

"Frankie thinks she could go off the deep end."

"Yes?"

"I've got a good business reason to go into this with you," Russell said cautiously. "If anything happens to Maria, it would interfere with your efficiency. I mean, it obviously hasn't happened yet, but it could."

"I'm under pressure," Gilette said shortly.

"Have you thought—it's none of my business—of sending her to a psychiatrist?"

"She'd be too scared."

"Frankie thought a big part of her problem is that she's plain homesick. Misses her father—"

"She wouldn't be seeing him if she were at home."

"Misses people with whom she can speak her language."

"She sees too Goddamned much of people who speak her language. Damned oily priest, I found him at the house once, she talks about him all the time, son of a bitch named Caffra. You want to see her problem, you talk to them."

"Not so loud, Nick. I'm not arguing with you."

"Look, I really liked her father even though he was a

Commie—spoke English like the British ambassador—but when these bastards fall out they wreck everybody's life. Just tell Frankie to tell her it's not my fault, it's not the fault of anybody in America. I can't give up everything in my life because Tito's got it in for her father."

"Frankie says she feels terribly guilty because she made you give up all the competitions you'd planned to enter."

"You've been finding out a lot about what goes on in my house," Gilette said angrily. He put his hand to his upper lip and rumpled it under the mustache.

"We want to help."

"Nobody can help!" Gilette almost shouted. The tables around them were silent, people looking away.

"Nick, please. Somebody can help."

Gilette settled into his chair. "All right. I'm sorry. You're my boss. What do you want me to do?"

"Frankie thought maybe you should talk to Father Caffra. Put your heads together. He must know some things that would help you handle it."

"All he knows is his damned church and his damned independence movement. That's all she tells me he talks about. If I weren't away so much—well, I don't want to complain about the job. If I were home all the time she'd probably drive me crazy with her father."

Russell sighed. "Okay, Nick," he said. "Tell me about IBM. And let's get another drink."

"No." Gilette rubbed his eyes. "I mean, yes, let's have another drink. But Frankie's right. You're right. I'm sorry I made a scene. You don't know what it's like. This was going to be my year. I had four invitations from rifle teams, anything I wanted. Work's going well, isn't it?"

"Sure, the work's going well."

"I'm sorry I made a scene. Tell me what to do."

"I don't want to get you mad at me again."

"I'm all right now."

"Okay. *Do* call Father Caffra. All you're doing is getting over a hump. It's going to work out for you; Frankie's sure of it."

"Bob—" Gilette said, and paused. Then, quickly, "It's never going to be all right, never again. I've gone too far."

"What does *that* mean?"

"Nothing. Nothing. I guess. I'll call Father Caffra, I'll pretend I think he's on my side. Maybe he knows something I can do."

"Great," Russell said, and lifted his new glass in a toasting gesture. *"Now,* tell me about IBM."

Calls came in to Harry Johnson all afternoon. One of the earliest was from Langley, responding *en clair.*

"Look, Harry, we didn't give you this Gilette because we didn't have him."

"Bull."

"No, we didn't. I've looked it up. He was checked out once, because he was that kind of shot; you don't run into too many of those. But you know how sticky DOD has been about the use of military attachés."

"It's happened."

"Oh, of course it's happened. But you have to remember how much legitimate work there is for a military attaché; and, of course, they've got their own agents. They're not supposed to be into operations at all."

"Forget it. What do your people know about Gilette now?"

"Nothing now." There was a pause. "When he was in Belgrade, we thought he was maybe a little unstable. And, you know, he had these contacts with the Jugs—married one later. But we stopped even thinking about him, because he got invited to Tito's hunting lodge. I mean, if it ever surfaced that somebody like Gilette, who'd been in the presence of the Marshal, was a marksman for us—Jesus, Harry! Remember how Khrushchev reacted when he found the U-2 pilot—what's his name? Powers—had weaponry on him.

And he wasn't even supposed to be on the ground, let alone in the presence of his nibs."

"You make a case," said Harry.

"But you still don't believe me," said the voice from Langley.

"I'll decide it later. We're going to put our hands on this guy."

"You'll find we're clean."

"For your sake," Harry said sourly, "I hope so."

"Don't try any funny business," the voice said, changing tone just perceptibly. "You can get in over your head very fast."

"I thought I already was," Harry said. "Take another look at Gilette for me, on the next level," he said. "Just to be sure. Everybody makes mistakes. If you and I get into a war with each other, the casualties could be horrendous."

"I hear you," said the voice, and the phone was hung up.

Then the agent with the Gilette assignment: Motor Vehicle had come through with a white Ford station wagon and a green Toyota hatchback. Harry made notes. The reputation in Croton was tops: Foreign wife, didn't go out much. House kept real well. Paid his bills, no member of the family ever in any trouble. A picture of Gilette had been found in one of the magazines, accepting a trophy; copies were being made, and would be distributed.

Wu checked in with word that the company had telephone and AmEx credit cards for its employees over the clerical level, and the cards were heavily used: "These brainy electronics guys: the nontaxable, nondiscoverable perk." Both Bell and AmEx were making an emergency run to find out about usage, but the output was likely to be so heavy you couldn't prove anything. Did Harry want the oil companies, too? Indeed, Harry did.

A call from Binghamton: "You know," said the deputy chief, "we've been thinking, we've really got three cities here.

There's Johnson City, there's Endicott. Would you like us to check the motel registries at those places, too? I'm sure their departments would cooperate."

"I think that's a splendid idea," said Harry Johnson.

In midafternoon, there was an anguished call from the Yugoslav ambassador: Gilette himself had just made contact with one of the most dangerous of the Croatian terrorists. "I'm working on it," said Harry. "We'll have him under surveillance tonight."

"Remember that I will know whether you do or not," the ambassador said bitterly.

The computer company called back with the itineraries since September 1 of the seven men whose clearance the FBI was reviewing. Harry took it down, but had no reason to look at it. The dates were in his head. Gilette had been in Hanover, New Hampshire, the day after the outrage in Concord; in Easton, Pennsylvania, the day of the murder in Allentown; in New Haven the day before the shooting in Stamford; in Cherry Hill, New Jersey, the day after the killing in Hoboken; in Endicott, New York, the beginning of this week. . . .

And Wu: AmEx had come through. The company card had been used in or near all the sniper sites on or about the days. The signature record would take considerably more time to check; Wu assumed—correctly—that Harry would want it checked. "Yes," Harry said with great satisfaction. "But there's no big hurry on that. The prosecution will need it, but I don't."

One more call: to Carla Whitmont. He caught her at home, on one ring. "Mrs. Whitmont?"

"Yes, I am speaking."

"Harry Johnson of the FBI."

"My God, Mr. Johnson, how can you call me? My husband says—"

"I don't care what your husband says. I'm not calling about that."

238

"But they must be—"

"I don't care what they must be, Mrs. Whitmont. I want to talk with you about a man named Nicholas Gilette."

He waited.

"I barely know him," she said finally. "I met him on Saturday night. I had a party. He was the houseguest of neighbors. They brought him."

"Whose guest was he? I need the name."

"Carl Ensor. He is some sort of banker in Philadelphia; my husband does business with him."

"I see you're still a very efficient source," Harry said, making a note and leaving a phrase on the tape he knew was spinning somewhere. "Have you seen Gilette again, since Saturday?"

The pause was long enough to provide the answer; then she said, "No."

"I am in a big hurry, Mrs. Whitmont. Where did you see him?"

"He came to a place where I teach an equestrian class, to watch me ride."

"Where?"

"Near Peekskill. Yesterday."

"What did he talk to you about?"

"Horses."

"Did he show you a gun?"

"Why would he show me a gun?"

"I thought he might. Did he talk about shooting?"

"A little, at the party. He had been duck hunting with Ensor that morning. They say he is very good."

"I hear that, too. Are you going to see him again?"

This time the answer was so quick as to be even more conclusively a lie: "No."

"Mrs. Whitmont, don't see him again. If you have made an appointment with him, do not keep it. Do not go to the place where you are to meet him. He is a very dangerous man."

Carla laughed her liquid laugh at the other end of the line. "I think so myself," she said. "So dramatic you are on the telephone, Mr. Johnson."

"It's not a joke," Harry said.

"Since we are not joking, and you are just calling me this way," Carla Whitmont said, "I have something that may be of interest to you. My husband was interviewed early this afternoon by a young man who works for some congressman. I saw him at his office right after this conversation. He was asked a number of questions to which he did not know the answers."

"How interesting," Harry said.

"At first the young man threatened him, said he knew a number of things, some of which, fortunately, were guesses and were not true. Then he began to talk about what he called making a deal. But he had not thought of the one element that might possibly make a deal acceptable."

"Which is?"

"A guarantee that Mr. Whitmont's wife would never in any way be publicly involved."

"Such a deal," Harry said conversationally, "would be very difficult to design. The people who might have made such arrangements years ago are no longer in a position to do so."

"I am aware of that," Carla Whitmont said soberly. "But I am concerned. The man who came today was an amateur. If they should send a professional . . ."

"Not likely."

"For both our sakes, I hope not. Surely, if this goes on too long, professionals will be called upon."

"I am doing the best I can, Mrs. Whitmont. I think the situation is controllable. And in the meantime, if you hear from Nicholas Gilette, you must call me immediately."

"At what number?"

"Seven seven hundred—the one in the telephone book, for

the FBI. We have no secrets, you and I, Mrs. Whitmont."

"Only my husband has secrets."

"It's the nature of his business."

"Yes; when it is important to him," Carla Whitmont said, "he can keep a secret."

But it was not, in fact, as easy as that. Shortly after Carla left his office, Tony Whitmont had been visited by his financial v.p. with bad news from Philadelphia, where Ensor was being difficult about the loan. The financial v.p. found Whitmont in the conference room, looking, glassy-eyed, at the portrait of his father, unresponsive to the message, and unwilling to call an immediate meeting to discuss the new situation. He wanted to let it go till Friday morning at the scheduled meeting, he said; he didn't feel up to concentrating on it just now. The financial v.p., returning to his office, activated the ladies' room network through his secretary, and found out that Whitmont had just been visited by a congressional staffer. Oh, Christ, the financial v.p. thought, we've got another of those damned investigations of the coffee market coming up, and he took down his copy of the last hearings at which he had testified, to make sure that when it was his turn to be interviewed he would say what he said before.

Bill Adams had tried to reach Harry while he was on with Carla, and had left word for him to call back. "I was just about to call you anyway," Harry said when he did so.

"We seem to have a problem I don't understand very well," Adams said. "Are you sure you did a good job in that talk with Spitts?"

"Tolerably good."

"Well, they're not satisfied. Congressman Barkham wants me to see Spitts, and also a young fellow named Francis, from the staff of the committee that's started this study of the Bureau. He wanted to make the appointment for today, and the best I could put it off to was tomorrow afternoon."

"Good," said Harry Johnson. "Because *I* want to see you this afternoon. Like right now."

"This is a rough day," Adams began.

"No, it's a smooth day," Harry said. "A fine day. We've got our sniper. What I want to come up about is to establish the arrest procedures."

"Hey!" said Adams. "You sure?"

"I'm sure."

That night, Gilette did arithmetic homework with Jack for the first time since school started, and saw with pleasure how quick the boy was. Maria, in European style, had got him into the habit of using graph paper rather than paper with just lines and big spaces, and it gave Gilette an idea. He told Jack the Christian Gauss story, and they worked out together—Jack saw it almost immediately—that you could solve the problem of adding the numbers 1 to 100 by drawing a square and a diagonal—and why the answer was easier to see on graph paper. Maria was in the windowless room against the hillside with the sewing machine, the washing machine and the ironing board, putting in shape one of the costumes from the old country to wear at the church tomorrow afternoon. When he looked in on her she was upset, sure he would object; but instead he said it looked pretty, and asked if he could see her in it when she finished. He urged her to stay at the church affair for supper. He was probably stuck with a business dinner; a sitter could feed Jack.

For the second night, Gilette kept an eye on the street through the intricately crocheted heavy white curtains his wife had brought in her dowry. There was the black Mercedes with two men: it came by twice, early in the evening. The second time, it slowed almost to a stop beside another car, a gray compact Plymouth, parked almost a block beyond the Gilette house on the narrow, one-way, hillside street.

Gilette thought he saw men in that car, too, and some minutes later a headlight from the traffic revealed that there were two heads, one of them looking back toward the Gilette house.

Gilette thought about his conversation that afternoon with Father Caffra, who had talked less about Maria and Croatia and more about him—his reputation as a sportsman, the contests he had won in Yugoslavia, how much the priest hoped that someday he would accompany his wife to one of their occasions, many people came who spoke English. They seemed to be watching *him,* Gilette thought, shuddering. Maybe it was Father Caffra's people in the gray Plymouth.

His sense that he could not defend his wife led him to a pit of concern about his chances of defending himself. Abruptly, he abandoned Jack's homework and went to the attic room, where he was safe. Here was his machine shop, the boxes lined with blue velvet that held the guns, the high shelf all around the four walls that held the magnificent variety of trophies—collegiate, military, AAU, NRA, German, French, Dutch, Italian, Yugoslav.

From one of the boxes he took the long rifle that had been his weapon in military competition, given to him by the unit as a gesture of reward. He raised it to his shoulder, and sighted out between the barren trees to the gray car. He caressed the barrel, and thought of beginning his long-contemplated project to rebore the gun, which he had been promising himself whenever the damned traveling let up.

But this was not the night to get Maria upset; he had promised to be with Jack. He replaced the rifle lovingly in its teak box, sprayed the room with the insect bomb, turned off the lights and returned downstairs.

XIII

First Come, First Served

Harry Johnson's Thursday began with a trip to Foley Square and the U.S. attorney's office, where he outlined in person the case for a warrant he had sketched on the telephone the night before. Expansive and discursive as Harry had never seen him, Adams had decided to make the arrest with federal agents on a federal charge, everything—well, almost everything—by the book. It was tempting to barge in, seize the man and the guns, and challenge the courts to put this particular killer back on the streets because some *i*'s weren't dotted and some *t*'s weren't crossed. Might get a constitutional amendment that way. But the A.G. would bust his buttons, and this was no time for the Bureau to get the President mad. "And, then," Adams said almost dreamily, "suppose we were wrong. . . . Everything looks clearer at a distance."

Surveillance of the Gilette home had begun almost immediately. The phone had been tapped—not, God forbid, by the government, but by a supposedly private company under contract for other services. A car was in place. When that car left to follow Gilette to work, another, staffed with a Croatian-speaking agent, would keep an eye on the house. Assuming the arrest warrant and the search warrant could be got from a magistrate fairly early in the morning, Gilette could be picked up while out to lunch—"I don't want to do anything in those offices if we can help it"—and the search party would take control of the house. Best to do it when Mrs. Gilette was home, poor creature.

Harry urged a compassionate attention to her needs, if only to avoid the public spectacle of a young woman crazed with the double blow of a father's death and a husband's arrest as a mass murderer. One of the first calls intercepted on the tap had been to a number quickly identified as the home of Robert Russell, Gilette's boss, a conversation about how happy Maria was with the prospect of some Croatian church social, and how her husband had admired her costume and urged her to stay at the church for supper. Mrs. Russell insisted that Jack come to her for dinner—then he'll have a party, too—rather than stay home with a sitter. Under the circumstances, Mrs. Gilette might be able to go to ground with her friend Mrs. Russell, before the vultures with their notebooks came around to pick the bones. The Croatian-speaking agent was given instructions to make these arrangements, if he could, once the house had been secured and the search begun.

All told, twelve men, including Harry's task force, were assigned, equipped with photos of the quarry, and briefed. It would be Harry's show: Washington and the local police departments would be told only after the fact. Interrogation would be at the Bureau's only Westchester County office, in New Rochelle; Harry would personally deliver the warrants to the agents who needed them and then set up in New Rochelle. Wu would make the actual arrest; the agent who had been about to let Gilette slide would be Harry's driver and would be available during the interrogation. Adams and Harry were both more than willing for Gilette to claim Miranda rights, get a lawyer and stand mute: between them, the physical evidence of the gun and the travel schedule would be plenty. Because the arrest would be made in Westchester County, Yonkers would probably have priority on the murder prosecution; the local D.A.s could fight it out among themselves. The federal charges, essential for a federal arrest, would of course be held in abeyance.

Much of which was unpalatable to the young, faintly supercilious U.S. attorney, a year out of law school, to whom Harry brought the formal request for warrants. There was not much in it for him: federal criminal process was being used by the FBI as a comfort station, he said. But the fact was, as Harry pointed out with as much patience as he could muster, that in the wake of the Kaganopoulos affair, the New York City police department could not credibly undertake the conclusion of the case; and none of the other cities was near up to the job. It was the Bureau that had made the case and would have to complete it, and with all respect, making the case was more important than the formalities of prosecution, which would be child's play. Eventually, the young lawyer relented and took Harry to the chambers of an almost equally young magistrate, who first observed acidly that the last warrants issued in this matter had brought discredit to everybody, then grumbled at the entirely circumstantial evidence—much of it strictly parol material out of the agent's own mouth—on which he was asked to act. Which side *are* they on? Harry wondered, not for the first time; but controlled himself and quietly made the obvious point that the purpose of the search warrant was to provide the hard evidence; and the magistrate signed.

By now it was after eleven o'clock. Harry returned briefly to the office to give the search warrant to a member of that team for delivery to Croton, then headed for Pleasantville; before he got there, Gilette went off to lunch with three other

246

men from the office, riding in their car. Harry located Wu's green Plymouth in the restaurant parking lot, gave him the documents and orders to pick up the suspect as he left after lunch, and take him first to the parking lot at the computer company's office building to search the suspect's wagon in his presence and remove any weaponry. Then Harry went to New Rochelle, tested his radio contact with the arrest group and the search group, and settled in to wait, going over the Gilette dossier yet again and making final notes for the interrogation.

Adrian Francis, back in New York now specifically to work on "the Harry Johnson business," came to Spitts's office early that morning to plan the tactics for the afternoon's meeting with Adams. He had told Congressman Barkham all about Oscar Riskovsky and received permission to beard the New York director of the FBI in his den; but he had not told anyone but Spitts about the stream of information he had been receiving from Langley, or about his conversations with Tony Whitmont. There was proof enough for Francis, who had been in Washington the day before and had been invited for a brief visit to Langley, where a young woman who did not identify herself played for him a few minutes of excerpts from recent telephone conversations between Johnson and Whitmont. But he had nothing in his hands; at best, talking about it within the committee risked advance notice to the Bureau, which might easily find some effective denial. What was needed was a pledge from Adams, in the presence of Spitts, that the FBI would make its own investigation. By monitoring closely what the Bureau did, Francis would have an engine the congressman could ride to his own destination. And the congressman would be very grateful.

It was Spitts who suggested that Oscar be included in the meeting. Francis disagreed: "I can't use a potential witness that way; it makes his testimony less convincing if it comes out." Besides, Riskovsky would be on Johnson's side and would minimize the case they presented to Adams. But the material on payoffs would be news to Oscar, Spitts insisted, and might very well break him: "He's a romantic, you know; an idealist. And the right man to tell the car story—just *because* he doesn't know why it's so important."

So Oscar was summoned, and propositioned; and on the assurance it was understood that he would defend Johnson (and himself)—and why, he asked, and was brushed aside, would Spitts and Francis want someone who believed in Johnson to be part of their effort to destroy him?—he consented.

Carla Whitmont began the day in a state of almost delicious uncertainty. She did not even consider the cancellation of the lesson, for the last session of the season was always the most satisfying, the girls *were* grateful, there were the testimonies of accomplishment—and for those who were not leaving the horses to winter in Putnam County, arrangements to be solidified. But the drink with Gilette afterward—Johnson's words were provocation and discouragement combined. She left herself the option, told Tony and Jay she might well be very late for dinner, might even wind up having dinner with the senior girls. She left early, stopped briefly at the school to discuss midwinter programs with the head of the phys ed department, and got to the farm in time to make herself a bite of late lunch in the kitchen and butter up the farmer and his wife on the importance of the responsibilities they assumed during the months when there was no visible presence from St. Ann's.

Leaving his home, Gilette noted that there was a dark-green Plymouth parked where the gray one had been the night before. He carefully—it took an effort—did not look into the car as he passed it: he had seen enough of the Yugoslav secret police during his time in that country to have an image fixed in his head, and right now he did not see why he should let them know that he knew his house was being watched. But it was not only his house. In the side mirror he saw the Plymouth pull out and follow; they were watching *him*. They did not even trust him to go right to the office; as he neared intersections from which he might have turned off his usual route, the green Plymouth came marginally into view in the mirror.

It would be intolerable to be followed—not just over a period of time, but today. As he drove, he pondered possibilities, and decided that today he would simply shake them after lunch; tomorrow, if they were still around, he might make some sort of protest. It was related, he was sure, to the Mandragora problem—probably the poor old guy *was* dead, and some announcement was about to be made. After the announcement, they would probably stay with him for weeks—maybe months—before they decided to save their money. Even days was too much, and the question was who to approach to get them off his back. Ensor: he would know; he'd call the Ambassador tomorrow and ask for advice.

Gilette was lunching with members of the design department, to work over the outlines of the shoe company's needs; he suggested a restaurant not far away, with an entrance from the parking lot on one side, from the street on the other. He had already left word that he was returning to Poughkeepsie that afternoon for a late meeting with his buddy there on elements of the IBM offer. He went off to the lunch in a car owned by one of the designers, pausing long enough at the door to the office building to make sure the men in the green Plymouth would spot him. Looking through the rear window of the car, he was pleased to note that the Plymouth was following him to the restaurant.

The lunch was a conclusion to what had been a fruitful morning meeting, rather social than business, and Gilette was able to excuse himself from it before dessert, pleading the need to get to Poughkeepsie. He should have remembered it, he said, and taken his own car; but they shouldn't worry, he'd get a cab back to the office. Standing inside the front entrance, Gilette waited until the driver of the cab he had called actually walked into the entrance, then he left, using the driver as a shield against any possible observation from the edge of the parking lot. The cab was not followed; there seemed to be nothing out of the ordinary in the company lot; and Gilette slid into the station wagon and drove off, alone at last, for his afternoon rendezvous.

It was two-thirty when Harry heard from Frank Wu in Pleasantville that the fish was out of the net. He called the computer company to inquire where Gilette was that afternoon—FBI, emergency, nobody hesitated to cooperate—and learned about an appointment in Poughkeepsie. He called IBM and found Gilette was not expected. By now the men in the design department had reported to the company their conversation with the two appalled and infuriated agents at the restaurant parking lot, and Russell had called Adams, who put him through to Johnson, asking his own anguished questions first. Johnson, who had just given orders to ask all state and local police to pick up the Ford station wagon and its driver—"probably armed, may be dangerous"—saw no reason not to tell Russell, who refused to believe any of it; and to ask him to alert his wife about the special kindness she would be asked to do her friend that afternoon. Russell could not imagine where Gilette might be going if not to Poughkeepsie. Johnson radioed the search team in Croton, first to look out for Gilette's wagon in case it came home, then to move in immediately once Mrs. Gilette returned from her daily trip to school to pick up John.

It was almost three o'clock; staring at the unfamiliar wall of the windowless office for official visitors in the FBI substation in New Rochelle, Johnson had a moment to think. There was only one other handle he could grab; he called Tony Whitmont: "Where's your wife this afternoon?"

"What do you want her for?"

"Just tell me where she is. It's important. I'll explain some other time."

"She has this horseback riding class she gives for St. Ann's School. Tuesdays and Thursdays. Starts around now—somewhere up above Peekskill, over the county line. You can't reach her."

"*Where is she?* Exactly."

Whitmont didn't know; the school would.

"Call the school; I'll hang on."

A couple of minutes later, Whitmont was back with the address, and Johnson was on the telephone to the Putnam County police: a car immediately, *here,* to look for the station wagon already requested in the all points bulletin.

In a police car on the Taconic Parkway, officers Stanley Larkin and Attilio Guadagno got a message from the communications center: Proceed to . . . turn off . . . . Guadagno took out the county map and pinpointed the road. The police car turned into the peaceful lanes of Putnam County, headed for the farm twelve miles away. It was almost three-fifteen.

Gilette had told Carla he would come at around four o'clock, to catch the last minutes of the jumping work in the fading November sun. He knew how to get there now; he drove at the speed limits, never over, through Bedford Village and then west, to the Bear Mountain roads and north again toward the farm. He was not being followed, he was sure; and no way they could pick him up now, on these country roads. He was more than half an hour early; he pulled the car up on the lane near the property, where he could see the jumping course through the trees. At first he simply watched, disappointed as Carla sat her horse beside the jump and coached the girls over. She called the girls around her and was saying something, gesturing; and then came the moment for which he was waiting, when she took the jump herself.

Gilette trembled, ran his hand over the inlaid leathers of the box, opened it, took out the gun, affixed the scope. Carla was still jumping the horse, this way then that, a rhythm of start and stop, up and down, her hand expressively moving toward the girls assembled on their horses beside the jump. He caught her in the scope, the gun still unloaded, and followed the motion of the horse and rider with his hands. Then she went to the side again, dismounted, set the girls' knees and feet, returned to her horse, watched the girls work out her instructions. Gilette still watched Carla, through the scope, and now he loaded the gun.

Again Carla shook her head at the girls and went to illustrating, and behind Gilette's blue eyes the calculating machine effortlessly began, and gathered momentum: range, velocity, pattern, elapsed time. . . .

Looking for the pinpoint on their map, the officers in the police car were driving slowly when Guadagno spotted the Ford wagon three or four hundred feet up the lane. "Right turn," he called, and Larkin spun the car hard. He thought he saw something metallic poking out the right front window of the wagon; foot hard on the gas, he hit the siren button. Almost immediately after the wailing call began, the metallic protrusion jumped, and the splat of the .22 was in the policemen's ears as their car jolted to a stop, Guadagno out of the passenger seat with gun drawn.

Larkin, a step behind, looked over in the direction that the shot had been fired, and saw a group of young women riding horses on a training track. Between the road and the track, a low branch of one of the trees had split in the middle, and its end was hanging like the wing of a wounded bird. The man in the driver's seat of the car had dropped the gun to his lap and was looking up at Patrolman Guadagno with an expression that could have been irritation or rage. "You made me miss my aim," said Nicholas Gilette.

Gilette cuffed and bundled into the rear seat of the police car, Patrolman Larkin called his headquarters, and was patched through to Harry Johnson, the county chief of police sitting in on the conference call. Larkin thought he and his partner should take a few minutes and get statements from the intended victims, but Johnson said it wouldn't be necessary: "I know who they are." He did request that they take a quick look at the tree and dig out the bullet if it had lodged there. As Gilette had been caught in the act of attempting a crime in Putnam County, local police had their own grounds to hold him; he thought it best that they simply book him on their own charges, and put him in their own lockup. Though he would have to check it with his superiors, Harry thought that with their permission he would probably wish to come up himself and help in the interrogation. Meanwhile, they had access to a box for test-firing the gun, did they not?—carefully, for others would wish to test-fire it, too.

Then Harry called Adams, who reacted with an emotional whoop. He did not want Harry to go upstate, he said; pending approval from Washington, he thought he wanted Harry back in New York, ready to star at a press conference. While Adams was requesting guidance from Washington, Harry called the search crew in Croton: they had taken possession. Maria Gilette, addressed in Croatian, had assumed they were from the church, to escort her. "Why have you come so early?" she said. "I am not dressed." The agent who had to tell her why—and he told her also that her father was dead, because he thought it best to get everything out of the way at once—thought this the most miserable piece of work he had ever done in his life. The little boy had told them about Daddy's gunshop in the attic, and two of the men were there now, making inventory. "Beautiful stuff up there. Just super." The Croatian spook was in the kitchen with the terrified and continually sobbing woman; Mrs. Russell was on her way and would take the boy. "Don't pull the place apart," Harry said. "We won't need that: he had the gun with him."

Larkin and Guadagno came back on the radio: they had the bullet; a backup car had been ordered with a man to take Gilette's wagon off to the police station. As soon as he arrived, they would leave the scene. Approved? Approved.

Adams was on the intercom. Washington did want FBI New York to announce; the Director himself was calling the Putnam County chief of police to make sure that no premature announcement was made by local authorities. The press department was already on the phone to the papers and television stations, proclaiming a press conference for five o'clock to announce a development of major importance in the sniper investigation. Harry should get his ass into town immediately. Wu and partner would go up to Putnam, not so much to participate in the interrogation as to monitor whatever the locals did—and to be present with the federal warrant in case some idiot local judge decided his duty required him to set low bail on the prisoner.

At five o'clock, then—after a fast ride down the Thruway and an infuriating traffic jam at the Triborough Bridge— Harry was at a lectern facing a row of floodlights and mini-cams, a forest of microphones, parallel lines of reporters sitting at the same conference table where forty-eight hours earlier the detectives from the local police departments had aired their complaints. Adams had picked him up at the elevator, and as they walked through the dingy corridor had told him that Gilette was already booked and would be held overnight for arraignment the next day; no hurry. The prisoner had been read his rights in the police car, but had insisted on talking about what a difficult shot he'd been trying; and comparing it with the jogger in Binghamton, the drunk ragpicker in Allentown, the girl jumping as she ran in Hoboken. People were the great challenge, because they moved unpredictably. He said he didn't want a lawyer. The White House had called in directly with a message of congratulations for New York; in a day or two Adams and Harry would have to have a talk about old subjects and new assignments. "*Better* assignments," he said, and squeezed Harry's elbow.

They entered the conference room together, and had to push their way through the crowd and the equipment, because both the access doors were in the rear. As they reached the lectern, lights switched on along both walls and in the rear with the intensity of an instrument of torture. Harry sat in the chair beside the lectern and took from his attaché case the yellow pad on which he had been scribbling through the ride down from New Rochelle, as Adams made the introduction:

"As many of you gentlemen know, the search for the sniper murderer has been coordinated in this office by supervising agent Harry Johnson, who now has an announcement for you."

Harry took the pad to the lectern and studied it briefly. "Acting on information supplied by this office," he said, and looked challengingly the length of the room into the lights and the cameras, "and pursuant to a federal warrant secured this morning from the district court for the Southern District of New York, Putnam County police officers Stanley Larkin and Attilio Guadagno—that's L-a-r-k-i-n and G-u-a-d-a-g-n-o—have arrested a man who will be charged with the several murders committed with a .22 rifle in the Northeast during the last ten weeks. The accused's name is Nicholas Gilette—G-i-l-e-t-t-e. He is a male Caucasian, thirty-three years old, married, with one child. His home is in Croton-on-Hudson, and he is employed as a junior executive in a computer company in Pleasantville. He is an ex-marine officer who served at one time as a military attaché abroad. He holds a number of gold medals for marksmanship in both collegiate and military competitions, including several international competitions.

"He was apprehended in the act of attempting another

murder, in a rural area. Therefore, Putnam County is holding him on that charge, and he will not be arraigned immediately on the others. The gun used in today's attempt is in the possession of the Putnam County police, and other guns belonging to Mr. Gilette have been taken from his house by federal agents. The bullet fired in today's attempt lodged in a tree and has been recovered. It is the same kind of bullet that killed the victims in New York, Concord, Allentown, Stamford, Binghamton and Hoboken. A box of similar bullets was found in Mr. Gilette's car. Ballistics tests are now being conducted. Any information about the results of these tests will have to come from the prosecutors. I believe that in current practice the results are not to be publicized prior to their introduction in court.

"A great deal of admirable police work has been done on this case by the local departments in the cities where the crimes were commited, and by agents from the criminal division of this office. Special credit should be given, of course, to officers Larkin and Guadagno, without whose alertness the sniper would probably have claimed another victim this afternoon."

Adams took the lectern and Harry stood aside. "Yes," Adams said, "we do have a photograph of Nicholas Gilette, about three years old. There are copies on the table by the door, and you may pick them up as you leave. *As you leave,*" he repeated despairingly, for a dozen people had jumped toward the door, and the television grips were improvising easels for display to the minicams. Adams gave up and waited for the uproar to ease. "Now I'm sure Mr. Johnson will be happy to answer whatever questions he can."

A new roar of conflicting voices filled the room. Adams pointed to the doyen of the corps, a grizzled beanpole from the *Times:* "Has the prisoner made a statement?"

Johnson looked at Adams, who nodded. "I understand, not at first hand, that he has had a conversation with the arresting officers. Unless and until it is absolutely clear that he has determined not to seek legal advice, no effort will be made to take what you call a statement from him."

One of the comely young ladies from the local television news staffs was next, and asked the hard question: "I'd like to know more details about what happened," she said. "You tell us that this Gilette was found in a rural area, shooting at somebody."

"Yes."

"Does your statement that the Putnam police found him on your information mean that you directed them to that rural area?"

Harry hesitated. "Yes."

"May I inquire," she said politely, "how you knew that this Gilette would be shooting at someone in a rural area of Putnam County?"

For a wonder, the others in the room were letting her continue. Harry said, "I didn't actually *know*."

"But you sent them there."

"Yes."

"Why?"

Harry smiled. "I had an informant," he said.

Another television reporter, a black young man in a blazer, picked up the same thread. "Do you know who he was shooting at?"

Harry said, "There were a number of people present in a group. We do not know at whom Mr. Gilette was aiming. There is no reason to believe that he knew. As the pattern of the sniper attacks has been random, and no one was harmed on this occasion, I see no reason to invade the privacy of these people."

"But you sent the cops there," called a voice from the rear.

"Yes, I did. I'm afraid you are now touching on that confidentiality of sources that we value as much as you do. There are aspects of detective work in a case of this nature on which I am afraid I will be unable to enlighten you."

Adams beside him said, "Is there anything else?"—and the press conference moved off in a more predictable direction.

Spitts, Francis and Oscar Riskovsky arrived at the FBI building together, and were impressed by the assemblage of television trucks all along the block. "I guess they've caught Dillinger," Francis said as they waited for the young man in the glass-walled booth at the box of an entranceway to verify their appointment with Adams.

"You know," Oscar said, "I've never been here before. Not very impressive, is it?"

"They're getting a new building," Francis said. "Your taxes and mine."

The legitimacy of their presence confirmed, the three men were taken up the elevator to the tenth-floor waiting room, an asphalt-tiled extension of the elevator corridor, and there they sat. The normal exit patterns of five o'clock swirled past them in the elevator area, and there was a good deal of back and forth; there seemed an air of excitement in the building. "Something is definitely going on here," Spitts noted.

"Lots," said Francis, and began outlining for them some of the recent discoveries by the House Committee's staff. Oscar was morosely silent. At five-thirty, Francis went to the receptionist to complain, cloaked in the dignity of the Congress. The girl was contrite. "Mr. Adams is usually very punctual," she said, "but there is a very important press conference which was not called until just a little while ago, and he had to be there. It should end any minute now."

And a few minutes later a new burst of people erupted from the doors at the end of the waiting area—technicians with cameras and lights, sound technicians with their little black trunks, faces familiar from the evening news shows. On their heels came Adams, who had left Johnson talking with people from the print media. Introductions were accomplished, including the ever-awkward left-hand shake with Os-

258

car, and as Adams led them around the other way, far from the conference room, he most courteously apologized for keeping them waiting. He ushered them to seats in his square office, and took his place behind the desk, maintaining a distance. "And now what can I do for you?" he said heartily.

"We are here," Francis began, "to demand that the Bureau institute an internal investigation of the conduct of supervisor Harry Johnson."

Adams shook his head, smiling broadly. "My best man," he said. "I really think you must be joking."

"Joking!" Spitts said furiously. "Best man! Do you think it's a joke that this 'best man' of yours infiltrated my law office? Riskovsky here was an informer for him throughout—"

"But I don't want you to believe—" Oscar interrupted, and was in turn interrupted by Francis.

"I'm told he's been on the take—"

"On the take!" Adams said incredulously.

"I've heard tapes of telephone taps—"

"Telephone taps! Who made them?"

"I can't tell you."

"Do you have the tapes in your possession?"

"No—I heard them."

"Who played them for you?"

"I can't tell you."

"I thought you fellows didn't believe in tapping telephones," Adams said. "And I'm sick and tired of made-up stories to the discredit of the Bureau; I know what you've been spreading around. On the take! You know what Harry Johnson's on the take for? A Presidential Medal." He looked at his watch. "I'll show you," he added, and reached out of his desk a remote control for the television set in the corner. He pushed a button, and a cartoon cat began extolling a dry substance.

"What the hell!" said Spitts.

"Just wait."

The news show began: "The FBI today announced the capture of the sniper who has been terrorizing the Northeast. The announcement was made by agent Harry Johnson, who had coordinated the wide-ranging search, at a press conference in the Bureau's New York headquarters." A screen behind the announcer showed Adams and Johnson arriving at the lectern; the screen advanced and filled the tube as Johnson made his statement.

"Sources close to the Bureau," the announcer intoned at its end, "say that advanced technology was important in the process that led agents to the alleged sniper. But Johnson himself said the arrest had been made possible by leads provided through an informer. More after this message . . ." and a box of laundry detergent danced determinedly onto the screen. Adams pushed another button, and the dancing box diminished to a dot.

"Is there anything *else* I can do for you gentlemen?" he said.

"I don't see what difference any of this makes," Adrian Francis began, but Spitts cut him short.

"Clown," he said. "Can't see what difference it makes. You think your congressman wants to throw mud on the miracle worker? Or you can get Oscar to say boo now in public? Or Whitmont even to talk to you again? You think your buddy at Langley won't call you a crazy scheming Commie liar if you so much as hint you spoke with CIA? Grow up, kid. Nobody has a duty to be interested in the things that interest you."

Spitts rose with some dignity from the government-issue armchair. The silence was broken by a bellow of laughter from Oscar Riskovsky. "Where," he sputtered, and laughed again, "where do I find Mr. Johnson's office? I want to congratulate him. I want to thank him. . . ."

Sue Johnson's plane from Denver had been delayed, and did not arrive at Kennedy until almost four o'clock. She called the office to tell them she wouldn't be in and to check on the market, and then went home to bathe and change for the evening. She turned on the radio as she dressed, and heard her father's voice, broadcast live from the press conference. Hurriedly, she wrote a note and taped it beside the button that called her apartment from the downstairs antechamber of the brownstone, in case she didn't get back before Oscar came to pick her up, and she grabbed a taxi crosstown to the FBI building. There, in the confusion of departing television crews and reporters, she was able to fly past the minimal security of the man in the booth and take the elevator to the ninth floor. She arrived at her father's office only seconds after he had walked in himself, to be run at and embraced by a joyously tearful Tilly, who had been "so frightened for you . . . so happy now."

"I hope I'm not interrupting anything," Sue said, seeing them in each other's arms. "Just wanted to tell you how great you sounded on the radio."

"Oh, isn't it *wonderful,* Miss Johnson?" Tilly said.

And Oscar was in the doorway, black eyes shining. "Sure is," he said.

"I wasn't supposed to see you till seven-thirty," said Sue. "Better early than late. We all gotta celebrate."

"Absolutely," said Harry, now disentangled from Tilly. "All four of us." Tilly nodded. "Where do we celebrate?"

"There's that fancy place on top of the World Trade Center," Sue suggested. "I take people there when I really need something they don't want to give me."

"Never been," said Harry. "They tell me you have to make reservations two weeks in advance."

Sue smiled a soft, slow smile. "Papa," she said. "Oh, Papa. You don't understand the modern world. Tonight your problem isn't getting a table; it's forcing them to let you pay your check when you're done. You are a *celebrity.*" She reached for the telephone and dialed.

As Harry was putting on his coat, Dr. Goldberg called.

"I *like* this case," he said. "When are you going to tell them he shot the dog?"

"Maybe never."

"You're such a big man now, you think you could get me in on the sanity hearings?"

"I can try. What do you want to do with the information?"

"Maybe I'll write a book."

"Over my dead body," Harry said.

"Everything is over dead bodies," said Dr. Goldberg. "This poor bastard—his dead body becomes a totem. Celebrate tonight. I say that sincerely."

Tony Whitmont, working late, had two telephone calls in a space of ten minutes. The first was from Carla, who had a story to tell, and told it all. She was shaken, embarrassed, "feeling foolish," and home. The second was from Carl Ensor, who was watching the evening news.

"My God, Tony, I can't tell you how I feel, introducing that man into your house!"

"Yeah. Do you know who he was shooting at today?"

"No, they didn't announce that."

"Carla."

"You're not serious?"

"Dead serious."

"Good Lord!"

"He sat beside her at our party," Tony said mournfully.

"But nothing happened."

"Thank God, no."

"Even so," said Carl Ensor.

"Even so," Tony echoed. "Well, you couldn't have known. I guess." There was a pause. "Incidentally," Tony added, "I have my weekly meeting on finance tomorrow morning. Can I tell my people anything about that loan we discussed?"

"Oh, we'll take care of the loan," Carl Ensor said. "Don't worry about that. And do give Carla my deepest—my most regretful—apologies."

At the restaurant, Harry was the subject of obsequious attention, numerous double takes, and several requests for autographs. He had three drinks before dinner, listened to Sue and Oscar, looked up the island at the skyline and the lights, relaxed—more, he thought, than in years. Won't last, he said to himself; nothing lasts.

Twice during the prolonged and lavish dinner, the wines chosen by the sommelier "with thanks from all peoples," Harry's beeper summoned him to the pay phones. Once it was Tony Whitmont, calling from home:

"It seems all right now."

"It is all right."

"Carla's very grateful."

"She should be."

"She thought—we thought—that perhaps we could give you some big prize, a lot of money at once. In honor of saving her life. Once for all."

"That's illegal," Harry said.

"But it's *nice* illegal," said Whitmont. "If it came out, nobody could say anything."

"That wife of yours is too clever. Forget it—all of it. I'm in line for some fancy new job, more money than I can spend, and the sort of thing I've wanted money for is going to be over, I guess. We all have to be very formal and legal now. You want to do something for me?"

"We surely do."

"There's a young man who's been working for me, very capable. College graduate, veteran. Lost an arm in an accident. No business experience, but smart. He's going to be out of a job. He'd earn his keep for you fast as an investigator in that crooked business you're in. Everybody needs a spook these days. Will you see him?"

"Better still. We're opening a new budget slot for a security officer."

"Oscar Riskovsky. He'll call you tomorrow."

He told Oscar about it at the table. "Time to settle in," he said.

"And the two of you will see each other," Sue said, "*socially.*"

"Only socially."

Then the second beep, in the middle of the main course; Sue and the maitre d' were both horrified. This time it was very brief: the computer center, reporting that Binghamton had passed on a registration from a motel in Endicott matching one of the names on the file: Nicholas Gilette. Nobody had stopped the computer search. Harry told his caller he was delighted, and they could now move that program off the computer. They were surprised; almost alone among the sentient citizens of New York, the myrmidons of the machinery hadn't heard.

"This is the life," said Theo Kaganopoulos, throwing himself on the bedspread in his wet bathing suit. "This is *the* fucking life! Turn on the TV, Fricka."

His wife did so and went off to the gold-plated bathroom. The news was in midcourse: "Concluding his tribute to agent Harry Johnson, the congressman said that methods similar to those used by the New York FBI in its pursuit of the East Coast sniper should be tried here in Hawaii, where the police now have a backlog of seventeen unsolved murders in one year."

"Hey! Fricka! That shit-faced FBI man found the fucking sniper! Who'da believed it?"

"Does that mean we can go home?" she called from inside the luxuries of the bathroom.

"Ah, sure, we can always go fucking home. Why should we—so long as the fucking government's paying the fucking bills? Don't you like it here?"

"Sure, Theo, I like it here."

"You fucking better." He got off the bed and went to the

television set to look for something that wasn't news.
"Hawaii!" he said. "Holy shit!"

Whatever is in the tables of organization and the congressional documents, the true controller of the CIA is a man in the Office of Management and Budget, permanently emplaced, beyond criticism because he is transparent to whatever President he serves. He has other responsibilities, too, and it was not until after midnight that he could turn his attention to the Gilette matter. He had, of course, no scruples about making telephone calls after midnight.

Phil was awakened by the special sound of the red telephone by his bed, and took it before the second ring. He was trained to wake up alert.

"Most extraordinary, that Gilette business," said a familiar voice.

"I agree; all of that."

"You sure we never had anything to do with him?"

"Absolutely. Never one of ours."

"Extraordinary."

"Comes out very well, you know. We had an intercept early this evening from the Yugoslav mission, giving the go-ahead to the foreign minister for his trip here."

"That *is* a plus, isn't it?" There was a pause. "I understand you fellows have had your troubles with agent Johnson."

"Um," Phil said. "Yes, we have."

"Got a little impetuous, I hear."

"Maybe."

"You haven't done anything irrevocable, I hope. The President hasn't had much good news recently, and he's really rather excited about this thing."

"No, nothing irrevocable."

"Nothing on paper? Nothing that can't be denied if it's absolutely necessary? Not that I think it will be."

"No. All by voice. Telephone on a secure line. We did

an electronic search to make sure that aide wasn't recording what he heard the one time we saw him."

"Good. I can be completely confident this episode is over?"

"Completely."

"I imagine you have some records somewhere. Paper. Tapes. Something in the computer?"

"Yes."

"Let's make sure all that disappears. It *never was.*"

"Yes."

"If I were you, I'd have trouble sleeping while any of that material still exists. Do it tonight."

"Yes, sir."